Praise for *Drowning*:

'Masterful' **Patricia Cornwell**

'*Drowning* is the first terrific thriller of 2023. Honest. It has at least a dozen legit cliffhangers and a dozen huggable characters you can't stop rooting for. T. J. Newman has the goods. Make that the greats!' **James Patterson**

'Stunning, emotional, and unforgettable. *Drowning* reads like *Apollo 13* underwater' **Don Winslow**

'*Drowning* is *The Poseidon Adventure* meets *The Martian*. It is another can't-put-down, edge-of-your-seat thriller from T. J. Newman, one of our most exciting new authors' **Adrian McKinty**

'*Drowning* is pure adrenaline and all heart. Gripping, relentless, effortlessly assured, T. J. Newman's thriller is tense and moving. You'll be grabbed from page one as the crew and passengers of a downed airliner fight for survival and rescuers race to reach them. *Drowning* is an incredible ride – strap in, brace, and remember to breathe' **Meg Gardiner**

'A stunningly vivid tour de force! Gripping. Shocking. Heartbreaking. You will not be able to come up for air until the very last page!' **Brad Thor**

'*Drowning* by T. J. Newman is a remarkable novel with extraordinary writing, story, and characters. T. J. Newman is a gifted writer and I stayed up all night reading it' **Dervla McTiernan**

Praise for *Falling*:

'Think *Speed* on a passenger jet – with the cockpit dials
turned up to supersonic' **Ian Rankin**

'Amazing . . . Intense suspense, shocks and scares plus chilling
insider authenticity make this one very special' **Lee Child**

'*Falling* is the best kind of thriller (for me as a reader anyway).
Characters you care deeply about. Nonstop, totally authentic suspense'
James Patterson

'Attention, please: T. J. Newman has written the perfect
thriller! . . . Terrific and terrifying, a true page-turner.
A must-read for summer vacation' **Gillian Flynn**

'. . . I only put it down for bathroom breaks . . .
Highly (get it?) recommended!' **SJ Watson**

'A jet-propelled thriller that will have you in its grip from
first page to last. A truly astonishing debut and an incredible
work of pure suspense' **Steve Cavanagh**

'T.J. Newman has taken a brilliant idea, a decade of
real-life experience and crafted the perfect summer thriller.
Relentlessly paced and unforgettable' **Janet Evanovich**

ALSO BY T. J. NEWMAN

Falling

DROWNING

T.J. NEWMAN

SIMON &
SCHUSTER

London · New York · Sydney · Toronto · New Delhi

First published in Great Britain by Simon & Schuster UK Ltd, 2023

Copyright © T.J. Newman, 2023

The right of T.J. Newman to be identified as author
of this work has been asserted in accordance with the
Copyright, Designs and Patents Act, 1988.

1 3 5 7 9 10 8 6 4 2

Simon & Schuster UK Ltd
1st Floor
222 Gray's Inn Road
London WC1X 8HB

Simon & Schuster Australia, Sydney
Simon & Schuster India, New Delhi

www.simonandschuster.co.uk
www.simonandschuster.com.au
www.simonandschuster.co.in

A CIP catalogue record for this book
is available from the British Library

Hardback ISBN: 978-1-3985-0766-1
Trade Paperback ISBN: 978-1-3985-0767-8
eBook ISBN: 978-1-3985-0768-5
Audio ISBN: 978-1-3985-1291-7

Printed and Bound in the UK using 100% Renewable
Electricity at CPI Group (UK) Ltd

MIX
Paper | Supporting
responsible forestry
FSC
www.fsc.org   FSC® C171272

For the weasels,
Grant and Davis

The term *last-ditch* is used to describe an effort that is made at the end of a long line of failures. It is the final attempt and is not expected to succeed.

In aviation, the emergency landing of an aircraft on water is called a *ditching*.

CHAPTER ONE

WILL KENT OPENED HIS EYES JUST IN TIME TO SEE THE ENGINE EXPLODE.

His arm shot up to protect the passenger seated at the window, but his daughter Shannon didn't seem to notice. The eleven-year-old girl just watched the flames spewing out of the back of the engine's tail cone and uttered an uneasy *whoa*.

Will sat up straight and looked over the tops of the seats. The emergency exit was two rows up. A flight attendant sat there in a rear-facing jump seat staring at the passengers. He could just make out her name bar. Molly. Will caught her eye.

Molly didn't say a thing. She didn't have to.

The aircraft shook. Panic gripped the cabin as everyone craned for a look out the windows. Flames. Chunks of metal ripping off, flying by.

Will leaned over Shannon for a better view. The engine was on fire. Parts of the wing were shredded. Below the plane, crystal-clear turquoise water.

Shannon looked to her dad. "Why aren't we turning back to Honolulu?"

Will had been wondering the same thing.

In the cockpit, every pilot's worst nightmare was coming true.

"We lost thrust in engine one," First Officer Kit Callahan radioed to ATC, her voice rising involuntarily as the plane dropped. "And all hydraulic fluid in all three systems."

"Say again, fourteen twenty-one?"

The air traffic controller sounded skeptical. Even the captain glanced over to see for himself. Any other day, all this second-guessing would have pissed her off.

Not today.

Kit triple-checked the ECAM, barely believing the display herself. System failures were listed in order of severity. Level 3 failures, the most crucial, were first, in red. Red filled the screen. Every time she cleared one, another would pop up. All were Level 3. The digital screen looked like it was bleeding out.

They'd been airborne for less than two minutes. Engine one was dead. So were the hydraulics. This extended beyond their training. Pilots don't run situations like this in the simulator.

There'd be no point.

"Fourteen twenty-one, ah, did you say all three? All three hydraulic—"

"Goddamn it, dead stick!" Captain Miller said.

No hydraulic fluid. No hydraulic power.

The plane was dead in the air.

Green. Blue. Yellow. The aircraft's three hydraulic lines. Two layers of redundancy in case of a system failure. It's *that* important. The display should have shown three green lines at 3,000 PSI. Kit was looking at three amber lines with 0 PSI. Her best guess was that when the engine blew, fragments of metal sprayed like buckshot through the hydraulic lines and drained the fluid. Any moving component on the aircraft—ailerons, flaps, spoilers, rudder—everything that let them fly the plane, had frozen in place.

The pilots couldn't command the Airbus A321 to do anything. They had no control.

"We can't turn back," Kit told the controller. "Requesting an alternate in front of us."

Will ripped open one of the plastic pouches he'd just pulled from the compartments under their seats. He passed it to Shannon.

She turned the pouch over, looking at the folded yellow life vest tucked inside.

"Are we going to crash?"

Several passengers looked at her. She'd voiced their worst fears.

"Shannon," Will said, shifting in his seat to face her. "We've lost an engine. I don't know why we're not turning back. It may be because we can't."

Will pulled the vest out and shook it open, slipping it over her head before cradling her face in both his hands.

"I know you're scared. But whatever happens, I'm going to be right here with you."

Will heard a seat belt unbuckle. He waited for the refastening click after the passenger realized there was nowhere to run. Instead came heavy footsteps. He looked up just as a red-faced, middle-aged white guy in a blue polo shirt blew past their row on his way to the back. Angry male voices began to rise in the rear of the plane as the guy in the blue polo shirt yelled at a male flight attendant who was seated in a swing-out jump seat in the center of the aisle.

"Sir!" the flight attendant bellowed. "Sit down! *Sir!*"

Suddenly, the plane dropped sharply. Everything went down—

—blue polo went up.

His head smashed into the ceiling. Will turned away as the man slammed back to the floor—just in time to see Molly the flight attendant unbuckle her harness and head for the back of the plane. Another jolt made the plane thrash violently. Molly flew forward. Her head smacked into an armrest, with her chin taking the brunt of it. Crawling on all fours back to her jump seat, Molly strapped herself in while blood trickled from a split lip.

Will refocused on Shannon. "Shannon. We stay together. You understand? No matter what. We stay together."

Shannon wasn't listening to her dad. Will followed her gaze. Blue polo was on his feet again, stumbling back to his seat amid the turbulence, moaning in pain. He held his head while blood poured down his face in thick streaks. As he passed their aisle, the plane dipped. He braced himself, then continued on, leaving behind a bright red hand-print stamped on the white overhead bin.

Shannon stared unblinkingly at the blood.

"We stay together," she repeated.

Molly Hernandez winced as she wiped the blood off her chin with the arm of her uniform sweater. She tried to look calm as she blinked at the passengers from under her straight-cut bangs, but her hands would not stop shaking.

Another seat belt unbuckled. Molly turned. A woman in a long floral dress got up to let the guy in the blue polo back into their row just as the plane lurched again. Floral dress lost her balance and fell into the man. Their heads smacked against one another and the woman grimaced in pain, a streak of his blood now covering her forehead. He sat clumsily, and with another jolt of the plane, she fell back into her own seat.

"Ma'am?"

I hate that guy, Molly thought, stewing. *Three people are now hurt and bloodied for no reason.*

"Excuse me—"

The only reason Molly had even gotten up was because she was worried about the unaccompanied minor. Flying all alone. Sitting in the last row of the plane. Poor kid had a front-row seat for all that scream-ing, all that blood—

A piece of the engine slammed violently against the plane. Every-one jerked away from the windows and Molly yelped. A few people screamed. Holy *shit* the passengers looked terrified. Holy *fuck* every-thing was happening so fast.

Molly closed her eyes. She was spinning out. *Calm down,* she thought, taking a breath. *Just review your commands. Heads down, stay down. Heads down, stay down. Release seat belts. Leave—*

"Excuse me! Ma'am!"

"What? What do you want?" Molly snapped at the woman sitting across from her. She immediately regretted it. "I'm sorry."

"Where's that vest?"

"Under your seat."

The woman bent over and her waist-length braids pooled on the floor. She struggled with the compartment under her seat until the plastic seal broke off with a snap. The woman sat up with the plastic pouch, ripped it open, shook out the bright yellow life vest, and threw it over her head.

"But don't—"

Grabbing the red T-handles, the woman yanked down like it was a parachute, inflating the vest with a loud hiss. Everyone watched the woman try to lean back in her seat. She now looked more like a raft than a passenger.

In the cockpit, Kit looked to the controls overhead. The whole panel was lit up. Every button in the hydraulics section glowed amber with a single word: FAULT. Above that, a large rectangular button labeled ENG 1 with FIRE printed on its plastic guard burned bright red. She double-checked the smaller buttons flanking it. They *should* have shown a glowing white SQUIB, meaning the primary and backup fire-suppression systems had been armed. Instead, the buttons were dark.

"Push button didn't activate," Kit said.

The pilots had no way to fight the engine fire or cut off the fuel that was feeding it.

Kit cleared the engine failure and a new Level 3 failure popped up on the ECAM explaining why the fire-suppression system hadn't activated. There, like a bright red, all-caps middle finger: ENG 1 FADEC FAULT.

"FADEC fault."

"Goddamn it," Captain Miller mumbled.

The Full Authority Digital Engine Control was a small computer affixed inside the engine that acted as the link to the pilots. Any action in the cockpit went *first* to the FADEC, *then* the engine responded. Engine one's FADEC was dead. Without it, there was no communication

between the two. The pilots couldn't tell the engine to do anything—
and they also had no idea what the engine was doing.

"I need eyes," Captain Miller said.

Kit punched a button.

Three high-low chimes sounded throughout the cabin as a red light lit
up on the ceiling above the emergency exit row. Will watched Molly
rip a phone from a cradle and press it to her ear without saying a word.

Shannon took her own phone out of airplane mode, brought up a
text thread, and began typing. Will noticed the contact. MOMMY, with
a pink heart emoji.

There was a loud bang. Will grabbed his armrests as the plane
dipped to the left. The phone flew from Shannon's hands, dropping to
the floor with a thud. Just as she bent to get it, the plane dove, and the
phone slid forward.

"No!" Shannon cried, reaching out. Like every eleven-year-old, her
phone was her life. Being without it was unthinkable. She grabbed at
her seat belt but Will's arm pinned her down.

"Leave it," he said.

"I want to tell her—"

"You'll tell her in person."

He was firm. He wanted her to take it as confidence that they were
going to be okay.

But he also knew she was smarter than that.

Further up, strapped into his jump seat in row eight, Kaholo Kapule did
what all the flight attendants were doing: holding the interphones to
their ears and not saying a word.

In emergencies, flight attendants are trained to wait. The pilots will
be busy. They'll communicate as soon as they can, *if* they can. Do not
distract or interfere by calling them. They will call you.

While Kaholo waited, that nice young couple was watching him with wide eyes, so the flight attendant gave them an easy half smile. They held hands, knuckles turning white next to shiny new wedding bands. Another couple up in first class was celebrating their fifty-fifth anniversary. Colleen, the lead flight attendant, had made an announcement for both.

"Who can see the engine?" came Kit's voice through the interphone.

"I can," Kaholo said, unbuckling his harness and standing for a better look. The passengers leaned back so he could see. The Hawaiian native could surf before he could walk, so even in an uneasy ride, he never had to hold on to anything. But as he bent and saw what was on the other side of the window, he instinctively grabbed a seat back.

Will stared at Molly.

She'd had that phone to her ear for nearly a minute now but hadn't said a thing. She was just sitting there. Listening.

Will leaned into the window. It was hard to assess the engine since he was sitting behind it, but flames now covered all that was left of it. Most of the outer cowling had been blown off or ripped apart by the airstream. Mechanical inner workings were exposed. The inlet cowl, the massive circular section of metal covering the front of the engine, clung to the bottom, swaying precariously, looking like it might fall any second.

Suddenly the plane dropped like a brick thrown off the roof of a building. A baby started to wail. The mother held her tight and sang a soft song into her ear. No one had a clue what was going to happen. Uncertainty brought fear. Fear created anxiety. They prayed. They cried. They texted goodbye to their loved ones.

But Will's attention had turned back to Molly. And so he was the only one who saw the blood drain from her face at something said to her by someone on the other end of that phone.

Molly's mouth parted. She blinked a couple times. Then, without saying a word, she hung up the phone and just sat there very, very still.

Will reached over and took Shannon's hand. He knew what came next.

A chime rang throughout the cabin.

"This is the captain. Prepare to ditch."

CHAPTER TWO

LEAD FLIGHT ATTENDANT COLLEEN BENNETT KNEW THE DITCHING EVACUATION
commands by heart—but not the ditching preparation announcement.
With no time to look it up, she had to improvise. She took a deep breath
and tried to steady her voice.

"Ladies and gentlemen, we will be making an emergency landing . . . on the water. There's a pouch containing a life vest under your
seat. Place the vest over your head and buckle the strap. Do *not* inflate
the vest. Only inflate the vest as you leave the aircraft."

Will could see that Shannon was scared. He tried to reassure her with
a look that appeared only to make her more nervous. He reached over
and tightened the strap on her vest.

In the cockpit, there was another high-pitched ping as a new notifica-
tion popped up on the primary flight display.

Kit had been flipping pages in the QRH for the third time but
everything in the emergency quick reference handbook they'd either
already done or couldn't do—so she tossed the binder in a compartment
behind her and leaned forward to read the new directive.

USE MAN PITCH TRIM

Kit looked to the captain.

"First time for everything," he said, moving his right hand to the trim wheel on the center pedestal and palming it with a light grip. Pushing the trim wheel forward or backward would move the cables connected to the elevator and rudder on the tail. Meaning, in theory, a pilot could adjust the plane's altitude and pitch.

The controls rattled. Captain Miller struggled to maintain the right amount of pressure on the trim wheel. On a small aircraft it's a difficult task. The system is sensitive and imprecise. It's easy to overshoot and then overcorrect. On a commercial jet it's all but impossible.

ATC came back with two alternates: Maui and Kona.

Kit stared at the endless stretch of water that surrounded them and replied to both options in the same way.

"Unable."

"Okay, stand by."

The radio went silent as the controller scrambled to come up with another option the pilots knew wasn't there.

They were four minutes into the flight. Zero hydraulic power. The plane refused to climb. They couldn't turn back to Honolulu. Maui and the Big Island were too far. Directly ahead were Molokai and Lanai—but those islands were nearly uninhabited and almost entirely mountainous.

There was nothing the plane could reach except the water.

At the back of the plane, a chunk of the engine slammed against the window, splintering the outer layer of windowpane. The unaccompanied minor screamed and turned to face Ed Vernon in his jump seat. The little girl's dark brown eyes became glossy. Bottom lip trembling, she blinked as two heavy tears slid down her cheeks.

Ed glanced at the lanyard around her neck. Printed across the fabric were the words TINY TRAVELER. Handwritten on the card in the clear plastic holder was her information. Maia Taylor. Eight years old. Her guardian's contact info for when they landed. And Ed's own signature, assuming responsibility for her.

Maia wiped her face with her sleeve. The hot pink plastic balls at the end of her pigtail twists swayed in the turbulence.

"Are we going to die?" she asked.

The radio crackled and the controller declared all runways at Honolulu were cleared and available for Flight 1421's return. Kit held her headset close to her mouth.

"Unable. We cannot turn around. We cannot climb. We have no hydraulic power. We have no control of this aircraft. Don't give us alternates. Get a rescue team ready to get us in the water."

The radio went silent.

Finally, there came static. Then only: *"Roger that."*

Kit tried to get her eyes to bring the white digital altitude numbers into focus in the turbulence, but she didn't need exact figures to know the numbers were getting smaller, fast.

"Flaps?" Captain Miller said.

"Still at two," Kit said, glancing down at the levers on the center console.

"Landing gear?"

"Up."

"Ditching switch?"

A pause. "Sure."

She reached up, lifted the guard covering the button labeled DITCH-ING, pressed it, and an ON light illuminated. If it worked, the cabin pressure controller had just sent a "close" signal to the valves, vents, and fans across the outer surface of the airframe.

She'd shut all external openings in an attempt to make the plane watertight.

This was what it had come to. The ditch switch. Manual trim. They'd moved past Hail Marys into fool's errands. Kit didn't know a single pilot who had ever used these systems outside of the sim.

If you're pressing the ditch switch, you don't live to tell the tale.

"Show me again," Will said.

Shannon leaned forward, laying her chest flat against her thighs. Her arms wrapped under her legs behind her knees and she held on to opposite elbows. Her knees cradled her cheeks and she looked down to her toes.

"Good," Will said. "So when the pilot says, you get in that brace position." Shannon nodded. "Keep your heels forward in case the seats collapse. And keep your tongue—"

"On the roof of my mouth so I don't bite it," Shannon finished.

"Good. And when the plane comes to a stop—"

"We get off the plane. Fast."

"Where's your exit?"

Shannon pointed at the exit two rows up.

"And if not there, where's your next closest?"

The man sitting in the aisle seat next to Will pointed behind them. "Back of the plane."

Will and Shannon both turned. The man shrugged.

"I'm following you guys."

From her window seat in the first row of the plane, Ruth Belkin took her husband's soft, wrinkled hand in hers.

"You know, Ira," she said, "fifty-five years isn't a bad run to 'death do us part.'"

Across the aisle from them, a young woman sat at the window with a phone to her ear. "Mom, it's me," the girl said, a finger jammed in her other ear. She turned toward the orange flames outside, which matched her red hair. The engine shook. Another rivet attaching the cowling shot off. The massive chunk of metal dropped an inch more.

"Mom, I'm on the plane and something's happened and I . . . I—"

Her voice broke.

"I don't think we're going to make it."

Ruth could envision the moment when the mother would see she'd missed a call from her daughter. The mom would check her watch, confused: *Shouldn't she be flying right now?* The mom would start the voicemail with a smile—but by the sound of her daughter's breathing alone, she'd know something was wrong.

Ruth listened to the girl cry, knowing sometime soon, her mother's sobs would join hers.

Ira took Ruth's hand in both of his and kissed it.

Kit could hear muffled sounds coming from the cabin and wondered what the passengers were doing in these final moments. She assumed they were crying. Praying. Trying to make phone calls. Calls to say *I love you. I'm sorry. I forgive you.* Including herself and the captain, there were ninety-nine souls on board. And right now, the other ninety-seven were back there trying to do what needed to be done before the end. Ninety-seven men, women, and children she was responsible for.

Air traffic control squawked. *"Coastal fourteen twenty-one, all runways at all airports are cleared and available. Emergency services are standing by."*

Kit felt a lump in her throat. ATC understood the situation. They knew the plane couldn't make an airport. ATC knew just as every pilot and controller listening on the radio knew.

Flight 1421 was going down.

But by stopping all traffic, by turning all attention to them, everyone was saying: *You're not alone.*

Kit cleared her throat. "Appreciate that. Unable. We're gonna be in the water."

The pilots stared at the approaching ocean as the radio crackled with dead air. Kit could imagine the controller looking to his colleagues. Knowing this would be the last conversation this flight crew ever had.

"Ah, roger that," the controller responded. His voice cracked. *"We got you on radar. Coast Guard is standing by for rescue and recovery."* There was a pause. *"Godspeed, fourteen twenty-one."*

"Coastal fourteen twenty-one, good day," Kit said, the traditional sign-off sounding more like a goodbye.

Neither pilot spoke. She'd never flown with the captain before this trip. He was fine, but they hadn't really connected. With some guilt, she realized she was glad it was him here now and not a friend. She wondered if he was thinking something similar.

"All right," Captain Miller said.

Kit understood. She pushed a button. A ping rang out in the cabin. When she spoke, her voice was calm. Firm.

"Prepare for impact. Brace, brace, brace."

Immediately, the four flight attendants began shouting their brace commands over and over—*Heads down, stay down! Heads down, stay down! Heads down, stay down!*—and all around the aircraft, the passengers placed their bodies into positions that would give them the best chance at survival.

Colleen watched the old couple lean forward with their hands still entwined. Kaholo saw the newlyweds kiss one last time, deeply, before both folded their arms on the seat backs in front of them. The guy in the blue polo sat back, crossing his arms defiantly, while the woman sitting beside him held on to her legs as her tears soaked into her long floral dress. Molly's voice was going hoarse as she called out her commands, all the while watching the woman in the inflated life vest praying loudly to baby Jesus. Ed closed his eyes as he shouted. He couldn't stand to see that poor little girl looking up at him anymore.

Will checked Shannon's brace position one final time before leaning forward to assume his own. As his body shook with the plane, his jaw rattled against his knees. Outside of the flight attendants' shouts, the plane had gone eerily quiet. He stared down at their feet.

Shannon's tennis shoes were white with pink and orange zigzags. There was a grass stain on one of the toes and the laces had gotten dusty from the playground at recess.

"I love you, jelly bean," he whispered.

Up front, a robotic voice began to bleat through the cockpit: *Low terrain, pull up! Low terrain, pull up!* As the numbers on the altimeter got smaller, the voice seemed to get louder. Kit turned the volume counterclockwise until it clicked off.

Heads down, stay down! Heads down, stay down!

In the cabin, the passengers and flight attendants were bracing. In the cockpit, the pilots sat up straight and prepared to fly the plane as far into the crash as possible.

The whitecaps on the clear blue water had individual features. They were so close.

Kit looked up. A memory she hadn't thought of in years came to mind. *"Help me, Jesus" buttons.* She was nine. She sat in the first officer's seat. Her dad sat in the captain's chair. He said all the bad buttons were on the panel overhead where you had to look up to push them. He said looking up reminds you to pray.

"'Cause if you're pushing the 'Help me, Jesus' buttons—you're screwed."

Kit looked at the glowing buttons and shook her head.

He would get the last laugh. He always did.

Captain Miller pulled back the power on the right engine. It spooled down in the way engines do seconds before landing. The voices in the back stopped. It was quiet. Calm. Still. The plane seemed light. Suspended in the air.

Then, six minutes and thirty-seven seconds after it had taken off, Flight 1421 crashed.

The bottom of the aircraft hit the water squarely. The ocean's surface was unyielding, like slamming into concrete. The water didn't give. The metal did. The aluminum alloy bent inward, absorbing the force, but the impact was too great. Gashes dotted along the bottom of the plane like Morse code as water burst into the cargo holds.

The plane bounced, going airborne for two and a half seconds, before slamming back down. *Hard.* The right wing clipped the water. Metal sheared like torn paper as it ripped off the airframe. Mechanical entrails poured out as the snapped wing created drag and slowed the forward motion.

If the nose had dipped, if the plane had cartwheeled, if *anything* besides what happened had occurred, the airframe would have broken apart. All lives would have been lost.

But it didn't.

The plane moved across the surface like it was being dragged by the tip of its nose. The left wing—still attached—was raised high in the air. Its engine—still on fire—was a streak of orange flames. The right side took the most damage. Every structural limit was tested. The metal outer skin. The windows. The doors. The seals. Both in the cargo bay and in the cabin. Most held. Some did not.

From the moment of impact until the plane came to rest was nine seconds. Somehow, the plane was still in one piece. The passengers who'd survived the crash thought it was a miracle. They thought they were the lucky ones.

They had no idea that the worst was yet to come.

CHAPTER THREE

SHANNON KEPT SHAKING WILL—BUT HE WASN'T RESPONDING.

"Dad. *Dad.*"

His body was slumped over and tangled up with the man in the aisle seat. Neither moved. The row behind theirs had been ripped out of the floor and collapsed forward, pushing their seats up, pinning her in at the window.

Shannon turned and looked outside. Water was lapping at the windows. The plane was floating on the surface. The tip and end portions of the left wing were gone. But the rest was still attached. So was the engine, which remained on fire. It all hovered over the water's surface because the plane leaned to the right.

She watched the chaos unfolding inside the plane and didn't know what to do. People were bleeding. People were crying. Some were dead.

And she was alone.

"Dad!" Shannon cried in desperation, shaking him harder.

But he didn't open his eyes.

Something tickled on Kaholo's forehead. When he touched the spot and pulled back his hand, he found his fingertips were covered in blood.

Kaholo looked to the left. The engine was still running. The blades were still turning. The fire was still raging. Kaholo squinted into the brightness of the flames, the water, and the sky. That's when it hit him.

Holy shit. We're alive.

He gazed around the cabin, then looked up. An image came into focus.

A laptop. Lodged into the roof of the plane like an axe without a handle. *As we get ready to take off, please check that your seat belts are fastened, seat backs and tray tables are up, and electronics are secured.* The safety demo rattled around his throbbing head as he stared up at what happens to unsecured electronics.

He unbuckled and stood, knowing he was about to see the results of unfastened seat belts.

Fifteen rows back, Molly was two steps ahead of him.

"Release seat belts! Life vests under seat! Put them on! Leave everything, come this way!"

The words were rote muscle memory, hardwired through years of training and repetition.

"Release seat belts! Life vests under seat! Put them on! Leave everything, come this way!"

Molly crossed to her primary exit, the L3 door. Looking out the porthole window, she assessed the conditions outside the left side of the aircraft. Water. Fire. Debris. She turned. R3, her secondary exit, didn't need a closer look. The plane was leaning and the entire right side of the aircraft was submerged. Molly looked down. On the floor, aircraft right, at the seam where the floor met the wall, were two inches of standing water.

That's not good.

There was a loud crack behind her. Molly spun and saw an overhead bin hanging down on one hinge, blood covering the corner that drooped. One lifeless body she thought could have been a severe concussion or even a heart attack was still strapped into his seat. Blue polo shirt guy, still bleeding, was fumbling with the clasp of his life vest. A few rows beyond him, a young man stood staring down at the woman in the aisle seat next to him. He wasn't wearing a life vest. He wasn't preparing to evacuate. He just stood there, frozen.

The buckle in Molly's fingers clicked and she pulled the loose strap tight around her waist. It hadn't been thirty seconds since the plane had come to a stop, but she'd seen enough and she'd made the decision.

L3 and R3 were unusable.

"Exit blocked, go back! Exit blocked, go *back*!"

Will heard something far away. A voice. But he was in too much pain to try to figure out whose. The voice stopped. Will groaned. Everything was dark. Everything hurt.

Suddenly everything was wet and cold.

Will's eyes shot open as he sat upright, coughing. He squinted in the bright light. Shannon stood next to him with her purple-sequined backpack in one hand and her now empty sticker-covered water bottle in the other.

Most people were already up and moving. Which was exactly what he and Shannon needed to be doing.

Shannon was watching him, waiting. It pained him to think of her alone the whole time he was passed out. It must have been so scary. Will grabbed her by the shoulders. "Are you okay?"

Before she could answer, a loud pop came from the engine. The flames bellowed.

"We gotta go," Will said.

At the front of the plane, Colleen shouted as she prepared to open her primary exit, L1: the door the passengers had used to board the plane in Honolulu.

"Stay back! Stay back!"

Every word out of her mouth was an emergency command that had been drilled into her so deeply over the years that now, the first time she'd ever needed to say them outside of a training exercise, the words came without having to think about it. She was on autopilot, which freed her brain to focus on the passengers in her first-class cabin.

The young redhead was missing teeth, and blood poured from a busted lip. The man sitting beside her opened the bin and grabbed a bag.

"Leave *everything*!" Colleen yelled.

He dropped the bag.

Colleen checked the control panel. Only L4 at the back of the plane was open. Her door would be the second. With a glance at the cockpit door—still shut—she anchored herself to the plane by grabbing on to the bulkhead assist handle with her right hand. With her left, she pulled up sharply on the red handle in the middle of the door.

"Stay back! Stay—"

There was a pop, then a thump. Sunlight seeped in from the cracked lining of the doorframe. After a pause, the pneumatic assist took over and the door swung out and open. The forward galley filled with blinding light and a draft connected the open exits at the front and the back, flushing the plane with cool, briny air.

Colleen extended a hand behind her as she watched the slide raft unfurling onto the water outside. "Stay back! Stay *back*!"

Ruth and Ira watched the flight attendant scream at the passengers lining up in the aisle and crowding into the galley behind her to stay back, but the crowd was surging forward like frightened animals.

As the first passengers left the plane, Ira stepped out of their row to join the line. A woman in front of him pushed him back.

"Watch it!" Ira yelled, falling backward into Ruth. They both stumbled, catching themselves on the seats as another wave of bodies pressed forward.

Ruth looked up as the lead flight attendant's voice grew more strained. "Inflate vest! Walk down raft! Inflate— No! Stay calm! Sir! Stay calm!"

Ruth and Ira watched as the frenzied crowd pushed their way out of the plane, taking the flight attendant with them. The last thing they saw of her was her hand slipping from the handle she'd anchored herself to. Her voice grew distant.

Ira turned to his bride and together they sat down.

"We'll wait," Ruth said. "Just until the main rush has passed."

———————

Will could smell the salty sea air and knew the doors were open. He threw the water bottle in the backpack and tossed the backpack under the seat. Taking Shannon under the arms, he lifted her over the man seated next to him and set her down in the aisle. Will followed, standing on the seat to step over the man. He was looking up and down the plane, deciding which way they should go, when he noticed Shannon staring at the blood dripping out from under the unmoving man's body.

"Don't look," he said.

Shannon glanced around at the chaos. "Where am I supposed to look?"

He dropped down so they were eye to eye. "At me. You look at me. All the time. Okay?"

Shannon nodded.

Molly stood in front of her doors waving her arms to redirect the passengers to the back of the plane. Those who were physically able began moving that way. Stunned, crying, shaking, they nodded as they passed, grateful that someone knew what to do.

She heard a low moan and looked down. A woman was trying to crawl out from under a row of collapsed seats. No one stopped to help; they just stepped over her.

"Move, move—" Molly said, pushing people out of the way. Dropping to her hands and knees in the middle of the aisle, Molly grabbed the woman by the arms and pulled. The passenger screamed.

"Hey! You! Lift here," Molly said to another passenger. The man grabbed the bottom of the seats and lifted with a grunt. The work was awkward in the cramped space, but Molly tugged at the woman inch by inch until her body was finally clear.

Catching her breath, Molly got a good look at the woman as she watched the carpet beneath the passenger's leg darken with blood. Her calf was sliced open to the bone.

"I need you—"

But the man who had lifted the seats was gone.

Using the hem of her long floral dress, Bernadette Kowalski wiped that asshole's blood off her forehead. She stood there, alone, looking from the front to the back, trying to decide which way to go.

If Barry were here, he'd have already made the call. Barry always made the calls. Which was partially why he was now her ex-husband. But it was also why she was struggling now, just as she had all week on her first solo vacation post-divorce. She was still unlearning her learned helplessness.

Glancing to the back, she saw the flight attendant with the bangs struggling to drag an injured woman to the open area in front of the unopened exits. As she watched, the flight attendant tore off her own sweater and wrapped it tightly around the woman's leg as a makeshift tourniquet—but she was doing it all wrong.

Molly looked up as the woman in the floral dress dropped to the floor beside her.

"No," the woman said. "Here, like this."

The flight attendant scooted back and watched the woman unwrap and retie the sweater. The injured woman groaned.

"You're a doctor?" Molly said.

"Nurse," floral dress said. "Bernadette."

"Molly."

"Molly, hold this. Hold here. Pull hard."

Molly took the ends of the sweater and pulled. The injured woman moaned loudly again, but over it, Molly heard a child's voice.

"Dad, look."

At the sound of footsteps, Molly glanced up to see the father from earlier heading toward them with his daughter right on his heels. The little girl stared at all the blood. It covered the floor. Their clothes. Their hands.

The father dropped to his knees beside Bernadette. "Let's carry her to—"

"No," Molly said breathlessly, shaking the bangs out of her eyes. "Go."

"But I can help—"

"No! Get her out of here!"

The father knew Molly meant his daughter, and with a reluctant nod, he got up, put the child in front of him, and started for the back. Molly watched them go, noticing the woman with the waist-long braids in the inflated life vest struggling with yet another life vest.

That'll work!

But the life vest began to slip down her arm. Working to untie the knot, Jasmine Harris glanced up at a man and a little girl as they passed. On the seat next to her was a stack of unopened life vests she'd found under unoccupied seats.

No arm floaties. What about around the waist? Like an inner tube.

That worked. Jasmine triple-knotted to be sure. She spun it around so it crossed her back, ripped open another pouch, shook out the vest, and pulled on the red handles. She wrapped that vest around her waist, too—triple-knotted—and went for another. No chance in hell she was getting out of the plane until she was as buoyant as a goddamn boat.

Andy Matthews tugged at the collar of his blue polo shirt. The line of people in front of him was taking forever. He looked to the queue at the back of the plane. It was just as long. He noticed a woman already wearing a life vest throw another one over her head. *Good call*, he thought, scavenging under seats until he found an extra. By the time he'd clipped the buckle on the waist strap, the line had barely moved.

"Fuck this."

Hoisting himself up on the seats, he began to climb over the rows, passing the people waiting ahead of him. His foot kicked a man in the head, but Andy didn't even notice. He just kept passing people, moving toward the exit.

Ryan Wang didn't react to the kick in the head. He just watched the man scramble over the seats to the front of the plane. Ryan knew he should have been feeling that driving instinct to survive. He assumed it was in him somewhere. But he didn't care enough to find it.

Ryan looked down. Not a scratch on him.

He had been conscious and his eyes had been open during the crash. He'd watched in disbelief as things flew through the air around him. Overhead bins burst open. Seats broke away. Metal crunched. People cried out. Fire roiled from the engine, as it still did even now. He'd been awake through it all.

When it had finally stopped, he'd turned to his bride in the aisle seat next to him, ready to share the insanity of the moment. Instead, he'd found her folded forward in her chair, her chest laid flat against her thighs.

Ryan saw the spot of impact immediately. The exposed part of her neck just above her shoulders. The open section of spinal column was red and bruised already. The heavy suitcase that had dropped on her lay in the aisle.

She was the brilliant doctor, not him. But even as a dumb finance guy, he knew she was gone. He'd only been a husband for a week. Now he was a widower. Ryan looked out the window and watched the engine's fan blades spin.

"Hey!" the male flight attendant yelled. "You gotta go."

Ryan nodded but didn't get up.

The guy just sat there. *What's he doing?* Kaholo thought before looking up front. *And where the hell is Colleen?*

There was a loud *pop*. The engine was still burning, and now it was shaking violently. The whole wing was bucking up and down.

Kaholo knew it was designed to be flexible. But that movement didn't look right.

Will and Shannon were last in line at the back of the plane.

The line wasn't moving.

Will glanced into the plane. Molly's exits were still shut. So were the two exits in front of hers. And every exit on the right side of the plane was underwater.

That meant they were only using two exits on a plane designed with eight.

Which meant there were only two slide rafts available.

Will had seen quite a few empty seats on the plane. But with only two rafts in use, he knew there was a good chance they were already full.

"Okay, Shan. You go first. I'm right behind," Will said, trying to keep his tone calm. "And you'll inflate your vest when?"

"Aren't you coming?" Shannon asked, looking beyond him. She wasn't listening. Will turned.

There, in the last row of the aircraft, standing on the center seat, was a little girl. Probably a year or two younger than Shannon—and the child was all alone. She wasn't crying, but she looked like she wanted to. The little girl nodded.

"At the end. The flight attendant told me to wait for him."

The plane creaked and Kaholo felt a snap under his feet. He grabbed on to a seat as the plane sank further to the right with a jolt. At the front, the passengers now had to climb *up* to get out the exit. Those last in line began to yell at those in the front to move faster. Someone pushed someone. They pushed back harder. Someone held a suitcase above their head. Someone said they had a baby and everyone parted to let the mother and crying infant through. She'd wrapped her own life vest around the baby's body and Kaholo cursed, knowing there were infant life vests stowed in the back of the plane, if only there were time.

"Kaholo!"

Kit was pushing toward him from the front. The flight deck door was open, and bright light flooded into the plane through the cockpit windows. The first officer stood up on a seat for a view of the whole cabin and Kaholo saw the blood covering her uniform.

"Is the engine still on?" she asked.

"Yeah," he shouted, turning to double-check. "It was shaking. Now it's *shaking*. And the metal's not orange like it was. It's yellow. Like a bright yellow. The—"

Kaholo stopped.

A fluid was seeping out of the cracks and holes in the wing. Wherever the liquid landed on the water became an iridescent slick—and it was spreading. Kaholo turned back to the first officer.

"We got a problem."

Will was holding his hand out to the little girl who was on her own when suddenly a high-pitched noise came from outside.

The loud mechanical whine became more and more deafening as the plane shook more and more violently until even the waterline on the other side of the windows was vibrating.

Will knew what was about to happen.

He pulled Shannon in and turned to cover her.

What was left of the engine blew. Burning metal shrapnel shot in every direction, torpedoing through the water, tearing through the wing, slicing open the fuel tanks. Razor-sharp metal embedded into the side of the fuselage. Lodged into the back of a man's head. Punctured the slide raft at the front L1 door. Jet fuel sprayed everywhere and fuel vapors filled the air.

All it took was a spark to ignite the fuel.

In an instant, a massive fireball exploded and the entire surface went up in flames.

CHAPTER FOUR

THE FIRE SPREAD IN EVERY DIRECTION AS RAZOR-SHARP PIECES OF THE PLANE LITTERED the water's surface like fallen leaves. The air reeked of smoke and jet fuel. Passengers who had evacuated early and managed to swim away from the plane were huddled together, holding on to a portion of the wing tip that was still floating. They thought they were far enough out—but the fire was stalking them. No one helped the nearby passenger treading water in his life vest who began to panic when he realized the heat was melting the plastic. Everyone watched as the vest popped and the rush of air acted as a bellows. The man went up in a blaze.

No one knew what to do or which direction to go. Neck-deep in the water, every direction looked like the wrong one.

Some of the passengers were screaming. Some went into shock, unable to do anything but tread water. Dead bodies floated facedown. The slide raft at the L1 exit that had been punctured in the blast was now nearly deflated. A few passengers clung to the section that was still buoyant, but every second it got smaller as the air seeped out. Most passengers who had been on the forward L1 slide raft were now in the water, and many were injured.

Inside, Will clutched Shannon as they listened to the screams that came in through the open door. A body, still burning, floated by, bobbing up against the airplane windows. Father and daughter could only stare.

Suddenly, the windows were pitch-black. The cabin went dark.

Everything got quiet. A hush fell over the plane. It felt like a floating haunted house. No one moved.

Then, a moment later, the wind kicked up. The smoke cleared. The cabin brightened. The screaming resumed. Active panic took over.

Will looked around as the realization hit him hard.

"No . . . no . . ." he murmured to himself, checking his watch. "Close it!" he yelled suddenly, running to the back of the plane. "Close the door!"

The flight attendant, Ed, took one look at Will and continued to direct people off the plane.

"Stop!" Will screamed, pushing his way closer.

"There's a line," a passenger said, shoving Will back with both hands.

Will tried to get around him and the other passengers, but the aisle and galley were packed.

"You don't understand!"

But no one was listening. They just thought he was blue polo shirt 2.0.

Will grabbed Shannon by the hand and ran back into the plane, passing Molly and the women on the floor. He yelled forward as they went, but the front of the plane was a tangle of bodies still scrambling to evacuate.

"Dad!"

Shannon stopped, ripping the interphone from Molly's jump seat. Will grabbed it and hopped up on a seat. The big rectangular button seemed as good a guess as any, and when he pushed it, a ding rang out.

"Shut the door!" Will said, his voice booming through the plane.

Everyone turned. A woman in a pilot's uniform covered in blood pushed through the crowd toward him. Will met her halfway.

"Sir, you need to follow instructions," she said. "We have to get the passengers off the plane."

Will looked at her. "If we leave this plane, we die."

"When you ditch, you evacuate. Period."

"This isn't the kind of ditching you trained for!" Will argued, fighting to keep his voice level. "Look at the fire out there. Look at that fuel on the water. That wind's going to pick up and everyone out on that water who's not already burned to death is going to suffocate in the smoke. And we will too if we don't close the door!"

The pilot studied him carefully, weighing his words.

"The plane will float. You know it will," Will said. "It's our only shelter."

"Don't listen to him, Kit!" Ed yelled from the back galley. "He's going to get us all killed! Protocol says—"

"Fuck your protocol!" Will screamed back. "You don't have a protocol for this!"

"How sure are you?" Kit said.

Will turned back to the pilot. He pulled Shannon in front of him and wrapped his forearm across her shoulders. "This is my daughter and she's staying with me. Inside the plane. That's how sure I am."

Kit and Will stared at one another for a moment before Kit moved around him.

"Close the door!" Kit yelled, running to the back.

"Are you insane?" Ed said, taking a woman by the arm and pulling her toward the exit. She stepped down awkwardly and a man caught her as she almost fell over the side of the raft. Ed grabbed at another passenger but the man pulled away.

"Maybe we should listen—"

"No!" Ed spat. "We evacuate. We move away from the plane."

"You won't have time," Will said. "You'll never get far enough."

"It's my job to evacuate—"

"My plane, my call!" Kit yelled. She sidestepped Ed and moved toward the door, but he pushed her back—hard—slamming her into the wall of catering carriers. The pilot's head smacked against the metal with a sharp thwack. Ed looked just as shocked as Kit did.

"I'm sorry—"

"The door closes," Kit said with authority. "Shut it, or leave."

Ed hesitated, then turned and stepped off the plane. Walking to the center of the raft, he sat down next to the passengers and didn't look back.

"In or out," Kit said to everyone left in the galley. "I'm the captain. I'm staying. But the choice is yours."

Only Will, Shannon, Bernadette, and Molly stayed.

"Close it," Kit said to Molly. "I got the front."

With that, the pilot ran for the front, followed by Will and Shannon.

After the last passenger left, Molly got to her hands and knees and lifted a plastic flap at the base of the door labeled FOR DITCHING USE ONLY. She pulled the handle underneath, which engaged the slide's quick-release feature—and the slide raft and all the passengers in it began to pull away from the plane.

Molly watched the bobbing raft drift further into open water as the fire moved closer to it. A wave hit the side of the raft, lifting it off balance. Passengers knocked against one another and water soaked their laps. The distance between the plane and the raft grew, and after one last look, she stood and, using the side of her fist, pounded against the door's gust lock until she felt it give. Molly pulled the door closed, grabbed the control lever, and pushed the red handle down until it latched shut with a heavy thud.

The flight attendant stood in the dim galley listening to the sudden quiet while her eyes adjusted to the light. She turned to find Bernadette staring back at her. The two were covered in a dead woman's blood and ten minutes ago they hadn't even known each other's names.

Together, they headed toward the front of the plane. Molly surveyed the damage as they went. Seats were ripped out of the floor. Bags were everywhere. Somehow the oxygen masks in a row had dropped—

"Did he leave without me?"

Molly stopped in her tracks. Closed her eyes and swore under her breath. Then turned to face the unaccompanied minor.

"Stay with me now," Molly said to Maia, faking calm. "We've got a good plan. And another little girl. She's about your age. C'mon."

The little girl hopped down from her seat to follow the women. God, she was so tiny. So young. Molly tried to shake Ed's words.

He's going to get us all killed.

Molly and Bernadette moved quickly, trying not to look at any unmoving bodies they passed. One was still belted to her seat. Another lay sprawled on the floor. Maia slowed as she stepped over a pair of legs.

The little girl squatted and peered under the seats. The body was jammed into the place where the bags usually went. There was a dark stain on the carpet under the head, and his hair was matted with blood. Maia extended a finger and pushed gently on the man's shin. He didn't respond, so she poked again, a little harder.

"Maia."

The child spun around, hands clasped behind her back.

Molly went over to her. "Stay with us. It's going to be okay." The flight attendant held out her hand and the little girl took it.

As they went to the front together, Maia looked over her shoulder at the body.

Anyone still on board was now in first class. Will turned away from the children and spoke in hushed tones to Kit, who nodded, listening carefully. Ruth and Ira bickered over which bag their medications were in. Molly counted heads. Bernadette assessed Jasmine's cuts, working around the multiple life vests. Shannon and Maia stood off to the side watching.

At the base of the door at the front of the plane, Kaholo was trying to pull the ditching handle and detach the slide when a man's hand suddenly emerged from the water and grabbed his wrist. Kaholo called out and Kit dropped to her knees beside him. Together they pulled the man in the blue polo shirt back into the plane. Dripping water everywhere, Andy crawled to the other side of the galley, breathing hard.

Kaholo pulled the handle. The slide detached, dropped into the water, and immediately began to sink. It was useless now, a deflated slab of plastic. Standing up, the flight attendant pounded the gust lock with the side of his fist, pulled the door toward him, and thrust the control lever down.

Behind him, everyone was talking at once. Kaholo stood next to the closed door with his hand still on the handle, breathing heavily. Water puddled at his feet as it ran from his soaked uniform. He punched the door. Everyone went quiet. He turned, and with his black shoulder-length hair clinging to his face, he moved toward Will. Kit stepped in between them.

"The fuck I just do that for?" Kaholo said.

"I told you," Will said. "It's the only thing that makes sense."

Outside in the water, a pair of arms could be seen clawing at the window from below. The fingers scratched at the clear plastic but the plane's smooth surface left nothing to grab on to. The hands dropped lower and lower until the passenger disappeared. Only the tops of the flames remained.

"Out there we die," Will said. "In here we've got a chance."

"What are you talking about?" Molly asked.

"We crashed just southwest of Molokai," Will said. "Molokai is across from Lanai. We're at the end of the narrow channel between those two islands. It's a giant wind tunnel. The trade winds blow from the north, every day, starting *right now*, which means everyone out there . . ."

He paused, swallowing hard.

"How do you know all this?" Ruth asked.

"I'm an engineer," Will replied. "I design offshore oil rigs."

"Oil rigs," Ira said. "You don't work on airplanes?"

"What he says makes sense," Kit said. "The conditions outside became more dangerous than inside. That's it. Look, we don't have good options. We have what we have. Rescue and recovery know where we are. They're already on the way. This is just a temporary shelter."

"What about them?" Ira said, motioning outside.

"Rescue and recovery will be here soon," Kit said, sounding like she was trying to convince herself, too. "We wouldn't be helping by joining them."

Andy scoffed, slicking his wet hair back. The gash on his head from hitting the ceiling still dripped red. "No offense, stewardess," he said, "but—"

"I'm a pilot," Kit said.

Andy looked her up and down. "Okay. Then the captain—"

"I *am* the captain."

Only the flight attendants seemed to understand what that meant. Kaholo looked to the cockpit. A limp, outstretched arm extended from the left seat.

"Wait, where's Colleen?" Molly asked, looking around.

Kaholo motioned to the closed door. "She got the door open and I never saw her again."

"She left?"

"No," Ira said. "People pushed her out."

"There were so many," Ruth said. "They were so scared. She never stood a chance."

The crew took that news in. Kaholo then looked to the back and—

"Ed left," Kit said before he could ask.

The crew of six was now three.

"Lots of people died today, not just your friends," Andy said. "I didn't want to be one of them so I got back in the plane. Because I thought you had a plan. Turns out you don't. You have this guy. Why are we listening to him anyway?"

"Because he obsesses over what can go wrong," Shannon said. "Ask my mom."

"But is he *right*?" Jasmine asked.

"Usually. That's what makes it so annoying."

"This isn't fair," said Ira. "Ruth and I never got a chance to even try to get out."

The lines were drawn.

As the tension escalated, Shannon looked up at her dad. Will wanted to say something to make it better, to fix it. Instead, he took her head in his hands and gently kissed the top of it.

Suddenly, there was a creaking underfoot and the plane dipped further to the right. The pooling water was steadily growing, and it now rose up the right wall of the plane by nearly a foot. Everyone shifted to the left, but that put them up against the windows and the horrors on the other side. There was no good place to turn.

Kit reasoned with them, asking for calm. The plane was still buoyant. It would stay that way until help arrived. Yes, the cargo bays were filling with water—but closing the doors had acted like inserting a cork. The pressure of the water entering from the cargo holds would trap the air inside the cabin and at a certain point, no more water could enter. The plane would float on the surface like a half-filled bottle on its side.

"Forget it. I'm not dying in here," Andy said, and made for the door. Kit blocked his path. He moved to go around her and shouldered her backward. Will and Kaholo were moving immediately.

"You made your choice," Kit said, taking another shove. "You don't get to choose for—"

Suddenly, the cabin went dark. Everyone froze. The emergency lights cast an eerie fluorescent pall. The window views of clear blue water, bright orange flames, and yellow life vests disappeared. Instead, all that could be seen was thick, black smoke.

"Jesus, goddamn!" Jasmine said after a moment, clutching her heart. "Where'd you come from?"

Ryan had appeared at the bulkhead divider to the main cabin.

"Dude, you okay?" Kaholo asked, recognizing him as the guy he had yelled at earlier.

Ryan stared at the front of the plane. He slowly tilted his head.

"Molly, go make sure no one else is back there," Kit said, stepping in front of Ryan. "Sir? Are you all right?"

He didn't answer.

Molly went to the back while Bernadette tried to ask him medical questions. The wafting smoke kept making the cabin dark and then light and then dark again. Maia started to cry, and Shannon went over to put her arm around the girl's shoulder.

Ryan ignored all of it.

"I think he's in shock," Bernadette whispered to Kit.

Ryan turned slightly, locked eyes with Kit, and then looked toward the front of the plane.

Will followed his gaze. Immediately, he knew things were about to get worse.

CHAPTER FIVE

CAPTAIN MILLER'S DEAD BODY REMAINED STRAPPED INTO THE LEFT SEAT AS FRACTURE lines splintered across the cockpit windshield. With each crack, the panes weakened under the pressure of the water on the other side. The faint tinkling of breaking glass filled the small space.

Then, in an explosion of shattering glass and rushing water, the window burst.

Will immediately turned away, arms outstretched, heading for Shannon and Maia in a futile effort to shield them. Kit and Kaholo broke toward the cockpit, but the powerful flow of water pouring into the plane knocked them down. They grabbed at the bulkhead. The galley countertop. The jump seat. Anything to help them inch their way forward against the water that flooded into the sealed plane.

Kaholo reached the cockpit first. With both hands, he pulled at the door to release it from the magnets that held it open against the interior wall. Once Kit made it to the cockpit, they pulled together until it finally broke free. The force of the flow caught the door, slamming it shut violently. Kaholo cried out and held up his hand, which was now missing several of its fingertips. Blood streamed down his arm.

Shutting the door was like plugging a hole in a dam. The door was bulletproof, Kevlar reinforced. It would hold. But it wasn't watertight. Kit panted silently as she watched the small streams of water trickling in from the jambs rise to the top of the doorframe as water filled the entire cockpit.

There was a loud creak from below. Everyone went silent.

The plane groaned, giving voice to the pain it was absorbing, and then ever so slowly, the tail lifted as the nose dipped.

They'd reached a literal tipping point.

Kit caught herself as she fell forward against the door. The plane's center of gravity shifted and everything went forward—including the water already trapped inside the plane. When Kit looked down, the water was knee high . . . thigh high . . . waist high . . . it kept rising.

Everyone clutched at whatever they could. A seat back. The overhead bins. The person next to them. Jasmine was the first to move. Heading to the back of the plane, she leaned her tall frame against the rushing water, which was now carrying everything that could float forward.

Maia stood in the middle of the aisle, screaming. Her arms were raised above her head, the water already chest high on the child. Will picked her up. He turned to Shannon. "Get to the back. I'm right behind you."

At the front of the group, Jasmine tossed a child's stuffed pink bear out of the way, and the strap on one of her life vests caught on something under the water. It yanked her back and, panicking, she pushed forward—but that only tightened the vest around her stomach.

"Let's move!" Andy hollered from behind.

Jasmine slipped and fell, hitting the water with a loud splash. She scrambled to her feet, thrusting her body forward to try to break free. But the plastic seam of the vest only cut deeper into her waist the harder she pulled.

"Stop! *Stop!*" Molly said, grabbing Jasmine's shirt and pulling her back. Dipping into the water, the flight attendant angled her head to barely stay above the waterline while she felt for where the strap was caught.

Andy cursed and started climbing over the seats to pass them. Jasmine kept trying to push forward.

"Stop it!" Molly said.

"Sorry . . ." Jasmine muttered, stepping back, breathing heavily as she watched the water rise.

Molly found the hitch, looped the fabric up, pushed the strap forward, and released it at the end of the armrest. "Go," she said, rising to her feet.

Everyone called out to one another or to their mothers or to their god as they scrambled up the aisle, heading for higher ground at the back of the plane.

Ryan stepped into a row to let everyone pass and stared down at his wife's body. Still belted into her seat, she was facedown in the water, her loose black hair swirling, her arms floating. Tears streamed down Ryan's face. The water rose higher around him. As Ira and Ruth passed, Ruth took Ryan's arm and pulled him away.

Only Kaholo and Kit were left at the front.

"Kit!" Kaholo yelled. "C'mon!"

Kit nodded absentmindedly, still staring at the cockpit door. She felt the cool water hit her torso and turned to follow Kaholo up the aisle. She was the last one to move, pulling herself up by the backs of the seats as she lunged against the water. She visually swept each row as she went, making sure they weren't leaving anyone behind.

She was still responsible for the airframe and the souls on board.

At the front of the plane, every window showed water. Clear blue water that was getting steadily darker.

The plane was sinking.

Outside the aircraft, the waterline rose against the fuselage until window views of blue water replaced blue sky for the twelve souls that were still trapped inside. As the last of the tail slipped into the water, bubbles whirled in the plane's downward suctioning draft. Against the vast expanse of the open ocean, the massive commercial jet was like a child's toy in a bathtub.

Kit was the last to reach the back galley. "Molly," she said, wide-eyed and panting. "Head count."

The front of the plane's interior was completely submerged. The waterline was at a sloping angle and it already reached the tops of the seats halfway to the back. The bright fluorescent emergency lights cast eerie shadows as the cabin got darker with each passing moment.

Molly pointed a finger at each passenger and counted out loud while making a personal inventory in her head. *Ira and Ruth, the old couple. Bernadette, nurse. Jasmine, life vest woman. Andy, blue polo asshole. Will, smart guy. Shannon, smart kid. Ryan, newlywed widow. Maia, unaccompanied minor.* Plus, what was left of the crew: Kit, Kaholo, herself.

"Twelve. We're twelve. Still twelve."

Maia wailed in pain, covering both ears with her hands. Kaholo dropped to his knees, wincing in pain as blood dripped down his arm.

"Here, do this," he said to the child while pinching his nose shut with his good hand. "Then blow like this." Kaholo's cheeks puffed out. "Gently."

Will realized his own ears were throbbing painfully, too. Maia mimicked Kaholo. So did Will and everyone else. Will's ears popped in relief, equalized to the changing pressure.

There was a creaking noise and the plane shuddered.

"*Fuck!*" Andy shouted, the word reverberating in the cavelike acoustics.

"Language," Bernadette said, nodding toward the children.

"Are you fucking kidding me?" Andy said. "We're about to fucking drown and you're worried about my fucking language? Fuck that. And fuck *you*," he said, pointing at Will. "If we'd left the plane we'd at least have had a chance."

No one argued, not even Will.

Suddenly, Molly pushed forward and flung open the last overhead bin. Stepping up onto a seat, she reached deep into the back of the bin. There was a rip of Velcro and when she hopped down, she was holding an oddly shaped device about the size of a football. It was bright yellow and had a long antenna secured to the side, which she deployed as she moved down into the plane toward the water. Submerging the device, she held it under for a few moments before letting go. It popped back up and bobbed along the surface like a buoy. A small blinking light was now lit up on top. Everyone held their breath.

"Water-activated emergency locator transmitter," she said to the group.

Nobody responded.

She added softly, "So they can find us."

That was all they could do. Let the authorities know where to find the bodies.

It was sinking in. They were going to die. Trapped in this plane with each other.

Maia started to cry. Bernadette dropped down to her eye level and wrapped her in a hug. Kit moved forward, putting herself in front of everyone as though she could block them from the inevitable. Ira muttered to himself while shooting glances in Will's direction. Ruth kept turning his face back to hers, whispering softly to her husband. Finally, Ira gave her his full attention and clasped her hands in his. Ryan watched them for a moment before burying his face in his hands. Jasmine tried to speak directly to the baby Jesus, but the conversation was one-sided and she let him know how much that pissed her off. Molly and Kaholo just stared. At each other, at the water.

Will picked up Shannon with a grunt, straddling her legs across the front of his waist. He hadn't held her like this in forever. Somewhere along the way, she'd gotten too big. When was it, he wondered, that he'd picked her up this way for the last time and hadn't known it?

Life is measured in birthdays. Graduations. Weddings. First steps. A first crush. A first kiss. Firsts, not lasts, are the tallies on a life's scorecard. But as Will tucked a piece of her dark brown hair behind Shannon's ear, he only thought of the lasts.

When was the last time he'd brushed her teeth before she started doing it herself? When was the last time he'd clicked her into her car seat before she was big enough for a booster? When was the last time he'd had to tie her shoes before she learned how?

The life of a child is about firsts. The life of a parent is about lasts.

"I'm so sorry, sweetheart," Will whispered, his throat tight. He felt cool water hit his ankles and stifled a gasp. He refused to look down. He had to be strong for Shannon. But she understood what was happening. She looked down. Then she looked around at everything. She was calm. Steady. Taking it in, figuring it out. Just like her mother would have.

Shannon smiled and Will saw her.

Chris.

Shannon's mother. His wife. Soon to be ex-wife. Suddenly Will remembered a last: the last time he'd seen Shannon cry. April, one year ago. He and Chris had sat Shannon down at the kitchen table and told her they were separating. Shannon wasn't a crier. But she'd cried then. He'd moved out that weekend.

Will realized a couple of his own personal lasts. And they were all regrets.

Suddenly, the silence changed.

Everyone looked around at each other, trying not to move or make any noise. After a moment, Kit spoke, her voice a whisper.

"The water stopped rising."

Will watched the waterline across the door of the lavatory without blinking until he was sure.

She was right.

With the exception of the emergency lights, the plane was dark. Outside, beyond the windows, was nothing. A deep blue nothingness that grew darker by the minute. There was no way to tell if they were moving. There was no way of knowing where they were. It was eerie, the stillness—and the waiting. Waiting for what, none of them knew.

Everyone was quiet for a long time before Shannon said what they were all thinking.

"We're sinking to the bottom of the ocean."

Then the plane slammed into something.

THREE HOURS EARLIER

CHAPTER SIX

ON THE EASTERN SIDE OF OAHU, A SINGLE-LANE ROAD WOUND ALONG THE LUSH TROPI-
cal foothills of the Koolau Range. At the top of the hill at the end of the
street sat a two-story home made from wide planks of honey-colored
wood with a forest-green pitched metal roof. Picture windows framed
mountain views out the back, while to the front, the surf of Waimanalo
Beach could just be seen from the second story. The neighborhood kids
called it "the treehouse" because of the way it nestled into the jungle as
though it had grown right out of it. But Chris and Will called it *ho'oa'a*,
which meant "to develop roots."

Chris stood up straight and wiped her brow with the back of a
gloved hand. A warmth covered her body as the first rays of light came
up over the hill and, as if on cue, a wild rooster crowed. She smiled at
a memory and turned, shielding the glare with her hand so she could
enjoy the view.

She loved this house. God, did she love this house.

Light was streaming in through specifically crafted windows on the
master bedroom's eastern wall. It covered the floor and blanketed the
foot of the bed—just as Will had designed it to. He'd explained that as
the sun rose, your feet would get progressively warmer, so you'd wake
slowly. Naturally. Chris was usually up before that could happen. But
the design was still good. All his designs were good.

Using a hammer, Chris knocked the claw end of a crowbar under
a plank of the second-story balcony and then pushed down until the
wood began to shed flecks of mud-colored paint as it buckled. Flipping

the bar around to position the straight end, she pulled up until the final bit of leverage forced the wooden slat to separate from the supports with a splintering rip. She chucked the piece over the railing and a couple seconds later heard it join the others on the pile.

They'd been here fifteen—no, sixteen—years this spring. One point four acres that backed up to a small hillside covered in dense tropical vegetation with towering mountain peaks in the distance. They'd seen the listing in the local paper and decided to check it out on a whim. All it had taken was that first winding drive along the property line for them to decide that this was the one.

Of course, once they reached the house, they understood not only why it was in their price range but why no one else had snatched it up already. But it didn't matter. They'd made up their minds.

They were home.

The original house, if you could call it that, was a two-bedroom, one-bath. It wasn't exactly a fixer-upper—that would imply it had been livable to begin with. The first seven months Will and Chris had the place, they'd had to sleep in a tent in the backyard.

Just married. No kids yet. Young, stupid, and without a clue about just how painful and cruel life could be. For seven months, he planned and designed, and she demolished and built. For seven months, they slept on an inflatable mattress that occasionally deflated in the middle of the night in a tent that leaked in one corner when it rained. Their budget allowed for dinners of Top Ramen and peanut butter-and-jelly sandwiches, which they ate by candlelight while scratching at their ever-present mosquito bites. And every morning, no matter how tired they were, they were woken up at first light by the wild roosters.

It was the best seven months of their lives.

Over the years they dreamed and designed and built that house as they dreamed and designed and built a life together. The kitchen expansion happened the year Chris started her company. The second downstairs bedroom went in while Will was finishing up his master's degree. With a grunt, Chris pulled up on the crowbar and another plank separated from the original deck—the deck she'd finished while eight months pregnant.

The additions to their home were like hashes on a doorframe marking a child's height. The marks are what get noticed—but what matters is what happens in the spaces between them. The experiences in those spaces, the cards life deals you, *that* is what makes a house a home. That's what makes a marriage. That's what makes a family.

It's also what breaks them.

When she thinks back now to the day everything changed, it comes as snapshots. Still images in vibrant Technicolor as clear as the moment they happened.

The reflection in the rearview mirror of the girls in their car seats.

Matching pink swimsuits, purple Popsicle smiles.

Chris's own hands on the steering wheel.

The sun-faded public pool sign.

Annie sitting on a yellow striped towel.

Her little fingertips adjusting her goggles.

Chris's own hand holding on to Shannon's outstretched arm.

Bright white sunscreen smeared across pale, smooth skin.

A flash of pink to the left.

Shannon's parted lips, watching her big sister head for the water.

"Walk, Annie."

Those two words and the sound that followed haunted Chris every single night. From a deep sleep, her voice calls out—*Walk, Annie*—and a split second later her eyes snap open at the sound of Annie's head smacking against the pool deck. The exact same dream, every night, for six years. Heart pounding, Chris lay in her sweat-soaked T-shirt staring up at the ceiling fan, reliving what came next.

People like to say time heals all, but Chris knew anyone who says that has never had to bury their child. Healing never came to *ho'oa'a*. The best she and Will could manage was to cope, and they did so by staying busy. Busy raising a five-year-old who didn't fully understand where her sister had gone. Busy working. Busy jumping from one thing to the next, neither Will nor Chris standing still long enough to notice what was actually happening. That they were drifting apart. That they were fighting constantly. That everything they weren't saying was destroying their marriage.

On the morning of what should have been Annie's first day of sixth grade, she and Will were sitting at the kitchen table drinking coffee, not saying a word to one another, when it suddenly dawned on Chris that after Annie died, they'd stopped making changes to the house. It wasn't a conscious choice. She hadn't even noticed it. But suddenly, there at the kitchen table, Chris realized that they'd stopped working on the house for the same reason they'd stopped working on their marriage, which was the same reason they'd kept Annie's room exactly as it had been the day she'd walked out of it for the last time.

If they dealt with their marriage or changed the house or cleaned out Annie's room, they'd be moving forward. Which would mean they'd be leaving Annie behind. And neither of them was ready to do that.

A breeze kicked up, bringing with it a morning greeting from the plumerias. Chris breathed in deeply, relishing the creamy clove spiciness of the simple white flower with the bright yellow center. For anyone born and raised in Hawaii, the scent was a constant companion all your life. She'd worn one tucked behind her ear at their wedding. Plumerias had made up the graduation lei she'd placed around Will's neck. They'd filled the bouquets by her bedside at the hospital when both Annie and Shannon were born. And one rainy September morning, she'd dropped a handful into the ground and watched them land softly on a cruelly tiny coffin.

Last year, several months after they'd separated and Will had moved out, Chris decided the first step she'd take on her own should start there, at home. She designed a new wraparound lanai with a thin, wide-set metal railing through which the thicket of plumerias below would still be visible. That had been Annie's favorite part of the yard. She used to lie on her back and sing to herself while spinning the star-shaped flower in her fingers. So Chris wanted to build a place just for herself where the flower's scent could be with her while she watched the sun rise or set.

Chris heard a car and looked over to see Will's silver Volvo winding up the drive. Leaning the crowbar against the wall, she removed her gloves and wiped her hands on her cut-off jean shorts. Once she was inside the house, the crisp AC was an instant relief from the thick Hawaiian air, and before she went down to meet him, Chris stood there for a moment to cool off, take a few deep breaths, and center herself. She wondered how the next little bit would go. She prayed for Shannon's sake it would be smooth.

Will shut off the ignition and sat in the driveway listening to the engine settle.

He needed a second before he went in. Not always. Not usually. But today, yes.

The trip was proving more triggering than he'd expected. All week he'd had no appetite. He wasn't sleeping well. He couldn't focus. And his mind was fixed on Annie in a way it hadn't been in years.

He didn't want to, but he couldn't help it. Being home, seeing the plumerias peeking out from the side yard, it instantly brought him back to that day. Before he could stop it, every single moment began to play out in such vivid detail that it was like watching a movie of the worst day of his life projected onto the car's windshield in front of him.

The tires squealed as he parked crooked in the spot. Thrusting the car door open, he forgot to shut it before taking off at a dead sprint for the entrance to the public pool.

Chlorinated water dripped off kids with wet hair as they watched the backs of paramedics working from their knees. Their mothers pulled them out of the way by the shoulders, parting to let him through. No one had to say it to know it. It was obvious the panic-stricken man in the button-down shirt and leather shoes was the father.

Chris turned when he called out her name. Shannon let go of her hand and ran for her daddy. "WALK," he and Chris both screamed in unison, and the little girl froze in place, her eyes wide with terror, not understanding what was happening. He picked her up and clutched her to his chest as the paramedics rolled Annie's body by them. Will looked to where they'd just been, but all that was there now was a pair of goggles next to a puddle tinted red.

Chris went in the ambulance. Will and Shannon followed. "Daddy, it hurts," Shannon had said, pulling at the car seat harness with arms covered in splotches of bright white sunscreen that had never gotten rubbed in. Reluctantly, he loosened the straps.

The hospital was cold. Shannon, still in a little pink swimsuit, shivered as they hurried down the corridors. A vending machine hummed. Overhead, voices paged doctors. And as they turned a corner, Will stopped short. Standing at the other end of the hall was Chris.

He called her name. She turned. And he knew.

Will shook his head as though trying to wipe the memory away. He could feel his heart pounding in his chest, and he could feel every cell in his body screaming that this was a bad idea. They should stay home. He should drive off. They shouldn't take this flight.

Instead, he opened the car door.

As Chris made her way down the stairs, she heard Will trying to open the front door, but it was locked. She waited for the doorbell to ring, but instead heard keys jingling on the other side. Reaching the foyer, she unlocked and opened the door to find Will standing on the porch with keys outstretched in one hand, the other balancing two to-go coffee cups one on top of the other while he used his chin to hold them steady.

"Hi," he said.

"Hi—oh. Thanks," she replied with a tone of surprise, taking the coffee he held out and shutting the door behind him.

"They were out of almond milk," he said as they went to the kitchen.

"No, it's great, thanks."

"You see that For Sale sign in the Allens' yard?" Will asked.

"Yeah, she got a big job in LA. Wild, right?"

"They've been here longer than we have."

"Oh—before I forget. Your half of Shannon's tuition . . ."

"Shoot. I left the check on the counter."

"Okay, just bring it later . . . hey. Will. Look, I, uh . . ." she stammered, forgetting the order of the sentences she'd practiced. Gesturing for him to come closer, she lowered her voice to barely above a whisper. "I wanted to let you know something."

"Okay," he said after a beat.

"While Shannon's away, I'm going to pack up Annie's room."

Will just blinked at her.

"Saturday? Is when I'm thinking? You could help. If you want."

"That stuff is hers."

"I know—"

"And now it's ours."

"I know . . . and how long is it ours? It's been six years. How long do we keep that room a museum? Is Annie there? Can I go in that room and see my daughter? No. I cannot. Does it help me? Maybe at the beginning. But not anymore."

"It helps me."

"Well . . ." Chris searched for what to say. "Then take it to your place."

"She didn't live there. She lived here. This was her home. This is where her things belong."

"I thought you guys weren't going to fight today."

Will and Chris both startled as Shannon came in from the hall. "Hey, jelly bean," he said, trying to muster some enthusiasm.

"We're not fighting, sweetheart," Chris said.

"Which is what you always say when you're fighting."

Chris and Will exchanged looks.

"Can I just save us the hassle?" Shannon said, standing on tippy-toes to grab a bowl from the shelf. "Dad, you don't want me to go on this trip because you're afraid. Afraid something will happen. Afraid I'll get hurt. Mom, you're frustrated because you think he's being selfish. Prioritizing his own feelings over my need to have a life. Dad, you'll be distant and somehow make it all about you. Mom, you won't really listen or even try to see his viewpoint."

Her parents stared, dumbfounded.

"Where'd you get that from?" Will said.

"You," Shannon said, pouring cereal into the bowl. "These walls are crazy thin. You know I can hear you. Plus, c'mon. I'm eleven."

Will and Chris shared a glance.

"So anyway," Shannon continued, "I'll go on the trip. And in two weeks I'll come back. And since nothing will go wrong, we'll forget all about it—until the next thing comes up that you'll freak out over."

Her parents were not sure of what to say. Chris's phone started to buzz. She angled her head at the caller ID. "Sorry, sweetheart, hang on," she said, putting the phone to her ear as she left the room. "Feeny. What's up?"

Will leaned on the counter, watching Shannon shovel spoonfuls of cereal into her mouth. "I want you to have a life."

"Sure," she said through a mouthful. "If a team of Navy SEALs follows me around everywhere."

"You'd be okay with that?"

Shannon rolled her eyes.

"I'm kidding."

"No you're not."

"Yes, I am," Will replied.

"Prove it. Don't come with me today."

"We already went—"

"Dad. You can stay with me at the gate until the flight leaves. The camp has people to meet me at the gate in San Francisco—"

"Shannon—"

"Dad. *Listen.* I'd be alone for, like, a flight. Kids my age do it all the time. Kiana and her brother do it every summer."

"I'm aware kids do it all the time and that's up to their parents. *I'm* the parent here and you're not just some kid to me."

"But you're the one always saying I'm so mature for my age."

Will laughed. "Well, you are! But c'mon, Shan. You're eleven."

At that, Shannon scooted her chair back loudly and stormed out of the room just as Chris came back in.

"What happened?" Chris asked as they listened to Shannon stomp up the stairs.

"She acts like eleven is forty."

"To her it is."

Will laughed again. "Okay. Well. The tooth fairy came last week."

Chris gave him a look. "She's growing up."

"But she's not grown."

"I'm not saying she is. But she's not in pigtails."

Will shook his head with a look of indignation. "How am I always the bad guy?"

"She's nervous," Chris said.

"For the flight?"

"For camp."

"She said that?"

"I'm her mother. She doesn't have to."

"Oh, thank you for translating. I'm just the father."

Chris had several comebacks ready to fire, but the last thing Shannon needed was the two of them going at it. "If you're saying she's the kid here, then *you* be the adult."

Will didn't agree but he also didn't argue. Which Chris knew was as much as she'd get, so she headed for the stairs. "If you want to load up, her bag's in her room."

Chris's bedroom door was open and she could see Shannon sitting on the side of the bed. Chris took a seat beside her on what had been Will's side, when Will still slept there.

After Annie died, every night for nearly a whole year, they'd hear the little girl creep into their room in the middle of the night. Shannon learned quickly that if she went to Mom's side, she would be comforted—but ultimately taken back to her room. But if she went to Dad's side, he'd pick her up and put her in the bed, where she'd spend the rest of the night sleeping in between them. It didn't take long until Will was the only one being shaken awake to hear, *Daddy, I can't sleep.*

Mother and daughter sat together in silence. Chris just waited, letting Shannon come out with it on her own terms. When she finally did, the girl's voice was small and quiet.

"None of the other kids' parents are going with them. I'm going to be the weird kid."

"Hey, hey," Chris said, wrapping her arm around her little girl and pulling her in close. "You could never be the weird kid. Not possible." She rocked her in a way she hadn't in a long time, and Shannon let her do it. "Maybe they'll be jealous. Like, *Wow, she's got a bodyguard.*"

"Mom."

"I know, sweetheart. I know it's frustrating. You gotta understand your father, though. He means well. He just wants to make sure you're okay."

"How? He can't be with me every second. It just— It makes me feel . . . little. Like I'm not allowed to be big. He doesn't want me to be anything but how I was."

"You should tell him."

"I do!"

"Not like that. I've never heard you tell him like that. He's not a psychic. He needs to know how it makes you feel. You've got five hours on this flight. Use it. Talk to him."

Shannon didn't agree but she didn't argue, and Chris knew that was the best she'd get. Like father, like daughter; there were just as many ways they were similar as ways they were different.

"Mom . . . why doesn't he trust me?"

"Oh, sweetheart, he does. It's everything else he doesn't trust."

Both were quiet for a moment.

"Sometimes I wonder what it'd be like if it hadn't happened," Shannon said. "I know he misses her. But I do too. And I feel bad that it makes him hurt when I just, like, live my life. But I can't not grow up. It's not fair."

Chris felt an ache deep in her chest. It physically pained her to hear her daughter say what she herself had thought a million times. She knew that pain. She knew exactly what it felt like. She knew the frustration of feeling so helpless in so many ways.

"No. You're right. It's not fair."

Will threw Shannon's sequined backpack over one shoulder and rolled her suitcase out of her room—but stopped short as he left.

Across the hall, the door was ajar.

The hinges squeaked as he opened the door the rest of the way. Standing at the threshold, Will was unsure if he wanted to go any further, so he just looked in. The bed was made with the pink comforter smoothed flat. The flimsy plastic desk chair was pushed in against the desk. The glow-in-the-dark stars stuck to the ceiling were soaking up the sunlight streaming in through the blinds. Will wondered if after all these years they still lit up at night.

Will set the backpack down and walked to the center of the room, aware that his steps were slower. Lighter. A fine layer of dust covered everything. The third-place trophy for the twenty-five-meter back-stroke. The glittery, colorful bottles of lotion and body splash. The handmade Popsicle-stick picture frame that held a photo of Annie he'd taken that time they'd gone camping. The one where she was laughing so hard her eyes were shut. The one where marshmallows and chocolate covered her face. He couldn't help but smile back.

Will's chest ached, and he fought the urge to climb into the bed and hold the unicorn pillow tight against himself, as though it might help ease the pain. He knew it wouldn't. He'd tried it before.

The sound of footsteps coming down the stairs brought him back to the present. Will picked up the backpack and exited the room, leaving the door open as he left.

Chris hugged Shannon from the stairs' first step, which made the girl's head come to rest on her stomach. Chris knew it wasn't real, but just for that moment, it felt like Shannon was smaller. Younger. Like time had done what she'd asked for once. Lingering in the impossible wasn't fair to Shannon, no matter how badly she wanted to, so Chris squeezed her little girl tight, her little eleven-year-old adult, and then, fighting against every urge in her body, let her go.

"Check in every night. Unless you're busy having fun. Then still check in every night."

"Mom."

Chris winked. "Just a text. At least give me that."

"Rock and roll, jelly bean," Will said, coming into the foyer with her stuff.

"You'll do great," Chris said, watching Shannon put on her back-pack. "Two weeks will fly by. I love you."

"Love you, too, Mom."

Shannon turned and stepped out onto the front porch, and Chris's mask faltered. For a split second, all the pain and all the fear bubbled to the surface. And in that split second, Will was watching.

The two held each other's gaze, at eye level from her position on the stairs, and for a brief moment, they were back to before. She felt the urge to reach out, to touch him, and she thought maybe his arm moved as though he felt the same. But neither of them did. He looked away first, joining Shannon on the porch.

"Fly safe," Chris said, watching them go.

Will stopped at the bottom of the steps. "Saturday? That's when you're thinking of doing this?" Chris nodded. He shook his head and continued down the drive.

"Will—"

He turned back. Chris motioned to Shannon. "She's capable of more than you think."

"I know she is. That's what scares me."

12:17 p.m.

16 minutes after impact

Approximately 6.5 hours of oxygen inside plane

CHAPTER SEVEN

FITZ HUNG OUT THE SIDE OF THE HH-65, LOOKING LIKE A COAST GUARD RECRUITING poster.

Six foot two. Dark brown eyes. Dark brown skin. Clean-shaven head with a thin mustache lining his upper lip. District 14 commander Jackie "Fitz" Fitzgerald was egoless confidence incarnate.

But Fitz had never faced something like this.

The tropical paradise had turned into a war zone. Smoke and the stench of jet fuel filled the air. Hazards and debris covered the water's surface. Fitz peered down on a disaster more chaotic than anything he could have ever imagined, and his stomach dropped.

The task in front of them wasn't going to be difficult.

It bordered on impossible.

"Tanner," Fitz said, hearing his own voice in the noise-canceling headset.

"Sir," came Mikey Tanner's voice.

Fitz looked to the two other hovering choppers full of rescue swimmers and found Tanner, the dive officer supervisor of the Regional Dive Locker Pacific.

"Bring 'em up," Fitz said.

The choppers nosed down and headed straight for the worst of it.

———

"US Coast Guard District Fourteen to all available boats. Anyone willing and able to assist with survivor recovery of a ditched commercial aircraft, report to the southwestern coast of Molokai. Over."

When the call had gone out over channel 16, some thirty seconds of silence passed before a boat asked for exact coordinates.

"Just come. You'll see it," another boat had replied.

And so they came.

Commercial fishermen. Private sailboats. Tourist catamarans. Dive boats. Fishing charters. They put their work, vacations, and honeymoons on hold. They didn't have rescue training. These weren't professionals. They were just people wanting to help.

The first craft on the scene was an eighteen-foot recreational speedboat. The two-man crew motored straight for the first survivor they saw. They circled around, cut the engine, and let the wind drift them toward the man in the water . . . and then repeated the maneuver three times before they got close enough.

This was the open ocean. Even on a glass day, the currents were fierce. And every minute, as the wind picked up, the sea state became more volatile.

The rescuers scrambled to the transom at the back of the boat. Grabbing the man in the water by the arms, they pulled him in.

It wasn't easy. It wasn't pretty. But the first survivor of Flight 1421 was out of the water.

As the boats continued to arrive, the tactic was clear: start far out, work your way in, pick up the stragglers. Every person saved was a victory. But even so, it was impossible for the volunteer rescuers to ignore the screams of the passengers they *couldn't* reach inside the flames. As they fought against the billowing black smoke and heat radiating off the fire, the truth was painfully obvious: there was hardly anyone in the water to save.

Most of the passengers from the plane were trapped inside the fire or already gone.

A young family in a sailboat threw a survival ring to a woman, but she made no attempt to grab it. The father dove in after her, taking the woman by the life vest and pulling her over to the ring. He tried to rouse her, but she only stared back vacantly. Tucking her arms around the floating ring, he noticed the bloody gashes that covered her body. The husband gave a thumbs-up and his wife and children pulled her to safety.

A massive tourist catamaran dropped anchor and became the de facto muster point. Crafts that could maneuver more easily started bringing her the survivors they already had on board, transferring them to the bigger ship, then going back for more. The mesh netting that usually held sunbathing tourists was turned into a medical triage station as the catamaran's crew began administering first aid.

Of the few who had survived, most needed far more than a basic first aid kit could provide. All of them were badly burned. The rest floated facedown in the water, already gone. A dive boat assumed the unenviable job of victim recovery. The divers' long fins helped in dragging the bodies to the boats.

The survivors were already shivering—the first sign of hypothermia. But this was Hawaii. There were no blankets on board. So the vacationers wrapped beach towels around their shoulders and rubbed their arms while others passed out water bottles and snacks. Everyone tried to do something. Anything. They were doing the best they could. But the desperate pleas from inside the wall of flames told them that it wasn't good enough.

Tanner's helicopter hovered over the worst of it.

He had thought they knew what they were heading into. But now that they were on site, the entire mission bordered on no-go.

The conditions were deteriorating by the minute as the fire continued to spread. Thick black smoke obscured their vision, and the wind made the smoke unpredictable. Just when they'd find a point of entry, the wind would shift, forcing the helicopter to evade. They'd get another opening, they'd start to lower down—only to have the propeller's downwash fan the flames, making them even larger.

Fire dotted the surface. The water moved, the fuel slicks moved. The flames moved, the passengers moved, the smoke moved, the helicopters moved. Nothing was stationary. People were treading water. Dead bodies drifted aimlessly. Tanner watched as one of them bobbed into a section of fire, then was gone.

The smoke shifted and a yellow slide raft appeared in the middle of the debris field. Passengers on board the raft leaned over the side, using their hands as oars to move away from the approaching fire, but the wind kept pushing them toward it.

All it would take was one strong gust, and the raft would go up in flames.

"We're going for the raft," Tanner said to the other helicopter. "Start grabbing the solos."

Fitz watched through binoculars.

Spotting survivors was nearly impossible. Luggage. Plane parts. Victims. Everything looked like something and nothing, and going after a dead end would waste time they didn't have.

Fitz swept the area slowly, then—

"Unit bravo. Your three o'clock," he said, not taking his eyes off the passenger in the water. "Female. Solo. Yellow vest, green shirt. She's using a suitcase for flotation."

There was a pause on the radio. Then, "Affirmative."

Like the claw in a toy claw machine, a rescue basket dropped from unit bravo. A Coast Guard rescue swimmer sat inside, leaning back against the orange foam cylinders that lined the stainless-steel frame. The basket hit the water with a splash but remained buoyant as the coastguardsman scrambled into the water, heading for the woman in a green shirt clinging to a floating suitcase.

Hanging on to the basket with one hand, the diver fought against the waves. He got her into the basket and gave a thumbs-up. The basket began to rise. The woman's arms shook as she gripped the metal bars. She was not even halfway up when the winds shifted, trapping the woman and the helicopter in a column of smoke.

The pilot choked, jerking the control stick involuntarily. The chopper dropped and dipped to the right. The basket slammed back into the water. Regaining control, the pilot righted the chopper, dodging out of the plume, lifting the basket back into the sky.

The woman gasped for air as she hovered just over the water's surface. A large swell rose up over her. The woman's head slammed against the metal frame as the wave tossed her forward and nearly out. The cable snapped taut and the woman was jerked across to the other side. The chopper pulled up and the basket lifted clear of the water, swinging violently through the air like a pendulum. As the rescuers finally began to reel the basket up, the woman lay prostrate, weeping and vomiting salt water into the ocean below.

Tanner's chopper maneuvered around the smoke until they found a window. Hovering as closely as possible, the rescuers dropped a tow line to the inflatable slide raft below. The passengers reached up to grab it—but the line was unsteady in the wind and the raft was unsteady in the waves.

One of the men stood on the wobbly inflated surface while other passengers held his legs. The cable was nearly at his fingertips. He rose up the final inch—just as a wave hit the side of the raft, knocking the man overboard. The others were struggling to pull him back in when a large swell came up the other side, blasting square into the raft.

It was exactly what Tanner had feared. The raft drifted backward. The fire took it.

Several of the passengers dove forward into the water and tried to swim away. A woman stood to follow but lost her balance and fell backward instead. Her body hit the water with a fiery splash just as another pair of arms, covered in flames, grabbed at the top of the raft.

"Drop me down," Tanner said, fighting to be heard over the spinning propeller. He snapped his harness into the hoist. "I'll drag the raft out—"

Just then, the heat melted the plastic and the raft burst. The rush of oxygen fueled the fire, and orange flames shot high into the air, mushrooming in a puff of black smoke. As the raft quickly deflated, the few passengers still clinging to it sank into the water.

"I can still—"

Before Tanner could finish, the wind caught the lip of the raft that still had air and flipped the whole thing over, tossing everyone into the fire and trapping them underneath.

Tanner punched the inside of the chopper. "Give 'em a chance!"

The raft had been holding twenty-five people. Only two were left to save.

Tanner unhooked his harness and motioned for the rescue basket. He slid on his mask and got inside, gave a thumbs-up, and was lowered from the chopper into the mayhem.

As he approached the water, the heat grew intense. Condensation began to build up inside his mask. He couldn't see a thing. Tanner ripped it off, spit into it, and rubbed the saliva into the plastic lens. As he adjusted his mask, he watched one of the two passengers drift into the flames and out of sight.

That left only one potential survivor.

The man was wearing an orange life vest. Everyone else's was yellow. As the basket splashed down into the water, he began a feeble attempt to swim over. The man's strokes were weak and his legs didn't kick at all. Tanner slipped over the side of the basket and swam toward him as the chopper adjusted with him.

"Put your hand here. Roll in," Tanner hollered.

The man moaned a response and placed his hand where Tanner pointed. Tanner grabbed his legs to help hoist him in and the man cried out like a wounded animal. As he flopped into the basket, Tanner understood why. The man's legs were covered in burns so deep the muscle and tendons were exposed. Tanner was shocked he was still alive.

The man lay flat on his back, taking up nearly the whole basket. Tanner hopped in and gave a thumbs-up. The basket began to rise. Tanner could feel the heat of the encroaching flames behind him as the man mumbled and tried to grab him.

"Don't move," Tanner said. "We're going to get you help."

But the man wouldn't stop. He rambled incoherently. Something about a little girl, something about his crew. The guy was in shock and he was becoming increasingly agitated. His face was bright red. His chest heaved. Tanner knew that cardiac arrest was a real possibility.

"Ed," Tanner said, reading the name bar on the uniform. "You need to stay calm—"

"No!" Ed screamed. "You have to listen!"

Fitz's helicopter hovered high above.

"Sir?" came the pilot's voice through his headphones. "*Redwood* and *Oliver Feast* are on site."

Fitz swiveled until he found the two approaching ships. The USCG fast-response cutters would serve as field medical triage for those so severely injured that even Honolulu was too far.

They would also serve as temporary morgues.

"*Angelica*?" Fitz asked.

"ETA ten minutes," the pilot said. The larger, slower, Legend-class cutter USCG *Angelica* would serve as the on-scene command center. Fitz told the pilot to circle one more time, then take them to the *Angelica*.

"Drop us. Refuel. Come back for survivors."

The pilot affirmed Fitz's order and the chopper began a final loop around the debris field.

Fitz looked across the chopper to Steve Milton, his second-in-command. They'd been through a lot together over the years. But nothing had ever left Milton with that grave a look on his face. Fitz assumed he looked similar.

Fitz pulled the plane's manifest out of his pocket and studied the list of names.

Mary was someone's daughter. Alfonso was someone's son. Nathanial was someone's neighbor. Xiang was someone's best friend. Colleen was someone's mother. He pored over the names and then focused on the number he'd written and circled at the top. Ninety-nine.

Ninety-nine people were on that plane. Ninety-nine people had gone into the water. Every action today would be in service of one goal and one goal only: get as many passengers as possible home to their families.

But as Fitz looked at the carnage below, he feared how low the number might actually be.

"Sir!" said a voice through the headphones. "We registered an ELT ping. We've located the plane."

"Roger. We need to—"

Suddenly, Tanner's voice broke in over the radio.

Fitz listened, looking up at Milton. Neither could believe what the diver was saying.

"Tanner," Fitz said, pulling the mic close to his mouth. "The plane's gone. It sank. I don't think I heard you ri—"

"Sir, there are survivors, still alive, inside that plane."

No. It wasn't possible. Even if it was, even if there had been people alive inside that plane when it went down, they surely weren't now. No one would survive that.

But.

If they had. If it was true. If there were actually people down there to rescue . . . then this had just become something else entirely.

CHAPTER EIGHT

CHRIS COULDN'T SEE A THING BEYOND RISING BUBBLES AND BRIGHT LIGHT.

She didn't need to.

See like the blind man.

She ran her fingers along the bead of fused metal and knew the weld was perfect. Just as her mother had taught her. Just as she would teach Shannon.

Chris released her grip, and the light from the burning electrodes at the end of the stinger went dark.

"Cold."

There was a second's delay for her comms to be received on the ship. After her tender Noah Murphy had gotten the message and flipped the knife switch to cut the power, the subtle buzz of electricity coursing through the stinger in her hand went still. Chris flipped the tinted welding screen on the front of her helmet up to double-check her work. It was, as expected, perfect.

"So—"

"Feeny. Drop it," Chris said, her own voice a metallic echo in her industrial dive suit.

"I just want to understand," Feeny said.

Peter Feeny floated beside her, scratching his barrel chest through his wetsuit out of pure habit. She'd seen him do it a million times. In the parking lot of that dive bar the night they first met. At work as they wriggled into their wetsuits. Before he walked her down the aisle at her wedding, and then when he took his place beside Will as the best man. At the hospital when he declared himself Annie's godfather while holding a newborn Annie for the first time.

"So Willy flew all the way to San Francisco just to drop Shannon off to then turn around and fly all the way back—tonight—by himself," Feeny said.

"Yup," Chris said.

". . . Why?"

Chris stopped assessing the ship's hull and gave Feeny a look.

Will was why. They both knew that.

The pair transitioned to the next portion of corroded metal, careful to sweep their umbilical cables to avoid entanglements. The thick braid of rubber-coated cables connected their suits to the ship, supplying them with not only power for their tools but air.

"How does Shannon feel about—"

"Feeny. Look around." Chris paused. "What's there?"

"Water?"

Chris held up her stinger. "What's in here?"

"Electricity."

"Are we doing, quite literally, the most dangerous job on the planet?"

"We are."

"So is now a good time to talk about my soon-to-be ex-husband?"

The two floated in weightless suspension for some time with neither saying anything.

"That was rhetorical, right?" Feeny asked.

Chris flipped her helmet's welding screen down.

Focusing back on the ship, she adjusted her grip on the stinger.

"Hot."

She waited for Noah to turn on the power—but the familiar pulse of electricity didn't come.

"Hot," Chris repeated.

She waited. No response. Feeny shrugged.

"Noah, electricity is an important part of the process. Flip the knife switch."

More silence.

"Topside, you read?" Chris said. "Is comms—"

"Sorry. I'm here," came Noah's voice in a rush of words. "We've been scrapped."

"Again?" Chris said. Now she was pissed. "This is our third reschedule."

"I know, but—" Noah said. "Look, just come up."

"No. I'm not losing another whole day. We're *in* the water."

"Chris—"

"Goddamn government gigs—"

"Chris, *stop*," Noah said, cutting off his boss. "Things just got bigger than us."

Chris and Feeny exchanged a look, then started for the surface.

The dive was shallow enough that they could rise slowly without needing to take a safety stop. As they headed for the surface with slow, deliberate kicks, the underwater world transitioned from a deep, dark navy to a brilliant sapphire, which then faded into turquoise. The undulations of the waves made streaks of sunlight dance across their dive suits. It was calm and quiet.

Then they broke the surface.

Chris winced, forcing her eyes open against the bright midday sun so she could take in the two enormous helicopters screaming by overhead. Painted bright orange with the USCG insignia, the thwack of their propellers was so close she could feel the vibrations in her chest.

As she and Feeny bobbed next to the gargantuan hull of the nuclear-powered, 101,000-ton Nimitz-class aircraft carrier, watching the choppers head out, Chris suddenly felt very, very small.

On deck of the USS *Theodore Roosevelt*, water pooled at Chris and Feeny's feet as their partners helped them out of their gear.

They were a small crew. Chris. Feeny. Noah Murphy was the new kid. Sayid Raval was the next most senior and he'd been with the company for twelve years. That's the thing about families. Once you're in, it's hard to leave. And Chris had always run the company more like a family than a business.

Sayid unbuckled the chrome-plated brass fittings on Chris's diving helmet and dropped the sixty-pound fiberglass shell forward.

"We at war?" Chris asked, sliding her head free.

"Don't know," Sayid said. "An alarm sounded and everyone just kinda took off."

Chris looked around the deck. The slowest any of the Navy sailors were moving was a jog. There was an organization to the frenzy, but it was still a frenzy.

"Did you ask?"

"No one will stop," said Noah.

A young sailor came hustling by, brushing past them. Chris could just make out the white embroidered name bar on his dark blue coveralls.

"Rogers," Chris barked. The young man hesitated, then jogged over. "What's going on?"

"You mean with the MRO, ma'am?"

"The what?" Chris said, registering his confusion at why she didn't know what that was. "We're civilian contract. Industrial divers."

"MRO. Mass rescue operation," Rogers said, sliding the glasses up his nose.

Sayid cut in. "Isn't maritime search and rescue Coast Guard jurisdiction?"

"It is," Rogers said, walking away. "But if it's big enough, the Navy assists. I have to—"

"But what happened?" Noah called out.

Rogers talked as he walked backward. "Commercial aircraft ditching."

Chris felt the blood drain from her face. In an instant she was back at the hospital, staring down the hallway at Will and a five-year-old Shannon.

Walk, Annie.

"What airline?" Chris hollered.

"Coastal," Rogers said over his shoulder.

"Was it Flight fourteen twenty-one?"

The rawness in her voice made the young sailor stop dead in his tracks. He turned, and Chris saw in his eyes what she already knew.

CHAPTER NINE

WILL STARED AT THE WATER-FILLED CABIN, WONDERING TWO THINGS.

What happened . . .

. . . what now?

The plane had been sinking. Everyone had thought this was it, they were done for. Then the water had stopped rising and no one had known what to think. Then out of nowhere—*BAM*—the plane had slammed into something. It was loud. Violent. Everyone thought, *This is the end.*

But as the seconds ticked on, they realized the plane was still sealed and the air pocket was still intact. Somehow, they were still alive.

Now the entire front portion of the cabin was fully submerged. In the back, only the galley was completely dry. The waterline cut across the plane's interior at a sloping angle: in the last four rows the water was only ankle deep, but moving forward, the water was up to the overhead bins by midcabin.

Will patted his pockets, finding his pen. Biting the cap off, he squatted in front of the lav and started scribbling on the wall. *If the angle of the waterline rises to—*

"How?" Kaholo asked.

"Kaholo. Stop," Kit snapped. "I don't know. I have no idea."

It was the fifth time he'd said it, and each time, no one had answered. No one knew how they were still alive.

Kaholo looked at her with a hint of surprise, as though he hadn't realized he'd been talking out loud. That confused stupor was a common look among the passengers, Kit realized, and it triggered a random memory of an article she'd once read.

A group of backcountry skiers had been stranded on a mountain-side by an avalanche. Six skiers had survived the avalanche itself. All six had extensive training and experience in outdoor survival. Of those six, only two survived.

Kit had read the article because she'd wanted to know what those two had done differently from the rest. According to the survivors, they'd assigned each other easy and specific tasks to do for one another. The jobs had not only given them a purpose, but it meant someone else was counting on them. It seemed silly now, they'd said after the fact. But that was what had made the difference.

Kit raised her hands to get everyone's attention. "Listen up. We need to get a little organized. Ma'am, you're a . . ."

Bernadette nodded. "Nurse."

"That's great. Anyone else a nurse or doctor? EMT? Firefighter?"

No one else spoke up.

"Okay. We're lucky we got you. Could you give everyone a quick once-over? Start with him, please." Kit motioned to Kaholo. He'd taken his uniform tie off and wrapped it around his fingers, but the blood had already soaked through.

Kit turned to Jasmine. "And could you maybe—"

Jasmine shook her head. "I'm a bartender."

"Well. I'm sure we'll need your services, too. But could you assist—"

Kit stared at the nurse and realized she didn't know her name. She didn't know any of their names. She'd almost died with them, still might, and yet she didn't know anything about them.

"Bernadette," the woman offered.

"Bernadette. Nurse," Kit said. "And . . ." She extended a hand.

"Jasmine . . . bartender?"

Will was directly to her right, squatting with his back leaned up against the outside wall of the lav, not paying attention. He looked up to see Kit waiting expectantly.

"Ah, Will," he said, standing. "I'm—"

"An asshole," Andy said.

"The reason we're at the bottom of the ocean," Ira added. Ruth swatted his arm.

"The reason we're still alive," Will shot back.

The three men sparred a few rounds before Kit was able to quiet everyone back down and continue assigning jobs. After Bernadette took care of his hand, Kaholo was to gather and organize as much emergency equipment as he could find. Portable oxygen bottles. Flashlights. Extra life vests. First aid kits. Andy, the medical device salesman from San Jose, and Ryan, the finance guy, were to go through the overhead bins and passenger luggage to see if there was anything of use. Dry clothes would be especially needed. Molly was tasked with getting everyone fed and hydrated.

"The water's warm enough and our space is small and humid," Kit said. "But hypothermia's still possible. Try to stay dry. If your clothes are wet, change. And I don't care if you're not hungry or thirsty—everyone needs to eat and drink something."

Ira and Ruth, the seventy-eight-year-olds from Long Island, were to help Molly with the food, to which Ira muttered something about being put on KP duty for the first time since Saigon in '63.

After all that, there were only the children.

Kit knew they were complete strangers, and yet, the two little girls stood side by side holding hands. She hoped the bickering adults noticed.

Kit took out her phone and was relieved to see the screen light up. She squatted down in front of the girls.

"Maia. Shannon. You two have a very important job. You are the official historians," the pilot said. "Once we're out of here, we're going to want pictures and videos of it all. It's up to you two to document everything."

Kit held out her phone and gave them the code to unlock it. Shannon took it with a solemn nod and the two huddled over the device.

"And I hope," Kit said in a hushed tone to Will, "you're doing something useful with this vandalization of company property."

"Put it on my tab." Will tapped the wall with the pen. "So there's the size of the air pocket. The number of bodies. The bodies' approximate BMI and rate of metabolism—"

"You're figuring out how long we have air to breathe."

Will tilted his head. "Six? Maybe? But probably closer to five. Rough estimates, but yeah."

Kit swore under her breath. Five hours to organize and execute a massively complex rescue mission.

"But it's not just oxygen I'm worried about," Will said. "The real issue is a buildup of carbon dioxide. We'll suffer CO_2 poisoning long before we run out of air. Did I hear you say oxygen bottles?"

"Yeah, Kaholo's collecting them."

"Good. We're going to need them."

Across the plane, Andy and Ryan were pulling bags down from the overhead bins that weren't submerged. They separated the clothing into two piles—adult and children—and made a third pile for anything that might be useful. A lighter. A mirror. A camera tripod. A plastic lei. A tennis racket. Tweezers. Reading glasses.

Ryan was going through a shoulder bag when he froze, staring down at a clip-on reading light as a powerful wave of grief washed over him.

Every night, long after they'd gone to bed, he'd wake to find Jenny still up reading. He'd squint into the little reading light, wrap his arm around her waist, tell her she'd be sorry in the morning, then fall back asleep. In the morning, the alarm would go off and Jenny would groan, then complain about how tired she was, and he'd laugh and say, *I told you so*. It happened every single night and every single morning.

But it would never happen again. She was gone. Forever.

Andy stopped rifling through an open suitcase on the seat in front of him.

"Do they know we need to be rescued?"

Ryan looked up. "What do you mean?"

Andy turned toward the galley. "Hey. They're coming for us, right?"

Only Will could see Kit roll her eyes. "Andy. I already said. They know exactly where the plane went down—"

"No shit," Andy said. "I mean, do they know *we're* down *here?*"

Kit and Will looked at each other.

"We need communication," Will said.

CHAPTER TEN

FITZ'S FEET HIT THE DECK OF THE USCG *ANGELICA* AT THE SAME MOMENT AS THE helicopter's wheels. A coastguardsman ran up, holding on to his hat as he ducked under the rotor wash.

"They're ready for you, sir," the young man yelled over the noise. "We've set up in th—"

"Tell me about the location of the plane," Fitz interrupted.

"We registered the ELT ping. Informed you. Since then, all movement ceased."

Fitz stopped. "The plane's stationary?"

"Yes, sir."

Fitz stared at Milton. Both knew there were relatively shallow channels between all the islands in the Hawaiian archipelago. Some less than a thousand feet. Could there actually be a chance that the plane had come to rest shallow enough that the pressure or temperature or depth wouldn't mean a guaranteed death sentence?

"Would you say less than ten miles off Molokai?" Fitz asked.

"Just about," Milton said. "Be curious to see what's under the water there."

Fitz went through the door Milton held open, telling the coastguardsman that he wanted all the information they had, and he wanted it *now*. The coastguardsman struggled to keep up with the men as they made for the ship's interior while Fitz gave orders over his shoulder. Deploy the ROV with side-scan sonar support to the plane. Use the GoPro video recording system, ultra-short-baseline wavelength transponder, and Hypack navigation and differential GPS to monitor and record the ROV's position on the seafloor.

"I want to know the second you have eyes on that plane," Fitz said. "We need to know if there are any signs of life inside."

Having changed out of their wetsuits, Chris and the team huddled around a phone in the locker room, watching the developing news coverage.

Tourists in a nearby Hawaiian sightseeing helicopter had captured the crash, and news stations were replaying the videos posted to social media on a loop. Aerial shots of the fire. Yellow life vests on the water. The dramatic sinking of the plane itself. Chris scoured each shot, desperate for a glimpse of Shannon or Will. But neither appeared.

Chris was numb. Until she knew anything for sure, she would force herself to shut everything out and just keep going. Shannon needed her. She was counting on her. Crumbling wasn't an option.

"Look," Sayid said. A group of sailors across the locker room suddenly left in a hurry. Chris pocketed the phone and they followed. As the team jogged to the door, Chris scavenged from a pile of personal effects left behind.

"Here," Chris said, tossing a navy windbreaker to Feeny.

"What for?" Feeny said.

Chris glanced down at his brown vintage T-shirt with the yellow writing that declared, I MAY NOT BE PERFECT, BUT PARTS OF ME ARE EXCELLENT.

"If they find out our connection to the plane, we're gone," Chris said, pulling a navy blue ball cap down low over her long, wavy brown hair. "Be subtle. Background. Just disappear."

Chris quietly opened the door and slipped into the room, followed by the rest of her crew. A meeting was already in progress. Everyone's attention was focused forward on the large TV screen displaying the video conference call. No one noticed them in the back of the room.

"—need us to do."

Chris had met the woman speaking before—Navy Fleet Master Chief Patricia Larson—and her initial impression was that Larson was the kind of person who held her cards close to the vest. Larson was running point in the room. The man on the screen, Chris didn't know.

"Appreciated," he said in a deep baritone. The man radiated *capable*. "Unfortunately, our efforts on the surface are nearly over."

"How many?" Larson asked.

"So far, we think less than ten," the man on the screen said. The room murmured in disbelief. "We don't have firm numbers yet. But by the time we could get there, it was practically over. We're looking at a profound number of fatalities."

Chris felt her legs go weak. Feeny put steadying hands on her shoulders. The news coverage hadn't had specifics. Up until that moment, she'd had no idea what kind of scenario they were actually looking at. The man on the screen cleared his throat.

"But," he said, pausing. "There might be survivors still inside the plane."

"The plane?" Larson asked.

"We have credible intel that it sank with some passengers still inside."

Chris didn't take her eyes off the man. She listened to him describe all the assets they'd already deployed underwater and the intel that would soon return. She took in every detail, making mental notes, already planning. By the time Fitz—apparently that was his name—was finished bringing the room up-to-date, Chris had made a vow.

If there were people still alive inside that plane, they *would* survive the day.

"Until we see exactly what we're dealing with," Fitz said, "*no* plan is *the* plan. The main question is, are there survivors inside the plane? If there aren't, I'm not rushing a high-risk operation for vessel salvage or body recovery. But if there *are* people, alive, trapped inside . . ." He shook his head. "We're going to have to get real creative, real fast. I think we're looking at the SRDRS."

"Agreed," Larson said.

The two started talking about things that went over Chris and her team's head. Noah immediately got out his phone, and moments later they were huddled up getting a Google crash course as fast as they could.

The SRDRS—Submarine Rescue Diving and Recompression System—was a unique jewel of the Navy's resources. The multicomponent system was a state-of-the-art engineering marvel designed to do one thing and one thing only: rescue submariners from a sunken sub. The component of the system they would use today was the pressurized rescue module—the PRM.

Or, as it was more commonly called, the Falcon.

The Falcon was a remotely operated rescue vehicle that docked and mated with the distressed sub. Once it attached, a hatch on the submarine was opened, and the submariners could climb up and inside the rescue module. With everyone aboard, the hatch on the Falcon would close, and the rescue vessel would detach and then ascend to the surface with the submariners inside.

"We need to adjust our mental framework, here," Fitz said. "It's not a plane. Not anymore. It was a plane when it was in the air. Once it hit the water, it became a ship. Now? Submerged? We need to think of it as a submarine. The Falcon is the safest and most efficient way to get people out alive. Truthfully, it's our only viable option."

Larson agreed. "The biggest consideration will be the differences in mating it to a plane and not a sub. But we'll figure it out. Hansen," she said as a young man jogged over. "Prepare the VOO for immediate launch. Call the . . ."

Larson trailed off, her attention turning to someone else. In the silence, Chris looked up from the phone. From the back of the room she could hear a voice but couldn't make out what they were saying. Larson listened, at first disbelievingly, then her demeanor became frustrated.

"Did you hear that?" Larson said to Fitz. He hadn't, and Larson scooted to the side so the camera could catch a young man with mousy brown hair and glasses who stepped forward.

"Say it again," Larson said.

"Petty Officer Third Class Danny Rogers, sir," said Rogers, raising his hand at the camera. "I was just say—"

"Quicker," Larson snapped.

"It's broken. Sir," Rogers rushed out, pushing the glasses up his nose. "The Falcon. She's broken. We used her last month in a training exercise and the pump in the transfer skirt—the, ah, part that removes the water from the docking point so that people can climb—"

"He knows what the transfer skirt is," Larson interrupted.

"Okay, then that . . . it broke," Rogers said.

Fitz took a second to absorb the information. "And without the pump, there's no way to attach it to the distressed vessel."

Rogers nodded. "Correct. Sir. The pump doesn't just remove the water between the two vessels. It creates a suction that attaches them together. It acts like a . . . a . . ."

"Plunger," Fitz said.

"Exactly. Since the Falcon is a rigid structure, you need the pump. But it's—"

"Broken," Fitz said. "So replacement parts would—"

Rogers shook his head. "It's a unique piece of equipment. None of its parts are universal. And every bit of it is manufactured by a company in Maryland. We put the work order in last month, but they've had supply chain issues for other parts that make those parts. So they don't have the parts to make the parts to, ah, well, fix the parts."

Fitz ran a hand down his face. "How'd this happen, Larson?"

"If I may, sir," Rogers offered. "We only have one SRDRS in the whole of the United States military and since its inception in 2008 it's only been put into use once. It's not exactly a high priority for the Navy. Especially because there's a redundancy."

"Good," Fitz said. "Talk to me about redundancies."

"Several NATO countries have their own versions of rescue systems like ours that can be rapidly deployed and flown anywhere around the world in seventy-two hours—"

"Three days? These people might not have three hours."

Rogers's mouth moved, but nothing came out. Larson thanked him, and he walked back to the side of the room.

"Then that's that," Fitz said. "Let's move on. We—"

"I can make it work."

Every head turned to Chris at the back of the room.

"Be subtle," Feeny muttered under his breath. "Background. Just disappear."

On the screen, Fitz craned for a look. "Identify, sailor."

"Chris Kent," Chris said, stepping forward. "I can figure out a way to make it work without the pump." She paused. "Sir."

By now Fitz, and everyone else, could tell Chris was no sailor.

"Larson, who is—"

"We had routine hull maintenance scheduled for today," Larson said. "She's a civilian contracted industrial diver."

"But why is she in the room?" Fitz asked.

"I'm qualified and vetted," Chris cut in before Larson could ask her the same thing. "The government wouldn't let me aboard if not."

"You're there to repair ships," Fitz said, growing impatient. "Not this."

"I can modify the Falcon. I can make it work."

"Ma'am, we don't just modify billion-dollar pieces of equipment."

"Is the price tag supposed to intimidate me? It's a machine in the water. It's what we do."

The room bristled at the disrespect.

"Look, Ms. Kent—" But Fitz cut himself off, his mind seeming to go elsewhere.

"No, you look," Chris said, watching him unfold a piece of paper and study it. Her voice rose as she lost her patience, too. "We don't have time to argue. We need to figure out how—"

"Shannon Kent. Will Kent."

Chris's breath caught, hearing their names in his mouth. The two stared at each other for a moment before Chris said simply, "Yes. My daughter. My husband."

The only sound in the room was the hum of the lights.

Feeny leaned over to Sayid. "I'll get the coats, meet you at the car."

Chris studied Fitz's face for any indication that he knew where they were, or if they were okay, or . . .

"Ma'am," Fitz said. His voice had lost its edge. "You shouldn't be here. You should be with the other families."

"Why?" Chris asked. "To wait for an update? From here?"

"Ma'am—"

"Can you tell me where my family is?"

Chris held her breath, knowing the next words out of his mouth had the potential to end her. That paper he had, was it a casualty list? Were those the names of passengers taken to the hospital? Were Shannon and Will on a list of survivors? Her heart pounded while she waited.

Fitz hesitated, then finally said, "No. I don't have their status."

Chris exhaled. "Then as long as that's your answer, I'm staying here. You already said it. If they were on the surface, they're gone." Chris's voice wavered, just for a split second. She cleared her throat. "And if they're at the hospital, then, hey, I'm not a doctor. I can't do anything there, either. But *here*. Now. I can actually *do* something."

"What if they're not in the plane?" Larson asked.

"Whoever's down there, it's someone's kid. Someone's family." Chris paused, looking from Larson to Fitz. "If I wasn't here, and I knew there was someone who could save my family, I would pray—god, would I pray—that she wouldn't let anything stop her. Not the Navy, not the Coast Guard. Nothing."

Chris turned her attention solely to Fitz.

"So if you think I'm going to betray those families, or my own, and go sit in a hospital, waiting for some Coast Guard mouthpiece to finally tell me what happened . . . then you must not be a parent."

It was a heavy-handed approach and very possibly the wrong tack to take with this man. But Chris had no clue what would sway him and no time to find out. She stood there waiting while Fitz seemed to size her up and weigh his choices. Chris could feel everyone watching her, watching him.

"Larson," Fitz said finally. "Get the SRDRS on a VOO. Deploy it to the crash site."

Larson was at a loss for words.

"We're *not* using it, you understand me?" he added, looking pointedly at Chris. "Far as I'm concerned, the SRDRS is broken. But I won't find myself wishing I had an option I don't."

"Yes, sir," Larson said.

"As for you," Fitz said to Chris, "you can stay. You are only to observe—"

"But—"

"—while we remember your skills and that you are in the room," Fitz said with a finality to his tone. "If your expertise is needed, we'll ask."

Chris knew not to push her luck. With a nod, she stepped back.

"All right, then," Fitz said. "The obvious course of action is to shift to a vessel recovery approach. If we raise the plane using a lift sling—"

"Not a fucking chance," Chris called out, wrenching her arm out of Sayid's grip as she stormed back into the middle of the room.

"We don't even know what we're dealing with," Larson said to Chris.

"We don't have to," Chris said. "Look, if no one's alive in there, then, sure. Do whatever you want. That's a salvage operation. But if people are alive, then it's a rescue mission. I'd bet my life that whatever conditions allowed them to survive are not going to hold up to cables and slings moving the plane around. I promise you, you lift that plane, they're done."

"How can you be so sure?" Fitz said.

"You convinced me," Chris said. "What was it? Think of the plane as a submarine? The Falcon is the safest and most efficient way to get people out alive? I think the exact quote was, 'It's our only viable option.'"

Fitz hesitated. Finally, he just shook his head. "Mrs. Kent—"

"Chris."

"Chris. What exactly do you propose we do?"

"I don't know yet. But get me the blueprints and specs on that vessel and I *will* figure it out."

CHAPTER ELEVEN

WILL AND KIT HUDDLED AWAY FROM THE OTHERS, TRYING TO SOLVE THE FIRST ITEM ON their long list of problems: how to establish communication with the rescuers on the surface.

"Hey, girls," Kit said. "Does my phone have service?"

Maia and Shannon stood in the galley next to the open food cart. Molly handed a pack of cracker sandwiches to Shannon, and the look on all three of their faces confirmed that the question was as dumb as it had felt coming out of her mouth.

Kit turned back to Will. "Good to see I'm still thinking clearly."

"It's not like you're under any stress."

The two were smiling through the rare moment of levity when suddenly, one of the plastic catering inserts crashed to the galley floor. They turned to the commotion and Will was on his feet instantly.

"Sweetie. Sweetie, look at me," he said to Shannon, dropping to his knees and taking her by the shoulders. The child's face was turning an unnatural shade of red. "What happened?"

Shannon didn't respond. She *couldn't* respond. Her mouth widened, but there was no sound.

"Can you breathe at all?" Bernadette asked, kneeling beside Will. Shannon nodded once but shrugged too. Bernadette stuck a finger in the girl's mouth to sweep for obstructions.

"What was she eating?" Will asked.

"Crackers. Cheese cracker sandwiches," Molly said, hugging herself like it was her fault. Shannon's face was beginning to take on a purple tint.

"These aren't cheese," Maia said, looking down at the plastic-wrapped snack.

"Shan," Will said, his words clipped with panic. "Is your EpiPen in your backpack?"

Shannon's eyes widened when she saw the peanut butter cracker sandwiches in Maia's hand. She nodded quickly. Will turned and splashed his way down the aisle. He was up to his neck almost instantly, and then with a deep breath, he disappeared into the water.

Shannon staggered back dizzily. Bernadette told her to lie down. Everyone stood around watching, not sure what to do.

"Give her space," Jasmine said. The passengers moved out of the way, stepping into the aisle and into the last rows of seats. Kaholo dug around in an overhead bin with his one good hand, jumping down a moment later with a first aid kit.

"There's not an EpiPen in there," Molly said to Kaholo as he ripped it open and began rifling through the contents. "I don't think there's one in the EMK either."

Kaholo tossed bandages and over-the-counter medication out of the way to make sure, but Molly was right.

"Is the EMK still at the front?" Kaholo asked, looking at the water.

The EMK—emergency medical kit—was an enhanced selection of medical supplies. There was only one on board, as opposed to the four first aid kits, which were more basic. The sole EMK was in the first overhead bin, all the way at the front of the plane, completely submerged.

"Unless you brought it to the back with you. I didn't," Molly said.

"Does it even have one?" Kaholo said.

"I don't think so. But I've never needed one."

The flight attendants stared at each other, trying to calculate whether they could swim down and find it. Bubbles burst over the area where Will was, but he didn't come up for air.

Will's eyes burned from the salt water but he kept them open anyway. He knew they'd sat two rows back from the midcabin emergency exit on the left side of the aircraft. He found the wide aisle of the emergency exit fairly quickly and, grabbing the base of the seats, pulled himself back two rows and began swiping his hands under the seats, where they'd stowed their carry-ons.

Will expected to find the backpack but instead found only empty space.

Panic instantly set in. Alone in the dark water, he could hear his pulse beat in his ears as his hands swept the area—but the backpack wasn't there. Was this the right row? Maybe what he thought was the exit row wasn't. Or maybe the bag had been washed away when the plane flooded. Maybe it had somehow made it outside during the evacuation and it wasn't even inside the plane anymore.

Will's chest began to burn. He thought of Shannon, also without air, waiting for her father to save her.

One EpiPen. That was it. Once he found it, she'd be fine. But he had to find it. If he didn't, she would die. He wondered what the limit was. What was the point at which it didn't matter if he found the EpiPen because she'd already be gone?

Suddenly he was thinking of the public swimming pool. Of the puddle tinted red with Annie's blood.

Will clenched his jaw. *Stop it*, he told himself. *Shannon doesn't have time for your fear. Find the backpack.*

Bernadette was adjusting Shannon's head, tilting it back to keep her airway straight.

"Should we put something under her neck? Like a pillow?" Ruth asked quietly to the group.

"A pillow?" Ira replied, motioning around the water-filled plane.

"I know, I know. I just— Oh, poor thing," Ruth said, and sighed.

"Try blowing across her face," Kaholo said.

Bernadette looked up. "Do what?"

"Blow on her face. It'll make her gasp for air. I swear. I surf, and if someone blacks out in the water and we can't do CPR, that's what we do."

"She didn't black out," Andy snapped at Kaholo. "She's in anaphylactic shock."

"What, you're a fucking doctor now?"

Bernadette leaned forward and blew across Shannon's face. They waited.

One second.

Two.

"Fucking told you," Andy muttered after Shannon's body didn't respond.

Kit watched everything unfold, desperate to do something. On a regular trip, the flight attendants would have been calling up front right about now. She'd have answered and started recording the details of the situation while the other pilot patched MedLink to get a doctor on the ground on the line—

"Molly!" Kit said. "Where's the air-to-ground phone?"

The flight attendant, now on her knees across from Bernadette with Shannon lying between them, glanced up. "The what?"

Kit spun around the galley, searching every screen, display, and compartment. Of course Molly wouldn't know what she was talking about. Company policy dictated the flight attendants relay information to the cockpit during a medical emergency and that the pilots be the ones to patch MedLink. But Kit knew, if she could just find it, that somewhere back here was an air-to-ground phone.

If the phone worked—which was a huge *if*—they could get a doctor to advise them. It would also mean an open line of communication with the surface. MedLink could patch them to whoever was leading the rescue effort.

That phone could potentially save not only Shannon but all of them.

"Is that . . ." Kaholo said.

Kit spun. Affixed to the wall above the jump seat aircraft left was a white plastic phonelike device with a rectangular screen and a stack of buttons that was a few more rows than a normal ten-key numeric key-pad. Unsnapping a latch, she pulled the phone from the cradle with a crack of dust and debris, freeing a spiral cord that was tucked behind the seat cushion against the wall. Kit quickly studied the device, then held down a green button at the top. After a couple seconds, the screen lit up.

A burst of air came from behind them and Will surfaced. He looked at the group, and when no one gave him a reason not to, he took a deep breath and dove back under.

Will exhaled just enough air to let him stay under the water. He could feel his heart beat against his chest. Every pulsation tapped out a steady rhythm—boom *boom*, boom *boom*, boom *boom*—like a ticking clock counting down the moments until he lost his second-born.

His hand found a thin strip of fabric. A strap. He followed it to a bag. A backpack! The water was too dark and fuzzy to see if it was purple or sequined, so he just unzipped it and thrust his hand in. Digging around, Will felt fabric. Then there was a plastic wrapper. Some sort of packaged food. None of that seemed right. He felt for the things he knew for certain were in Shannon's bag. A water bottle. A paperback book. Neither was there.

This wasn't it.

Boom *boom*, boom *boom*, boom *boom*.

Kit rotated the phone under the door's emergency light. The small, dim screen had digital blips here and there that made it difficult to make out the information.

"Would your manual say anything about how to work this thing?" Kit asked.

"I don't know. Maybe?" Molly said. "But my manual's in my bag at my jump seat."

Kit understood what Molly meant. The flight attendants' manu-als, just like the pilot's, had once been massive eight-hundred-page behemoths they had to lug around on every trip. Now they were all digital. Molly's manual was on her company-issued iPhone—which meant it was submerged in water, and therefore useless.

Kit stared at the jump seat in front of her, thinking.

"Who was back here?"

"Ed," Kaholo said, jumping up as he realized where Kit was going. "Look in there."

Kit opened a little cubby next to the side wall of the plane. Inside, she found a stack of magazines, an open bag of chocolates, and a half-drunk bottle of water. She moved them around, looking deep in the back, but found nothing.

"Here!" On the other side of the galley, Kaholo slid the compartment under the coffeepots shut using the back of his wrist. With his good hand, he raised an iPhone with the company logo printed on the blue protective case.

Bernadette looked to the water, desperate for Will to pop up with the EpiPen. Shannon's face was now fully blue and her eyes were closed. "Damn it," the nurse said. She pinched the girl's nose shut and placed her own mouth on top of Shannon's. She exhaled two long puffs of air, then looked to Molly. "Go."

Molly interlocked her fingers, placed her palms flat on the little girl's chest, and began compressions, counting off numbers under her breath with each pump.

"One, two, three, four, five, six . . ."

"It's password protected," Kaholo said. "Five numbers. Zero zero zero zero zero? One two three four five?"

"Try it," Kit said.

After a moment Kaholo looked up and shook his head.

"Do it too many times, the phone locks," Jasmine said.

Kit and Kaholo looked at each other.

"Five numbers . . ." Kit said. "Five nu— His ID."

Kaholo ripped open the drawer, wincing as it hit his injured fingers, and grabbed the lanyard with Ed's ID. He punched the numbers into the phone.

"We're in."

". . . twenty-eight, twenty-nine, thirty." Molly sat back on her heels and wiped her forehead on her shoulder while Bernadette leaned forward and gently tipped Shannon's head back. When she was done with the breaths, Molly interlocked her fingers again and placed them on Shannon's chest.

"One, two, three, four . . ."

"Almost got it," Kaholo said, his face lit up by the screen as he searched the manual. Kit tapped the MedLink phone in her hand nervously.

"I think . . ." Kaholo said. "I think—here! Okay. Okay, 'press and hold "SND" for five seconds.'"

Kit pressed the button. Five seconds ticked in time with Molly's counting.

Kaholo continued. "'Press "RCL" to access preprogrammed numbers. Use up-slash-down button to choose MedLink.'"

Kit pressed the "RCL" button, then studied the dim screen. Pressing the up and down buttons, the digital directory shifted—but the blips made it impossible to make out the words. She had no idea which option was MedLink.

Kaholo looked up when she didn't affirm the direction. Kit met his gaze.

"I don't know what button to push."

There was a burst of air as Will broke the surface. Panting, he splashed up the aisle holding a purple-sequin-covered backpack, dropped to his knees, and ripped it open with shaking hands.

Tossing a water bottle and a book out of the bag, he fished around inside before finding a bright yellow plastic cylinder with an orange cap. He wedged a nail under the blue safety cap, popped the top off, then jammed the orange tip into Shannon's thigh. It was quiet enough in the plane to hear the click of the injection's release as the needle left the device. Will didn't move for several seconds, the pen pushed firm against her leg, making sure all the epinephrine had entered Shannon's system.

Molly and Will both breathed heavily, which made it more obvious that Shannon wasn't. After a few seconds, Molly returned her hands to the little girl's chest.

"One, two, three, four, five, six . . ."

Will took his daughter's legs in his lap and rocked them back and forth, muttering quietly to her. "I can't lose you, Shan . . ."

"Twenty-seven, twenty-eight . . ."

"I can't lose you, too."

". . . twenty-nine, thirty."

Bernadette leaned forward, tipped the child's head back, and blew a long puff of air into her mouth. She paused, inhaling deeply—just as Shannon gasped.

Will cried out, taking his daughter in his arms as everyone else crumpled in relief.

Soon, Shannon's face was returning to its normal coloring. Maia came to stand by her side. The little girl raised Kit's phone up high above Shannon and Will and snapped a picture. Maia smiled. Kit gave her a thumbs-up.

Kit looked at the phone in her hands. No labels. No numbers. No way of knowing which one was the right one.

She took a breath, punched a button, and held the phone up to her ear.

CHAPTER TWELVE

THE TELEMEDICINE SPECIALIST ADJUSTED HER HEADSET TO TRY TO FIX THE STATIC, BUT it wasn't on her end of the line. She was only halfway focused on the call anyway. Like everyone else in the 24/7 ground-to-air medical advisement global response center, she stared over the computer screens on her desk to the wall of TVs. The footage coming out of Hawaii was insane. An actual ditching. This never happened.

The static on the call started to clear. She could now somewhat make out the woman's voice on the other end of the line.

"Sorry," she told her, "could you repeat your flight number?"

CHAPTER THIRTEEN

CHRIS STOOD, ARMS CROSSED, WATCHING ROGERS'S FINGERS FLY ACROSS THE KEY-board. With a final stroke, designs for the entire SRDRS system appeared on four large monitors on the wall. Chris came around the table to join Feeny, Sayid, and Noah as they stared up at the screens.

"So it's clear," Rogers said, "they are *not* using the SRDRS. This is, you know, just so you can see—"

"Yeah, yeah, of course," Chris said without taking her eyes off the screens. "So our focus is here." She walked to the monitor displaying the Falcon and ran her hand along the bottom of the transfer skirt. "First question. How do we get this to attach to the plane? Can you bring up—"

Rogers was already typing. Before she could finish her thought, up popped a standalone image of the transfer skirt. The team studied the images and immediately started throwing out ideas. The possibilities ranged from good to bad to outright ignoring the laws of physics. Everything was on the table.

Chris turned. "What's the material on the lip of the skirt?"

Rogers hesitated, sliding his glasses up, before he just crossed his arms. Feeny glanced over at Sayid.

Rogers cleared his throat. "That's classified."

Chris stared at him. "Classified?"

Rogers nodded. "Classified."

Chris walked slowly to Rogers, never losing eye contact. The ticking clock on the wall was the only sound in the room.

"Okay. Maybe not exactly classified," Rogers said, squirming. "But look, I was told—I was told to only give you access to what the public, or, you know, a civilian contractor, would be allowed to have."

"So this is it?" Chris said, motioning to the screens. "Rogers, I could get all this by just looking at the damn thing. Without details, how the hell are we supposed to make it work?"

"With all due respect—you won't. Look, if there are people alive, then the entire United States Coast Guard *and* Navy will come up with a rescue plan. You should let them handle it. Ma'am."

Chris was now directly in his face. When she spoke, her voice was low and calm.

"They don't yet know their plan will fail. We'll be ready when it does."

Rogers and Chris stared at each other for some time. He looked away first, checked the time on the clock, then glanced up at the designs.

"Exactly," Chris said. "You get the big picture. You know what we're up against. You have ideas. And I know you know this can be done. But it won't if you don't help us."

Rogers looked at the designs and then over to Feeny, Sayid, and Noah.

"Dude," Feeny said. "We're talking about *saving lives* here. And besides, you get court-martialed or discharged or whatever, look, Chris'll give you a job. You won't even have to update your résumé."

Rogers's hands worked at his sides for a beat before he typed on the keyboard and hit "Enter."

Chris turned, and up on the screen was a complete and detailed schematic of the US Navy's Submarine Rescue Diving and Recompression System.

Fitz watched the medics work on a body laid flat across the floor of the helicopter. A moment later, the helicopter lifted off from the ship's deck, heading for the level-one trauma center at Queen's Hospital in Honolulu.

"Just him?" he said to Tanner with a nod at the chopper.

Tanner—breathing hard, water dripping from his mustache—nodded. "We only pulled one. Severely burned. I'm not sure he's going to make it. The other chopper, they brought up two. But," he said, unfastening the quick-release buckles on the leg straps of his rescue harness, "one of the two was body recovery."

Tanner unclipped the chest strap, slid out of the black and red rescue vest, and tossed it aside. Shaking his head like a wet dog, he sat back against the side railing. The rest of his team were across the deck taking off their gear, unzipping their wetsuits, sipping out of water bottles. No one spoke.

"Two was all there were?" Fitz said.

"Alive, yes. There were bodies. But it was too risky. I couldn't send my guys in for victim recovery alone. As soon as the fire burns out, we'll go."

"You're sure they were gone?"

Tanner stared at the deck. Fitz could tell the diver had seen things today he would never unsee. Tanner nodded once.

Fitz cleared his throat. "We lifted seven from the civilian boats—"

"*Seven?* A whole plane full of people and we got seven."

"A couple more are waiting to be picked up," Fitz said. "But, yes."

Tanner sighed and after a long moment only said, "Okay."

A female coastguardsman ran up and thrust a stack of papers into Fitz's hands. She immediately started to walk backward toward an interior corridor. Fitz and Tanner followed.

Fitz studied the pages, flipping through the colored bathymetric maps. The topographical images of the seafloor showed a peninsula-like figure surrounded by squiggly lines and numbers. Sections of bright color butted up against one another, with the key in the lower right-hand corner designating a depth for each color. But the areas surrounding the colored sections of seafloor had no assigned depths. For their purposes, once the shelf dropped off, it was just *down there*.

Fitz knew the ocean covered over 70 percent of the Earth's surface and contained approximately 97 percent of all the planet's water. Of that, scientists estimated only roughly 20 percent had been explored. Anyone who worked in the water knew most of the ocean was a completely unknown frontier.

Ocean depths were broken into five zones for an easy shorthand. The surface down to approximately two hundred meters was known as the sunlight zone. This was the warmest part of the ocean, where sunlight could still reach, and it was also where the vast majority of all marine life lived. When people thought of the ocean, this was what they were thinking of. It was the only portion of the ocean that nearly all humans ever interacted with.

Five percent. The sunlight zone made up only *5 percent* of the ocean. After that . . .

Twilight.

Midnight.

The abyss.

The trenches.

Or, as that depth was also called, the hadal zone. Named after Hades, the Greek god of the underworld.

Ninety-five percent of the ocean was contained in the lower four zones. Each a world so dark, cold, and uninhabitable that mankind's most advanced science and technology had only allowed them to obtain merely a hint of basic understanding about it.

Yet here we are on the surface, Fitz thought. With warm sunlight and an oxygen-rich environment ideal for humans. And people were *still* struggling and dying. What chance of survival did anyone underwater have if those above barely stood a chance? No one had said it out loud, but Fitz knew they were all thinking it.

Wherever that plane was, it probably wasn't coming back.

That was until Fitz was handed that bathymetric map.

In the upper right-hand quadrant, someone had handwritten an X and circled it.

"Is this . . . ?"

"The plane. Yes," the female coastguardsman said. "The ROVs just reached it. We're getting a first look now."

Fitz glanced at the key to find out what orange meant.

"Fifty-five?" Fitz said, his voice rising in disbelief. Tanner grabbed it to see for himself. "They're at fifty-five meters?"

Tanner looked up. Fitz knew he believed it, too.

If there were people alive in that plane and they were only at fifty-five meters, they might actually stand a chance of surviving.

Tanner held up the map. "What is this?"

"Penguin Bank," she said, leading the men into a room that hummed with activity. "It's the eroded summit of a sunken volcano that's now a broad, shallow shelf off the coast of Molokai. At its deepest? Less than two hundred feet down. The plane hit a part that's only about a hundred and seventy-five feet. Now, obviously that's still deep, but—"

"But it's survivable," Fitz said, moving toward the screens at the front of the room.

Three monitors showed different scenes of water, seafloor, and clouds of sand and silt reflecting in the ROV's lights. The cloudy images dissipated to clarity. Fitz leaned forward on the table. "I'll be goddamned."

The passengers froze at the sudden flash of light outside the plane. Everyone looked around at one another in the barely lit cabin, an occasional drip or splash the only noise, as they waited for something else to happen.

"Is it just me or—"

Everyone shushed Jasmine as light swept through the plane again, illuminating rows of seats and floating objects in an underwater glow. Rushing to the left side of the plane, they all squeezed into the few dry rows remaining at the back and pressed their faces up against the windows.

Outside, beams of light cut through the darkness like lasers. Bits of sand and silt floated in weightless suspension, seemingly trapped in the oscillating light.

In the galley, Kit bent to look out the door's porthole window. "I'll be goddamned."

Fitz couldn't believe what he was seeing.

Everyone in the room was staring at the screens, occasionally point-ing out a detail or asking a question. Underwater footage like this typi-cally showed barnacle-covered vessels degraded by time and salt water. By contrast, the plane looked brand-new. Badly damaged by the impact, yes, but the ROV's lights reflected off clean and shiny paint. The rivets were a rustless, bright silver. The windows clear and intact.

"This is the left side of the aircraft, correct?" Tanner asked, pointing at one of the screens as the ROV swept down the length of the plane, approaching the nose.

"Gotta be," Fitz said. "It's the right wing that broke off. See?" He pointed at a different monitor where jagged, torn metal and shredded mechanical entrails stuck out of the stub of a broken wing.

The third camera was at the back, sweeping up to the tail to find Coastal Airways' logo, while the first camera had now moved to the front, approaching the cockpit. As it circled the nose, Fitz squinted and leaned in.

"Is that—"

Everyone jumped as fish scattered in the light to reveal one of the pilots still strapped to his seat, his gray, bloated body already a food source. Chunks of flesh were torn and ripped off to expose muscle and bone. His lips and cheeks were gone completely, teeth and gums jutting out beneath dark sockets that had once held eyes. A couple people in the room turned away.

Milton burst into the room, extending a phone.

Fitz barely glanced over. "It'll wait," he said.

"Trust me, boss. You want to take this call."

Fitz absentmindedly reached for the phone as he tilted his head as the camera did, examining the damage to the cockpit.

"This is District Fourteen commander Fitzgerald," he said to a scratchy line, never taking his eyes off the monitors. Camera three had just passed the tail and was beginning to sweep down the back end of the plane.

"Commander Fitzgerald, this is Katherine Callahan," came a distant female voice, "captain of Flight fourteen twenty-one."

Fitz turned back to Milton.

"Told you you wanted to take the call."

"Captain Callahan," Fitz said. "Can I ask where you're calling from?"

Camera three reached the aircraft door and the bright light reflected off the window, momentarily turning the screen completely white. The ROV rose. When the light shifted, a woman's face appeared in the porthole window. The room erupted. The woman smiled in return, clearly hearing them on her end.

"I think you already know, sir."

"Yes, ma'am," Fitz said with a stunned shake of the head. Milton clapped him on the back. "Yes, ma'am."

As the camera made its way down the side of the plane, the rescuers saw their mission made clear pressed up against the windows. There were women and men. An old couple. Two little girls. All wearing huge smiles.

A newfound sense of purpose and hope filled the room.

There were lives to save.

The passengers in the plane shifted, moving back to let others come forward to the windows for a look. In one window appeared a man wearing an open button-down flannel shirt. Standing in front of him was a young girl with long, wavy brown hair. The man put his hands on the girl's shoulders and they both smiled. There was a familial comfort to their touch.

And the little girl was an exact younger version of Chris.

Fitz held a hand over the phone. "Someone go call the mama bear to let her know."

Fitz turned his attention back to the screen and his smile faded. With all focus on the faces at the windows, he hadn't noticed that the other two cameras had pulled back to show a wide-angle view of the plane.

"Did I lose you, Commander?" asked the pilot.

"No, we're here. Look, don't worry. We're coming to get you."

But the room had gone quiet. Everyone stared solemnly at all the screens, which now showed the full picture of what they were dealing with.

The plane was intact, with survivors inside.

But it was positioned nose down, teetering on the edge of a cliff.

2:00 p.m.

1 hour and 59 minutes after impact

Approximately 4.5 hours of oxygen inside plane

CHAPTER FOURTEEN

EVERYONE IN THE PLANE FELT SAFE NOW.

Will knew better.

He leaned against the lav door, tapping his fingers nervously as he watched Kit nod and repeatedly say *mmm-hmmm* into the phone. He needed to know what was being said on the other end of the line. What were they planning? How were they going to screw this up? Decisions were being made that could save his daughter . . . or kill her. And he was on the outside looking in.

Kit stared at Will's tapping fingers, then at him. Her look was pointed. Will raised his hands in mock surrender and went to join the others.

For everyone else, the initial excitement of knowing they'd been found had settled into a hesitant relief of knowing they'd be rescued. Will was always shocked by how easily people believed that things were going to be okay just because someone said so. As if it had slipped their minds that they were still trapped in a plane at the bottom of the ocean.

Everyone milled about and sat in the passenger seats while snacking their way through the food cart, throwing out questions like, *What's the first thing you're going to eat when we get out of here?* And, *Who's the first person you're going to call?* Shannon had recovered from her allergic reaction, and she and Maia were now giggling, drinking cans of Sprite and ginger ale. Will caught his daughter's eye as she took a sip. He faked a smile.

Will wasn't one to trust easily. He also believed most people weren't half as smart as their job title said they were. So while everyone else seemed fine with trusting the competency and abilities of their rescuers, Will would need some convincing.

"If that's what you think works, okay," he heard Kit say.

"What's okay?" Will asked, turning back. "What's their plan?"

Kit covered the phone's mouthpiece. "Rig the plane with lift slings and use a deck crane to bring it up by the tail."

Will stared at her blankly for a beat, then grabbed the phone out of her hand.

"If you do that, you'll kill us."

He'd said it louder than he'd meant to. All the passengers heard.

"No, *you're* going to kill us—" Ira said.

"Your heart," Ruth said. "Ira, calm—"

"He doesn't speak for us! Don't listen to him."

"Let the experts do their jobs, asshole," Andy said.

Will turned away as a man's deep baritone came on the other end of the line. "Who am I speaking to?"

"The kind of engineer you should be calling for advice right about now. Who's this?"

"The Coast Guard, the Navy, and the guy in charge."

"Really?" Will replied. "So you're the genius behind this bullshit? Look, this isn't a Cessna. It's a jet. Have you ever brought up something this big?"

"Yes."

"Fine," Will said. "But were there people—alive—trapped inside?"

"*Exactly* what I said," came a female voice on the other end of the line.

Will could barely hear her. Her voice was distant, like she was at the back of the room.

"Here's the thing," Will said, taking a step back and lowering his voice. "When the plane hit the bottom, I made a mark at the water-line."

Kit looked up.

"What's he saying?" Ira asked. Kit held out a hand—*Hold on.*

Will looked to the lav. Down near the floor, water had passed the line he'd made by about two inches.

"We're not as watertight as I'd hoped," Will said. The other passengers leaned over the last row of seats, trying to see the line.

"The cockpit door. The crack at the bottom," Kit said.

Will nodded. "That's where it's coming in, yeah."

"I can't hear other conversations," said the voice on the phone. "Talk to me."

"This air pocket's pretty simple," said Will. "Air is trapped at the top of a rigid structure—the plane. And I assumed the water had stopped rising because the air had nowhere else to go. Like a diving bell. But the water *is* still rising. Which means somewhere on the tail or back of the plane, there are cracks and holes and fractures and who knows what kind of weak spots that are allowing air to escape. Air goes out, water comes in.

"Now, it's slow, okay?" Will said quickly, more to the panicked passengers than the man on the call. "I'm not super worried about the rate at which the air is escaping. But what *terrifies* me is you guys moving this plane around. Attaching and wrapping cables and slings to a part of the plane that is clearly compromised is a bad, bad idea."

Fitz didn't respond.

"You rupture a weak spot? Lots of air escapes. You shift the plane too far, too fast? The pocket floods. Know what happens if the air escapes or the pocket floods? We die."

"I understand what's at stake," Fitz said.

"Do you? 'Cause we're all pretty scared and I don't hear that same level of fear up there. And that worries me."

The cabin was silent for a moment as everyone processed what Will had said. Ira was the first to speak.

"If he was so smart, we wouldn't be here in the first place," Ira said.

And with that, the arguing reignited along now-familiar battle lines. Will dropped his head, then looked over at his daughter. Even she looked conflicted. He could tell it pained her to be stuck in the middle of two sides that both made sense, with the added complications of love and loyalty. It was the same face she made when he fought with Chris.

"No, *listen*."

There was that woman's voice again on the other end of the line. As she spoke, her voice got closer, like she was making her way forward.

"We move them, we destroy what's keeping them alive," she said. "It's like moving a person with a spinal cord injury—"

"You don't," Will said. "You'll just make it worse. You cannot *move* the plane—"

"We have to get them *out* of the plane," said the woman.

"Thank you! Her. Listen to her," Will said. "You'd be fools not to."

"Careful, Will," she said. "Don't think I won't quote you the next time we fight."

Will nearly dropped the phone.

"*Chris?*"

Shannon looked up.

"Is our girl okay?" Chris said.

Will stammered, lost for words. It was her. It was actually her. Shannon came over.

"Mom?"

Will smiled down at his daughter, trying not to cry. "Shannon's fine," Will said to Chris.

"Tell her I'm going to get her home."

A wave of relief washed over him. "Your mom's up there," Will said in a tone of voice he hadn't used since before the engine had exploded. "It's going to be okay."

As the passengers in the plane looked at one another, confused, the deep baritone cleared his throat.

"We need to keep moving," he said. "Will, put Kit back on."

"Yes, but, Chris. Chris, listen—" Will said.

"She's gone," a different female voice said.

"What do you mean?" Will said.

"She went back to work."

Will smiled and handed the phone to Kit.

Fitz leaned into the speaker in the center of the table to hear the pilot's hushed tones. In a sealed plane, he knew this was as private a call as they'd get.

"There's no bedside manner," Kit said. "But so far Will's been right. Tell me you have a backup plan."

"I want to level with you, ma'am," Fitz said. "This *is* our backup plan. This rescue mission is . . . uniquely challenging."

Fitz could feel Kit waiting, hoping that there was a "but" coming next.

"But we *will* figure it out," was all he could honestly give her.

"Understood," Kit said, her voice flat. "What do you need from us?"

"Nothing yet," Fitz said. "But I need to know—do you trust him?"

"Will? I do. He's smart. And I know he wouldn't put his daughter in harm's way."

Fitz felt Milton's eyes on him but ignored it. "That says a lot," Fitz said before clearing his throat.

"Do you trust his wife?" Kit asked.

Fitz paused, thinking. "I know she won't stop until her daughter's safe."

Both ends of the line went quiet as it dawned on them that someone topside and someone inside the plane were both acting on the greatest motivation in the entire human experience.

They were parents fighting to save their child.

"We're going to get to work," Fitz said, finally. "But keep this line connected."

"One last thing," Kit said. "The surface rescue. How many . . ."

"We're still working," Fitz said, sensitive to the emotion in her voice. "I don't have a number for you yet, but I want to be honest, Captain Callahan. When I do, the number is going to be smaller than any of us hoped."

Fitz paused, letting her have a moment. He knew those were her passengers and her crewmates. Her responsibility.

"But," he said, "I can tell you this much for certain. The only reason you're all alive is because you stayed inside that plane."

CHAPTER FIFTEEN

FITZ STOOD AT THE BACK OF THE ROOM WATCHING THE DIVERS PLAN FOR A MISSION SO challenging it bordered on impossible.

"This is useless," Tanner said, moving his hand across a screen showing ROV footage of what used to be the wing but was now only a stub of jagged, torn metal. "No surface area. The plane would slip out the second we tried to lift it."

"There's nothing to clip into, anyway," said another diver.

"Exactly. Underwater salvage wasn't figured into a plane's design."

"Then we use the tail," said another diver. "Wrap the tail, lift it from the back. Vertical. The air would shift but keep."

"Nope," Fitz said, stepping around to the monitor that showed the tail section. Both the horizontal and vertical stabilizers were either torn off completely or significantly damaged. "Nothing to anchor to. Just like the wings. Plus, damage-wise, we don't know the full extent. And we won't until we're down there. Any structural issues letting air escape— they're there. So this whole area, it's a no-go."

Everyone stared at the monitors trying to figure out how to rig the battered and broken plane with lift slings and cables so they could raise it to the surface.

The wings were out. The tail was out. That left only one option.

Going under the plane.

Fitz flipped over one of the maps and began to sketch. "I'm more Picasso than da Vinci," he said. "But you get the idea."

Fitz held up his rough depiction of the plane. Lines came down from the surface, wrapped under the fuselage, crossed, and came back up the other side.

"Use the lift slings like a ribbon crossing under a present," Tanner said. "But instead of looping to tie a bow at the top, attach the lift slings to a cable and crane hook."

"Exactly."

"And if you gave a little slack to the front slings . . ." Milton said.

"Plane noses down, air pocket holds."

Everyone in the room agreed: it could work.

Tanner angled his head, studying the seabed the plane sat on. "That's not soft-bottomed soil. What's our surface?"

"Unfortunately, that," Fitz said, sliding a geological study across the table. "Hard reef and volcanic rock. We can't sweep the wires. We're going to have to tunnel."

Tunneling would add time—and risk.

A baby-faced six-foot, six-inch diver known to the team only as Runt raised his hand.

"Do we know how long these people have?" Runt asked.

"Best we figure, a little over four hours," Fitz said. "If we're generous."

As the ROVs continued to circle the plane, every once in a while a face would appear in a window to watch the machine motor by. They looked calm and safe inside the plane. Fitz wondered if they were tricking themselves into thinking they actually were.

Andrea Harris, the only female diver on the team, pointed at one of the screens. "How solid is the edge of that cliff? The one we're drilling into?"

Fitz looked at the plane's positioning: nose hanging off the edge of a cliff, sloping down, tail raised in the air. Beyond the cliff, it just dropped off.

"We don't know," Fitz said. "It's one of many things we don't know and don't have time to figure out. The only thing we know for sure is that this is the best idea we have."

His mind flashed to Chris. At this moment, she too was huddled up. Working the problem. Coming up with another plan. Fitz hoped they weren't going to need it. This lift plan *should* work. But looking at the divers, his confidence flickered.

He could see it on their faces. The uncertainty of it all. It was risky and dangerous. But what he'd said was the truth.

At this moment, this was the best idea they had.

Tanner leaned forward on the table.

"I've never asked you to do anything I wouldn't do myself," he said. "I'll be the first one in the water. Anyone wants out, now's the time."

None of the divers moved or said a word.

"Do they know they're on the edge of a cliff?" Runt asked.

Fitz and Milton shared a look.

"No," Fitz said. "These people don't need to know all the ways they could die."

CHAPTER SIXTEEN

MOLLY SCROUNGED AROUND IN THE DRINK CART UNTIL SHE FOUND WHAT SHE WAS looking for.

"Will this work?" she asked, unfolding a piece of paper and passing it to Ruth.

"Perfect, sweetheart," Ruth said, flipping the catering bill over to the blank side. "Do you have a pen?"

Ira shuffled over. "What are you doing?"

"Nothing," Ruth said.

"What do you mean, nothing?"

"A woman's heart is a deep ocean of secrets."

Kit looked up from across the galley. "Did you just quote *Titanic*?"

Ruth chuckled, taking the pen from Molly. "If you're asking, you know."

"I was sixteen when it came out. I saw it five times in the theater."

"My daughters were seventeen and nineteen. We went seven times. I've been thinking about it all day."

Kit laughed. "Me too."

"Well, could you not?" Ira said. "It didn't work out too well for the people on that boat."

"How would you know?" Ruth asked, taking a seat in the last row. "You refused to see it."

"Blasphemy," Bernadette said. "Why?"

"He thought it was a too-long movie about a stupid boat," Ruth said, unlatching the tray table.

Ira blew air out his lips. "I never said that."

"That's a direct quote and you know it."

Ira huffed some more but didn't argue. Ruth's cursive handwriting had filled nearly half the page before he couldn't take it any longer. "Damn it, Ruth—"

"I'm saying what I need to say in case I don't get the chance to say it, okay?" Ruth said.

"How will—"

"I'll seal it in a bottle. If we don't make it, well, they'll find it eventually."

"Ruth, we're going to be fine," Kit said. "It's going to be fine."

"Oh, I know. Just something to pass the time," Ruth said, winking at the little girls.

Water dripped. Ruth's pen continued to scratch.

"You have any more paper?" Ira asked the flight attendant.

Fitz and Milton stood at the railing as their ship, the USCG *Angelica*, cruised past the crash site to position itself over the plane. They watched as the USCG *Redwood* encircled the crash site's debris field with hard boom and absorbent materials, knowing that it wasn't just the scene of a tragic accident. It was also an environmental disaster and site of a future investigation.

Mercifully, the plane had sunk at an angle that placed it just far enough east that both the surface and underwater missions had operating clearance. But watching the crew of the *Redwood* work, Fitz thought of the victims within that perimeter. Victims they couldn't recover until the fire burned out. And he thought of all the parents who were at this moment frantically trying to connect with someone, anyone, who could tell them where their child was.

Fitz knew he was looking at the answer for some.

Voices rose across the deck. Fitz and Milton turned. The divers were drawing straws to see who would operate the drill.

"I don't get it," Runt said, holding up the shortest straw as the divers razzed him.

"I worry what they're teaching the youths these days," Tanner replied, laughing.

"Does this mean— Oh, c'mon."

Another diver gave a smiling Runt a good-natured shove as he tried unsuccessfully to barter his way out of his bad luck.

Fitz wanted to call them out for screwing around, but he knew the divers understood the gravity of the situation. They weren't being disrespectful. They were staying out of their heads so the weight of duty didn't crush them.

"Twenty-one," Milton said.

"Seriously?" Fitz replied.

"That means he was born in 2002, you believe that?" Milton spat into the water. "No wife. No kids. Practically a kid himself."

Fitz looked at the smiling young man and thought of Runt's parents. His family, his friends. Of how risky this operation was going to be and how this kid would be the first through the door. Fitz turned away, looking back to the flames.

A coastguardsman came jogging up. "Sir? We're ready."

The door opened. Chris, Feeny, Sayid, and Noah all looked up. Rogers stood up at attention. It was Larson.

"They're about to start," she said in a low voice, like it was privileged information, like she was doing Chris a favor.

"Okay," Chris said, staying seated. She'd already said all she needed to say about how bad of an idea she thought the plan was.

"You don't want to watch?"

"At best, it doesn't work. At worst, I'm watching my family die."

"And if you're wrong?" Larson asked.

"I assume someone will let me know."

After a moment, Larson went to leave but stopped, turning to watch

Chris lean over the table and point at something on a drawing. Chris asked Feeny a question, but before he could answer, Larson said loudly, "My hands are tied."

Everyone looked up.

"Coast Guard's mission. Fitz decides what goes. It's not my call."

"It's okay, I get it," Chris said. "You have to ask Daddy for permission."

Feeny's eyes widened and the men in the room looked down, pretending to be engrossed in the schematics on the table.

Larson smirked and stood a little straighter. "Then give me a plan so good I have no choice but to break rank."

Kaholo held up the airsickness bag, studying his own handwriting.

"Does *necessary* have two R's or one?"

He sat on an armrest with his feet propped on the seat across the aisle. With a pen in his good hand, he held his injured hand upright to lessen the throbbing.

"One," Ryan said, passing Bernadette his pen, having finished his message. "One R, one C, two S's."

After a long pause, Kaholo said, "*Necessary* has a C?"

Jasmine chuckled, folding her own note. "If your friends and family are going to run a spell check on your 'He gone' note, I say don't write it."

She unscrewed Shannon's sticker-covered water bottle, folded the boarding pass she'd written her note on one more time, and dropped it in with the others. Screwing the lid back on, Jasmine turned it upside down like a snow globe, watching the messages drop down and then back.

"Done?" she asked, seeing Andy folding his paper.

Andy had sat there in front of the blank sheet for a long time, not writing anything, while everyone ignored his occasional quips about how dumb this was. Finally, he'd scribbled something brief.

"Whatever," he said, passing his paper to Jasmine.

Will finished his note while eavesdropping on Shannon and Maia, who sat in the last row.

Maia was writing to her parents. Telling them how much fun she'd had visiting her grandma and grandpa in Hawaii. How she'd seen this big turtle and that pineapple was her favorite flavor of shaved ice. The child was writing a postcard, the concept of final words lost on her.

But Will was only half listening. His mind had wandered to Chris.

With a smile tugging playfully at his lips, he thought of the moments before he'd realized the voice on the phone was hers. The back-and-forth. Cutting each other off to finish each other's sentences. It felt like before. How they once were. A team. Partners. God, he missed that.

He'd assumed that was gone. He'd thought they were over. But as Will's pen hovered over the paper while he decided how exactly to phrase what he was thinking, he thought maybe—

"Who's Annie?" Maia asked, reading over Shannon's shoulder.

As if he'd heard a record scratch, Will snapped back to the plane.

Shannon blushed, quickly glancing up at him before looking away. Will felt the other passengers' eyes on him, and he blushed, too.

"My sister," Shannon said. "She died."

Maia looked from the note to Shannon, not fully understanding. "Why?"

"It was an accident. She hit her head."

The plane was utterly silent.

"My dad's sister died," Maia said after a bit. "But I was a baby. I didn't know her. Did you know your sister?"

Shannon nodded. "I was five. A lot I don't remember. But some stuff I do. Like playing with this little green tractor together. And swinging on the swings at the park. And she used to stick raspberries on her fingertips, then wiggle her hand around. It made me laugh so hard one time I spit milk out my nose. And I remember this scratchy blanket at the hospital they made me wear because I was cold."

Will held on to the backs of the seats, unsteady on his feet. He'd never heard any of this. But he'd also never asked. He looked to Maia, who was giving Shannon her full attention, and was so grateful to her for this moment. Maia was curious. She cast no judgment. She didn't bring her own baggage to the conversation, as always happened with him whenever Annie came up. Adults have their own intimate understanding of loss, and Will hated how they always tried to force a connection by invoking their personal experiences with grief. Will just wanted someone to listen. Like Maia was doing for Shannon.

"There's this lotion in her room," Shannon continued. "It was hers. It has glitter in it and it's in this teal bottle and it smells like coconut and sometimes I go in there and I smell it. I remember her then. Not, like, really remember? But it smells like something I know."

"Did she look like you?" Maia asked.

Shannon smiled. "Yeah. She had blue eyes, though. Like my dad. Mine are green. Like my mom's. In our baby photos I can't really tell if it's me or her sometimes. My mom says I cried a lot less, though. I guess she was a fussy baby."

Will smiled. That was true; god, could that baby cry. Ruth reached up, placing her hand on top of his, and squeezed in the way only a grandma can.

"Do you miss her?"

The question was for Will. Maia's wide, innocent eyes stared up at him, waiting.

How could he even answer that? What words could he string together to answer truthfully a question as absurd as it was innocent?

Will cleared his throat. "I do. Every day."

He looked down and met his daughter's eyes.

Suddenly, Kit held out her hands with a shushing noise.

Everyone froze, looking at the pilot and each other . . .

. . . as soft, distant sounds came from somewhere out in the water.

The sounds of a dive had long become white noise to Tanner. The swoosh of air on the inhale, the bubbling release on the exhale. Normally, he didn't even notice it.

Today, it was deafening.

Everything seemed darker. Brighter. Closer. Further. His senses were heightened in a way he hadn't experienced since he was a child.

When he was eleven, on his first dive, the first breath he took underwater made his eyes go wide as adrenaline spiked up and down his body. The regulator almost dropped from his mouth, but he got control of himself, quick.

Because he had to.

Because in the disorienting thrill of that very first breath, he got it.

I'm not supposed to be here.

It was why he'd kept diving. Why he'd made it his life. He had been hooked from that first realization that he could do something that shouldn't have been possible. He could breathe underwater. The fins he wore could make him something larger and more capable. His wetsuit gave him an aquatic animal's skin, sleek and protective. Diving pushed the boundaries of what the human body could do—should do—and like a true adrenaline junkie, he'd never stopped chasing the high.

But today brought him back to the flip side of that very first breath. Back to the sister emotion of that excitement.

Fear.

I'm not supposed to be here also meant *I can't survive here.*

None of them should have been there.

And if something went wrong, the options for recovery were virtually nonexistent.

The beams of light from the divers' headlamps faded into the darkness below them. The deeper they went, the darker it got, and even though they'd been squinting into the bright afternoon sun a few minutes ago, it now felt like a night dive.

To Tanner's right, a diver laid the guideline. In the diver's left hand, a reel spun the neon-yellow nylon line that trailed them down from the primary tie-off on the ship. Once they reached the target, they'd anchor the line to the aircraft. There would be no secondary tie-off. There was nothing between the ship and the plane.

Even though his ears were equalized, the subtle pressure in Tanner's head was constant. A normal recreational dive's limits were around eighteen meters, or sixty feet. A more advanced diver called it off around thirty meters. Those with specialized training for deep dives went down to forty meters.

The plane was situated just over sixty meters.

Two hundred feet.

Tanner had been on dives that low before. But they had been dives. Not rescues. His mind reeled as he considered the logistics of the mission. At depths this low, the increase in atmospheric pressure made a single breath like taking five on the surface. Which meant that their tanks would run out of air five times as fast. Which would need to be considered for their ascent.

Going up always took longer than going down on account of the deco stop—the decompression stop—a three-to-five-minute pause at five meters. This gave the body time to off-gas. Which meant letting the excess nitrogen that had accumulated in the body's blood vessels and tissues by breathing compressed air at high atmospheric pressure dissolve naturally. Without that acclimation, nitrogen bubbles could become trapped in the joints or the bloodstream.

Decompression sickness. Or, as it was commonly called, the bends.

The results of the bends ran the gamut from pain and discomfort . . . to death.

In addition to the deco stop, they would also have to make a deep stop, which meant thirty to sixty seconds spent in neutral buoyancy at 50 percent of the depth of the dive.

Tanner checked the dive computer on his wrist. It calculated the depth and pressure of the dive and told them when and how fast to ascend. So far, the screen was covered in white and blue. When the values turned red, or when it started vibrating on his wrist to get his attention, *that* was when Tanner would need to worry.

The computer read fifty-four meters. They should have been getting close. Tanner peered down below them, looking for the plane. But there was nothing. Only darkness.

Until . . .

Tanner narrowed his eyes.

A dim, hazy orb of light was slowly getting brighter. Coming closer.

The ethereal light had an alien presence to it, and Tanner registered a sensation that something was there that shouldn't have been. As the divers continued down, Tanner felt their collective energy shift. A sense of awe and disbelief overwhelmed them.

Like a ghostly apparition, the hazy outline of the plane sharpened with each kick closer. The divers' headlamps reflected off the metal, illuminating the darkness to the point that the divers had to squint. They were right on top of it, dropping down from directly above, and even against the enormity of the ocean, the plane seemed positively gargantuan. Tanner felt a tingle in his stomach similar to how he'd felt the time a humpback whale had once swum by him unexpectedly: a heady mixture of wonder, gratitude, and terror.

He'd dived to sunken ships before. Abandoned creations of man that had been reclaimed by nature, their metal and wooden frames rusted and decayed, destroyed by time and harsh marine elements. By contrast, the plane looked like it had just rolled off the factory floor.

The metal shined. The airline's livery was vivid greens and blues. Even the damage that was there—the missing right wing, the shredded metal, the destroyed left engine, the scars from the fire—seemed to shimmer with a vibrancy that almost gave the plane a living quality. It no longer seemed like a machine. It felt alive. Like they were approaching a wounded, dangerous animal.

Tanner stroked at the water, positioning himself to the right of the plane. He let his feet slowly drop beneath him as he went vertical in the water and exhaled the air in his lungs. As the bubbles went up, his body went down, and when he needed another breath—he stopped short.

He floated there, eye level with the plane's windows, staring into the eyes of a little girl who watched him from inside the plane, like he was a fish in a bowl.

CHAPTER SEVENTEEN

TANNER THOUGHT HE HAD PREPARED HIMSELF FOR THE SIGHT OF A COMMERCIAL AIR-liner hanging off a cliff at the bottom of the ocean. .

He was wrong.

The video feed from the ROVs had given him only an abstract idea. An idea condensed down so it could fit on a small tabletop screen. But now, seeing the enormity of this thing in person, two hundred feet down, from within the quiet confines of his scuba gear, it was almost too much to comprehend.

This wasn't just another mission. This was the mission they would tell their grandchildren about. Or, maybe, this was the mission that would cause PTSD for the rest of their lives.

Or, maybe, this was the mission they wouldn't come back from.

Tanner watched a cloud of sand billow up when the weight Runt dropped at his feet hit the seafloor. Runt clipped a line to the weight, then attached the other end of the line to the harness around his waist. He needed to anchor himself to counter the jackhammer's kickback.

Runt looked up and gave the "okay" hand sign, and the mission began.

One of the divers handed Runt a jackhammer. Runt swept the tool's pneumatic hose to ensure it was clear, then set the tip of the chisel into a flat section of rock.

Step one: dig an access trench.

The best location was on the right side of the aircraft, forward of the detached wing: far enough back from the cliff's edge, still underneath the body of the plane, just before the tail started to lift. Runt looked up. All the divers flashed the "okay" hand sign. He nodded and gripped the tool. Bubbles rose from his regulator in an extended exhale.

Runt squeezed the handle, and the chisel started to pound the rock. Loud, machine-gun-like sounds filled the otherwise silent space. He drilled for five seconds. Stopped. Checked his progress. Tanner swam forward as the debris settled to see for himself.

The jackhammer was driving into the seabed easily.

Too easily.

It would make for quicker drilling and rigging. But it also meant the foundation was weaker than they'd originally assumed.

Several divers removed the blasted chunks of seafloor from the trench and tossed them aside. Once it was clear, Runt stepped up and drilled some more. After a while, he stopped, and the divers removed the pieces. This process would repeat until they had cleared enough space.

While they worked to clear the trench, one of the coastguardsmen swam over to the plane. Inside, the passengers were pressed together, two, sometimes three, to a window. At one of them was the pair of little girls. The diver hovered weightlessly in front of them.

With an oxygen tank across his back, tubes winding around his body, fins, a mask, a regulator mouthpiece, and a bright red rescue-swimmer wetsuit, he was an intimidating tangle of equipment. Bubbles rose around him as he floated in front of the window, unable to speak, unable to smile or show any kind of emotion. The little girls stared back with wide eyes.

The diver took the regulator out of his mouth and leaned his head back. He stuck his tongue out, puffed out his cheeks with a forced exhale, then stuck out his tongue again, puffed out his cheeks, stuck out his tongue, puffed out his cheeks. He turned back to the window to see the girls giggling as they watched the bubble rings rise. The circles expanded as they went up, until they broke apart, and when the last one was gone, the children looked to the diver with huge grins. He smiled, then put his respirator back in. Giving the girls a salute, he returned to his team, a trail of bubbles rising in his wake.

Will surveyed the cabin. Kit was behind him in the galley on the phone with Fitz. Everyone else was glued to the windows on the right side of the aircraft, watching the divers work. Will ran his thumb back and forth across his bottom lip, eyeing the waterline.

The jackhammer started up again and the surface of the water began to vibrate. When the hammering stopped, the water stilled. After a couple minutes, the hammering resumed and the water's surface once again began to undulate. This time, something off to the side caught Will's attention.

He took a couple steps down into the plane and looked to the left, where the waterline cut across the windows. When the jackhammering stopped, the waterline moved, angling down. Will's head turned with it, trying to see if it was him, not the plane. When the hammering resumed, the waterline moved again, now angling up. The change was small. But it was real.

"Can I?" Will said to Kit a moment later in the galley, extending his hand.

She passed him the phone and he stepped deeper into the galley, away from the other passengers. "Question," he said. "What is the exact positioning of the plane?"

Fitz and Milton exchanged looks. Milton stopped sipping his coffee. In front of them, the monitors showed ROV footage of the divers' progress. Fitz cleared his throat.

"How do you mean?" he asked.

"What exactly did we land on? The plane feels . . . unstable."

Fitz stood up straighter. "Describe 'unstable.'"

"The plane rocks when they drill. Back and forth, like a seesaw.

That shouldn't happen if we're stable. So what aren't you telling us?" Will waited. "Fitz? Hello?"

Fitz had stopped listening. On the monitors, Runt passed the jackhammer off. Another diver handed him the drill. The ROV was positioned behind the young man, filming the flat section under the plane where Runt would now drill the hole. From the wide angle, a majority of the plane was visible. Fitz leaned in.

The plane was rocking in small back-and-forth movements, just like Will was describing.

"Tell them to stop!" Fitz screamed.

CHAPTER EIGHTEEN

THE PASSENGERS POUNDED THE WINDOWS, SCREAMING AT THE DIVERS, WHO COULDN'T hear them.

"Stop!" Will cried, watching Runt drop the weight into the two-foot-deep access trench, then step down after it. Will waved his arms frantically.

There was no way to stop it.

Runt centered his weight, placed the razor-sharp auger drill bit against the vertical slab of exposed seabed under the plane, and squeezed the handle. Instantly, the spinning auger began to bore a wide hole into the reef as chunks of volcanic rock flew in every direction.

The divers were spaced out in the water, focused on the steady progress Runt was making. The drill wasn't as loud as the jackhammer, but it was loud enough that none of them heard the voice in their earpieces screaming at them to stop.

Out of the corner of his eye, Tanner spotted a blinking light coming from the plane. He looked over and saw one of the little girls turning a cell phone flashlight on and off. In the window in front of her, Will was making a frantic slashing motion across his throat. Before Tanner could even wonder what they meant, he felt a vibration in his fins.

Tanner looked down. On the seafloor, rocks and shells were beginning to bounce.

Instantly, he got the message.

Kicking as hard as he could, Tanner swam to Runt. He knew Runt couldn't feel anything other than the drill's vibrations, and just then, the noise of the drill seemed to get even louder—but the power had already been cut.

Runt looked to his fellow divers.

The noise wasn't the drill.

It was coming from beneath them.

The ground began to tremble. Bubbles rose from fissures in the seafloor. There was a crack, and a small chunk of the cliff broke off, tumbling down, disappearing into the abyss.

Then the whole edge of the shelf began to crumble.

Water sloshed around the cabin as the nose tipped forward. The metal airframe groaned. The passengers shrieked as the floor shifted. Clutching at seats, they scrambled out of the rows, heading to the back.

"Shannon!" Will cried, grabbing her hand and pulling her along. Together, they went with everyone back, back as far as they could.

But they were trapped. There was nowhere to go.

Will clutched Shannon to his body, feeling the galley countertop digging into his back. He felt the plane slipping further down. He closed his eyes.

The seafloor beneath Runt broke loose and dropped out from underneath him. Letting go of the drill, he pushed off the ground to swim up—but the weight he was attached to fell with the shelf. The line pulled taut. Runt went down.

Runt's gloved fingers grappled for the drill, barely managing to grab the hose with one hand, but the weight tied to his waist kept pulling him down. With one hand struggling to hang on to the hose, the other worked its way around the harness, feeling for the weight's quick-release latch.

Looking down, Runt didn't see the approaching drill at the end of the hose. As it slammed into his hand, he lost his grip. His other hand shot up, grabbing the hose just in time. Abandoning the quick release, he clung to the hose with both hands—when suddenly the line snapped taut and the hose hit Runt in the face, knocking his regulator out.

Runt snapped his mouth shut, holding on to what little air was left in his lungs.

The other divers swam through the sand and debris, paddling frantically in an attempt to get to the beam of Runt's headlamp, but he'd had a head start, and he'd sunk fast.

Runt dangled off the end of the hose. The veins in his neck protruded. His chest burned. He could feel his regulator bumping up against his leg. Carefully, he took one hand off the hose to grab it but nearly lost his grip on the hose entirely. Tiny bubbles escaped from his lips as he clutched the hose with both hands again.

Readjusting, Runt removed the other hand to go for the weight's quick release. This time, he found the latch easily—just as stars began to dance in his vision.

His head was growing woozy. The gloves were too thick. The pull from the weight, too heavy. But Runt tried, fumbling to free himself. Desperate to save himself.

The divers were nearly there. The one in front kicked as hard as he could. He stretched out for Runt's hand. Runt reached up to take it—just as his eyes rolled into the back of his head as he blacked out.

Runt's other hand slipped from the drill and he went into a free fall.

The divers chased him down. Their teammate, their brother. The further down they went, the darker it became. The weight slammed against the side of the cliff, creating a cloud of sand and silt. The divers lost visual. But they kept on, following him down into the abyss.

Finally—there. The single beam of Runt's headlamp.

But the sliver of light was too far.

The diver in front, the one who'd almost had him, felt someone grab his tank and pull him back. He spun to find Tanner holding on to him, the rest of the divers floating just above. Tanner shook his head and made a motion for the surface. The diver waved Tanner off and went after Runt.

But as he turned, the last trace of Runt's headlamp disappeared into total darkness.

2:48 p.m.

2 hours and 47 minutes after impact

Approximately 2.5 hours of oxygen inside plane

CHAPTER NINETEEN

WILL SLAPPED THE PHONE AGAINST THE PALM OF HIS HAND A FEW TIMES. PUTTING IT
to his ear, he found the same scratchy reception.

"Speak louder," he said, cupping his hand around the mouthpiece.
"I can barely hear you." A voice said something, but he couldn't make
it out.

"Here," Kit said, and Will passed off the phone before he could give
in to the urge to slam it against the wall.

"Are you okay?" she heard Fitz ask. He sounded like he was at the
bottom of a well.

"We're okay," Kit replied, looking around at the group. "But you
guys really screwed our situation. The water rose. Big-time. We lost half
our air. At least half."

The plane was pitched forward, far steeper than it had been before.
The water was higher. The air pocket had shrunk. The phone's connection had deteriorated. And the divers were nowhere to be seen. The
situation was grave.

Fitz's voice was going in and out with the bad connection. Kit
closed her eyes and jammed a finger into her ear as someone stepped
on her foot.

"*Sorry*," Molly mouthed. Everyone was now crammed in the back
galley and the last two rows of the plane. Even there, the water now
came up to their knees. More suitcases were rifled through, more dry
clothes were passed around.

Kit tried to make out what Fitz was saying but could only catch a couple words at a time. "Speak *up*," Kit said. She had no idea if Fitz could even hear her. "We're wet. We're scared. We need to get out of this plane. Whatever you did made—"

Suddenly, Fitz's voice boomed through the earpiece loud enough for everyone to hear.

"—know we made the problem worse and we lost a good man, god-damn it!"

Something crashed on the other end of the line and then there was only static.

For a long while no one in the plane said anything. No one wanted to be the first to talk.

Kaholo saw movement outside. Bending, he pointed out the window. Everyone crowded around.

The divers were back. But they didn't come to the plane and they didn't continue their work. Moving slowly and methodically, they simply grabbed their tools and started for the surface.

"There's only five," Shannon said.

There had been six.

Kit listened to the scratchy feed, not sure if anyone was still there. "We didn't know," she said softly. "I'm so sorry."

"Why don't y'all hang tight," came a man's voice Kit didn't recognize. "We're going back to the drawing board and, uh, we'll let you know."

As the passengers watched the divers rise up and out of sight, it hit home. Not just that their odds of survival were getting worse, but that other people were putting themselves at risk to save them—with real consequences.

Shannon leaned against Will with her arms wrapped around his waist, her head resting on his stomach. He stroked her hair, staring at the roof, thinking: *I was right*. But the thought of saying *I told you so* repulsed him.

"I'm glad we wrote those notes," Bernadette said.

"Oh shut up," Andy said.

Jasmine crossed the galley and started opening the carts, rifling through the plastic bins of snacks and sodas, until she found what she was looking for. Without a word, she slid out a plastic carrier and set it on the counter. The little glass minis clinked together, and like Pavlov ringing a bell, all the adults' heads turned.

"Standard bar, you call it," Jasmine said, taking stock of the liquor bin's contents. "Vodka. Gin. Bourbon. Scotch. Tequila."

"Gin," Andy said, and Jasmine tossed a little blue bottle his way.

"Tequila," Kaholo and Molly said in unison.

"Hold on," Kit said as Jasmine passed the tequila. "You do know the first thing that happens for crew when we get out of here is a drug test, right?"

The flight attendants stared at the pilot, bottles unopened.

"They'll separate us. Do a Breathalyzer. Make us pee in a cup. Ask for a minute-by-minute account of your last forty-eight hours." Kit looked back and forth between the two. "Look, we crashed. People died. There *will* be an investigation. The airline. Airbus. The NTSB. They're going to want to know what happened. And right now, I guarantee you, the airline's C-suite is on their knees praying they can blame this on *us* and not the plane or maintenance or something *they'll* be liable for. If they find alcohol in your system, you won't just be fired on the spot. You might actually be held criminally responsible for what's happened."

The flight attendants took the information in. Then, with a loud crack, Molly twisted the mini open, tossed her head back, and downed the alcohol in one go. Wiping her mouth with the back of her hand, she didn't react to the burn and she didn't break eye contact with Kit either.

"In my professional opinion," Jasmine said, "what Molly's trying to say is: 'I wish a bitch would.'"

Kaholo opened his bottle. "Lot of ifs. The main one being *if* we get out of here."

"I said *when*." Kit's voice was resolute.

Kaholo raised the mini in a toast and downed his, too.

Ira and Ruth passed a can of Coke and a single mini of vodka

between them. Will nursed a scotch. Ryan, bourbon. Kit and Bernadette didn't want anything. Jasmine said she didn't drink. And for the
kids, Jasmine set two clear plastic cups on the counter and delighted the
girls by swirling the bright pink of cranberry juice psychedelically with
orange juice.

"I call it a, uh, a 'kiss on the beach,'" Jasmine said, squeezing a lime
wedge garnish in each of the kiddie cocktails.

Everyone was quiet for some time, clinging to what little relief the
drinks brought, but knowing nothing would fully stave off the sense of
impending doom.

A young sailor poked his head into the room and held up a phone.

"For you, ma'am," he said. "Fitz."

Chris took the phone and followed him into the hall. She watched
the sailor open the door to the deck, squinting into the bright light as
he left. Holding the phone against her chest as she waited for the door
to close behind him, she could feel her heart beating against her hand.

"This is Chris."

"All of the passengers are okay and the plane is ultimately fine," Fitz
said. "But you were right. We moved the plane into a worse position.
The air pocket inside shrank. And—" Fitz cleared his throat. Paused.
"We lost one of our divers. The mission was a failure."

Chris exhaled, unaware she'd been holding her breath. "Damn it,"
she muttered.

There, alone, in the quiet hallway, Chris realized how scared she'd
been. How much fear was right there, just below the surface. All day,
she'd allowed nothing in. Not fear, not hope. Nothing. Any emotion
could jeopardize what needed to be done, and *that* was the only thing
that mattered. Getting them home. She'd deal with how she felt about
it once they were out of that plane.

But it was undeniable. She was terrified. So just for a minute, she
let it in.

She was quiet. So was Fitz. And together, they just breathed, until Chris could think of nothing to say except the truth.

"I would have loved to have been wrong."

"Me too," Fitz said.

With a phone to his ear, he leaned against the railing on the starboard side of the ship, looking to the horizon. As far as the eye could see, it was water. Only water.

"I understand what's driving you, Chris," Fitz said. "More than you know."

Chris waited for more. Fitz waited for the lump in his throat to go down.

He thought of exactly fourteen months and five days ago. Of how he'd kissed his wife on the forehead, keys in hand, and said he needed to get some air. Of how he'd looked through the front window as he backed out of the driveway at all their friends and family, dressed in black, nodding respectfully, speaking softly, holding paper plates full of potluck casseroles and baked goods. He remembered how several houses down, he'd pulled over, opened the door, and thrown up on the street where he'd taught Michael to ride a bike all those years ago.

"My son's name was Michael."

The sun had been setting and the coroner had been walking to his car when Fitz pulled into the parking lot. The man stopped when he saw Fitz in his black suit and loosened tie. With a small nod, he headed back toward the building.

"*Are you sure?*" the coroner had asked, his hands resting on top of a closed manila file.

Fitz had nodded from the other side of the desk.

"He suffered," Fitz said, squinting into the sun's reflection off the water. "He didn't die on impact. He was alive. Fifteen minutes. Maybe more. Michael was alive that whole time. And alone."

When he said his son's name now, a hollow ache expanded in his chest. His name was all over that manila file. Michael Andrews Fitzgerald. Printed with his height and weight and age beneath pictures of his body in the mangled car, the drunk driver slumped over in his own car in the background, dense Hawaiian vegetation surrounding them on both sides of that isolated two-lane road.

It haunted Fitz every single day: The thought of Michael alone and scared. Knowing he was dying. Pleading for help. Did he cry out for him? For his mother? Did he blame them for not being there when he needed them most?

"If someone had just gotten to him sooner," Fitz said. "Every day. That's the first thought when I wake up, the last thought before I go to sleep. If someone had gotten to him sooner, would he still be alive?"

A flock of birds flew overhead in a V and Fitz looked up. One bird broke formation and dove, disappearing into the water. Moments later, some distance away, it popped up and bobbed on the surface with a fish in its beak.

Fitz still wasn't sure he would ultimately survive it. The pain that came with losing his only child, every day, threatened to break him. But today had been different. For once, his pain had a purpose. His actions could spare another father that moment when someone in uniform stands before you and says the unimaginable. Today, Fitz could be the one to get there in time.

"The diver we lost was a year older than Michael was," Fitz said. "He was twenty-one. Michael was twenty. They were just kids."

The bird's beak stopped moving with one final upward push as the white feathers on its long neck went up and down with a swallow. Spreading its wings, it flapped twice, slowly, rising from the surface to rejoin its flock.

"When I look at Shannon, I see Michael. I see Michael in every one of those passengers," Fitz said. "And I just— I wanted you to know that."

Listening to Chris's silence on the other end of the line, Fitz realized how vulnerable he was being—and immediately regretted it.

He hadn't told his wife where he went the day of the funeral. She didn't want to know any details of the accident. And he hadn't told anyone else because he didn't want to have to explain why. Fitz knew what only the unluckiest know. That until you've lost a child, you have *no idea* what loneliness and guilt and shame and grief even are. The last thing you want to do is talk to someone who doesn't get it.

This had been his secret. His alone. But now it belonged to both of them, him and this woman he didn't even know. Chris was probably trying to think of the right thing to say, the right words to fix it and make it better. But Fitz knew no words could ever fix this.

He heard Chris sniff. She took a breath.

"I'd have done the same thing," was all she said.

Fitz felt the lump in his throat return. He stared out at the horizon and for a brief moment, he wasn't a stalwart military man. He wasn't the commander in charge of the largest rescue operation in recent history. He was just a parent, alongside another parent.

Chris cleared her throat. "Shannon is my youngest."

Fitz froze.

No one else would have noticed it—but he did. That fraction of a second Chris hesitated before saying the word *is*. Shannon *is* my youngest. He knew that pause. That split second when you wonder with confusion and pain—*Do I use present tense or past tense?* Immediately after comes the guilt. The shame that you even considered moving their existence to the past. They were robbed of their future. How could you put what little you clung to every day—what little was left in the present—in the past?

Fitz's heart already ached for Chris without her having to say another word. He didn't know, but he knew what came next.

"Annie is my oldest," Chris continued. "She was eight when she slipped. It was an accident. We were at the pool. Paramedics came. But they couldn't do anything."

Chris went quiet. Fitz waited.

Staying with her in silence, he held space from a distance, waiting for her as she'd waited for him. But as the moments ticked on, he knew she was done. She wasn't going to open up any more than that. He got it. You go too deep, sometimes you don't come back. With everything they faced, Chris couldn't afford that—rather, Shannon and Will couldn't afford that—and Fitz respected her need for solid ground. He cleared his throat.

"I'm sorry we understand each other," he said.

"Me too," she said, and sighed. "But now we know where we both stand. You know I won't stop. Not until my girl is home. I won't feel this way. Not again."

"I understand," Fitz said.

He waited, letting the moment settle before it passed. Finally, he asked, "Is your plan ready?"

"Yes."

"Am I going to like it?"

"Nope."

CHAPTER TWENTY

"WHAT'S THE BAD NEWS?" ANDY ASKED.

Kit cocked her head. "What do you mean?"

"You said you had good news. I'd rather hear the bad news first."

"What? No, there's nothing. Look, the good news is, Will's wife has a plan—"

Andy and Ira groaned. Will was on his feet.

"Chris has something?"

"Wait," Jasmine cut in. "I thought she was an *ex*-wife?"

"Separated," Shannon said quickly. "They're just separated."

"Kit, what did Fitz say?" Will pleaded. "What's her plan?"

"Will, I don't know," Kit said. "All he said was her team was on the way to the crash site—"

"All of them?"

"Team?" Bernadette said.

"The guys she works with," Will said. "Her company. But wait. What's the plan?"

Kit put her hands up. "Look, Fitz just said they're going to hear them out. Nothing's been decided."

"They need to do whatever she says," Will said. "If she's got a plan, we've got a plan."

Andy rolled his eyes. "This company she works for—"

"Owns," Shannon said. "She owns the company."

"Whatever. The company does what exactly?"

"Industrial diving and marine-related construction," Will said. "You need something complex done underwater? You want Chris."

"That's what you do, too?" Kit asked.

"No, I'm an engineer," Will said. "I design stuff from a comfortable chair with a cup of coffee. She goes out and makes it happen."

"She married you, she can't be that smart," Andy said.

"She's not smart," Will snapped. "Smart is me. Smart knows things. Memorizes things. Smart can be taught. What Chris has is something else. She has this way where she just *gets* it. Her ideas. They feel . . . inevitable. Obvious. So you go, *How'd I not see that?* But you never would have. Because your brain doesn't work like hers. No one's does. She's beyond intelligence. Or even intuition. She's . . ."

The plane was quiet. Shannon was beaming.

"They don't have a word for what she is," he said finally. "They're all inadequate."

Ruth leaned her head against Ira's shoulder. "That's love," Ruth said.

"That's respect," Kit said.

Something flashed in the pilot's eyes that reminded Will of Chris. Strong women know loving someone is easy. Respecting them is a choice. And for some reason, Will went to a memory he hadn't thought of in ages: Chris, turning from inside her front door to wave goodbye as he drove off after their first date. He couldn't read the look on his future wife's face, but he knew it meant something good.

He'd never told Chris—but that was the moment he knew he loved her.

"If she's that great, why'd you leave her?" Andy asked.

Shannon looked up, waiting for the answer.

How could he explain when he didn't really know? He asked himself the same thing all the time. Annie's accident had been the trigger. But in the years since, the distance and the pain . . . why *had* they been so insurmountable for them? The answer had felt right there, like a name you can't remember, a face you can't quite place. But for whatever reason, it had eluded them.

What Will did know was that he'd never felt like more of a

failure—as a husband and as a father—than every time over the last year when he'd parked in their driveway and watched Shannon cross their front lawn to climb into the passenger seat so they could head to his apartment for the weekend. His whole life, that kind of moment had been the one thing he never wanted to put on his child.

After they lost Annie, their shared bottom line was an unconditional love for Shannon, so they made it work. But the older she got, the harder it became. The fighting and making up were too frequent. A constant resentment simmered between them just below the surface. And then, one morning, after they'd gotten into a nasty fight over nothing really, Will muttered sarcastically under his breath as he left the kitchen, "*Of course you're right. Self-righteous martyrs always are.*" To which Chris shot back, "*At least I see past myself. You see yourself as the victim, not Annie.*"

They'd stared at each other, surprised by their words. For all their faults, they prided themselves on never fighting dirty. They never name-called or took cheap shots. They always fought tough but clean. So with the sting of their comments still hanging in the air, it was clear to them both that a line had been crossed.

As Chris stared at him from the other side of the kitchen, her eyes pleaded with him.

Let's take it back. Please. It's not too late for us.

But he didn't. And neither did she.

And so later that week, after sixteen years together, he moved out.

Why? Why didn't he go to her? Hold her. Apologize. Why didn't he tell her how much he missed Annie and ask her what her own grief felt like? Why was it easier to push Chris away than to admit that he was scared? Scared of losing Shannon. Scared of losing Chris. Scared that if anything ever happened to either of them, it would end him. Why did he assume he would get another chance to do it all better? Why did he think there would be another opportunity other than the one right in front of him?

Those were his thoughts as the plane was sinking.

"Why did I leave her . . ." Will said, more of a musing to himself than an answer to Andy. "Isn't that what we're all doing right now? Looking back on our whole lives, asking ourselves what we would have done differently?"

The plane was silent for a long time. Shannon wrapped her arms around Will's waist. He could feel her heartbeat against his body.

"I lied," said Ira.

"About what?" Ruth asked.

"About *Titanic*. I lied," he said. "Ruth, I have you. I have two daughters. If we were there, if that'd been us . . . The thought of putting the three of you in a lifeboat. Never knowing what happened. If you were okay. And I knew—" The old man's voice cracked. "I knew—if I watched—I just—I couldn't—"

Ruth wrapped her arms around her husband, shushing him quietly as he cried.

Will tightened his own arms around Shannon and looked out the window at the dark water, imagining Chris at this moment.

Somewhere, up above, she was figuring out how to get down to them. How to get them out. How to get them home.

He knew nothing would stop her.

He knew Chris was on her way.

CHAPTER TWENTY-ONE

LARSON EXITED THE CHOPPER FIRST. ROGERS WAS ON HER HEELS. THEN THE COAST-guardsmen and Navy sailors already on the deck of the USS *Powell* exchanged looks as they watched the four civilians who followed after them.

Flip-flops and straw hats. Long hair and tank tops. Bright colors. Big sunglasses.

They were as far from military as it got.

The USS *Powell*, a T-ATF-166 Powhatan-class fleet ocean tug, was the VOO—vessel of opportunity—that carried the Falcon. Command had shifted there as soon as it arrived on site. Fitz and his team had just started inspecting the SRDRS when they got word that the Navy contingency was on approach.

"Chris," Fitz hollered over the fading thwack of the rotors as the chopper flew off. He stuck out his hand and greeted a woman he'd never met who understood him better than most ever would. As she brushed the hair out of her face while introductions were made all around, he couldn't help but notice the tan line on her bare ring finger.

"Is that her?" Chris asked. Without waiting for an answer, she headed toward the stern.

Attached to the back of the ship was a bright yellow behemoth of machinery. Towering nearly fifty feet high, the deployment system was a complex maze of metal pipes and hydraulic-powered rigging that cradled the Falcon. Once activated, the system would rock forward, slowly lowering the rescue module into the water.

Chris and her team peered up at the oblong cylinder, focusing on the large metal bubble attached to the bottom of the vessel: the transfer skirt.

This was the point of attachment between the plane and the rescue module. This was the location—if everything went according to plan— where the passengers would climb out of the plane and into the rescue module.

Chris handed Fitz a piece of paper from her back pocket. Unfolding it, he studied the page briefly before turning it right-side up. After a few moments, he turned the paper back upside down.

"We have two problems," Chris said. "One: there's no way to dock this thing to the plane. And two: there isn't a hatch to open to allow the people inside the plane to get out." She pointed at the part of the draw-ing Fitz was studying.

"For problem one," Chris continued, "weld flat pieces of metal equi-distant around the base of the transfer skirt—the mating point with the plane. Think of a kid's drawing of the sun. A circle with rays coming out of it all the way around."

"Okay."

"The circle part is the bottom of the transfer skirt. That's what'll sit flush against the plane. And the rays all around that sun's circle"—she traced the short lines with her finger on the paper—"are the metal feet we're going to weld to it."

"But how does that make the Falcon attach to the plane?" Fitz asked.

Before she could answer, two more choppers were seen on approach, both dangling massive cargo payloads.

"Let's talk inside," Fitz said, already having to yell over the noise.

As everyone headed for the ship's interior, Milton stared at all of the equipment on approach.

"We weren't sure what you had," Feeny told him. "So we brought it all."

———

"The concept is simple," Chris said.

It was standing-room only. The Navy's own dive team had joined the Coast Guard's dive locker. Fitz, Milton, Tanner, and Larson all sat at the table. A speakerphone with a connection to the plane lay in the center. And a phone showing the image search results for "1800s toggle-head whaling harpoons" was being passed around the room.

"You put a sharp point on the end of a toggle bolt," Chris continued. "You harpoon the whale. Pull back. The toggle engages and the sharp end locks in place in the whale's flesh. Now, imagine these weaponized toggle bolts attached to—welded to—the slats of metal we're going to put around the transfer skirt."

Only Rogers nodded in understanding.

"Aircraft skin is made of aluminum alloy," Chris said. "It's tough. But it's extremely thin and lightweight. Which means it's easily penetrable. So with these attached along the bottom of the skirt, the Falcon will literally impale the surface of the plane and lock itself into place."

"What about the gap?" Larson said. "After the toggle goes in, won't there be a space where water could leak into the plane?"

"Yes," Chris answered. "Which is why each attachment, each of the feet, will have a rubber gasket. It'll act like an auto-locking rubber seal between the plane and our modified parts."

No one responded.

Chris tried to read the room. She knew they got it. But there was an expectant pause. Like they were waiting for her to say more. Or to say that she was just kidding and then present the real plan. Before they could be shot down completely, Feeny picked up the pitch.

"That's how we attach to the plane. That's problem one," Feeny said. "Problem two. How do we get people out of a sealed plane?"

Chris stepped back and Feeny took the floor.

"Obviously, there's no hatch on the plane like a sub would have," he said. "So we'll need to make one. I'll be inside the Falcon. Once we're connected, I open the Falcon's hatch, drop down into the transfer skirt, and then cut a hole in the roof of the plane."

"Won't there be water trapped in the skirt?" Larson said.

"Yes. But not enough to be a problem."

"As he cuts the hole, it'll drain into the cabin," Chris said. "But their air pocket's big enough. It should be fine as long as we move quickly."

"So once I get the hole cut," Feeny continued, "the passengers climb up and in. I close the hatch on the Falcon. We head for the surface."

"Hold on," Fitz said. "If I'm understanding, the Falcon is essentially embedded in the plane. How does it detach?"

"It doesn't," Chris said. "We cut it free."

"We?"

"Sayid, Noah, and I will dive with the Falcon. When it first mates, we'll spot-weld any points that aren't a perfect seal. Plug any holes or cracks. Then, once the passenger transfer is complete, we cut it free. Cut the metal slats that have been welded to the transfer skirt, leaving them stuck in the plane."

"Has something like this ever been done before?" Larson asked.

"I don't know," Chris said.

"How are you going to test it?"

"Test it? This *is* the test."

"Is it safe?" Fitz said.

"Of course not," Chris said. "Safe doesn't live here anymore. There is no more safe."

Larson slid her chair back to confer with the lead Navy diver, Brandon Caputo. Tanner leaned forward across the table to speak with Fitz. Everyone talked at once, and everyone had an opinion. Chris checked her watch.

After a few moments, Fitz raised a hand.

"All right, all right," Fitz said loudly over the noise. "Let's keep— Chris?"

Chris was headed for the door.

"I'm done wasting time," Chris said. "Unless you got any questions better than the last two, I'm getting to work."

"But—"

"Remind me," she said. "What are your other options?"

The only response was the squeak of the door closing behind her.

CHAPTER TWENTY-TWO

EVERYONE WAS STARING AT HIM LIKE HE WAS NUTS, SO WILL REPEATED HIMSELF.

"I said, we need to take the plane apart."

If topside went with Chris's plan, he explained, they'd need access to the aluminum outer skin. The plastic panels that lined the top of the plane's interior had a dropped-ceiling design, not all that different from the lightweight tiles commonly used to hide pipes and duct-work in most office buildings. So all they had to do was push up, and the lightweight panels would pop out of place, to then be angled and pulled down.

"We do that," Andy said, "and the roof will give. This is suicide."

"It will hold," Will said.

"Says the guy who got us into this mess."

Will pointed at the ceiling. "Andy, you really think those flimsy plastic sheets are what's keeping the water out?"

"Guys. C'mon," Kit said, jumping in before it could escalate. "The interior is cosmetic. Not structural. So, Kaholo, Jasmine. You're the tall-est." She pointed to aisle seats opposite each other and the two of them stepped up.

"That'd be easier if you took the vest off," Andy said.

"You let me worry about me," Jasmine said, having to pull down the inflated yellow pillow to see over it.

"Push up on three?" Kaholo said, reaching up to the last plastic ceil-ing panel with his good hand. "One, two, three—" The concave panel made a cracking noise as they both pushed up, but it didn't budge.

Kaholo counted again and they repeated the movement. This time, the panel lifted slightly on Jasmine's side.

Ryan hopped up with a foot on each aisle armrest in the row in front of them. Using Shannon's water bottle, which held their messages, to extend his reach, he helped push up on the center until there was a loud crack and the panel broke out of the frame completely.

Everyone watched the three of them jostle the piece around so it could drop down—but the overhead bins blocked clearance.

"Here, watch out," Molly said, and Kaholo moved out of the way. Molly opened the overhead bin, hopped up on the seat, and started fiddling with the plastic hinges inside. A flash of light went off and Molly looked up in surprise just as the sound of a photo clicked.

"Actually, can I borrow that?" she said to Maia. Taking the phone, Molly turned the flashlight on and shone it into the bin. Moments later there was a snap and the bin's lid fell out of its hinge.

"How'd you know how to do that?" Kaholo asked.

"I once worked a flight that took a two-hour delay for a broken bin. When maintenance finally showed up, it took him like two seconds to fix it," Molly said as the second hinge clicked and the lid detached entirely. "I had him show me how to do it so that'd never happen to me again." She passed the lid down and Kit took it, tucking it into the lav and out of the way.

"Employee of the month," Ryan said.

Molly laughed, stepping across the aisle to the seat on the other side. "Not really. I had tickets to a concert that night and missed the show. I was pissed."

That side took even less time, and without the overhead bin lids to block it, the ceiling panel came down easily.

"Did this maintenance guy teach you anything about that?" Ira said.

Everyone stared up. Thick green and pink insulation blankets lined the exposed cavity. On top of that ran a dense and complex network of wires.

"Boy, this would be a bad situation if we were surrounded by water or something," Jasmine said.

"Do you know which wires control what?" Will asked Kit.

Kit shook her head. "Not a clue."

"Well, the Falcon will dock right there," Will said, pointing directly overhead at the tangle of wires. "At minimum, they have to move. If we can't move them, we'll have to cut them."

"Are the wires live?" Ira asked.

The question hung, unanswered.

"Airbus was supposed to be sending over the designs," Kit said as she went for the phone. "I'll ask if there's anything about the electrical system."

Will followed but pointed at the insulation. "Can you all figure out how to remove that while Kit and I troubleshoot the electrical? But don't cut anything just yet."

"No shit," Andy said.

Kit was in the back with her ear to the phone. She looked at Will and shook her head. "They don't have schematics for the electrical yet."

Kit picked up the interphone and pressed the big button. A loud ding rang throughout the cabin. "Test," she said, and her echoing voice followed.

"Communication and emergency systems run on separate power sources," Kit said. "That's why the emergency lights work but not the regular cabin lighting."

"How do we have any power at all?" Will asked.

"A plane's electrical has redundancies. Some systems are battery or generator stored. But even that doesn't really make sense. I honestly don't know how or why we have any power and I've been terrified that it's going to cut off at any second."

A loud crack came from the cabin as Kaholo and Jasmine managed to rip an entire overhead bin out of the ceiling.

"Jesus!" Andy said, ducking as the bin was passed over his head. "Any second, that water's coming in—"

"Help or shut the fuck up, Andy," Kaholo said.

Will stared up at the widening exposure of wires and insulation and considered what little power was still on. Strips of emergency lights and the overhead signage at all the exits were it. Without that, the plane would be pitch-black.

"We need to shut off any other power before we cut any wires," Will said.

"Well, sure," Kit agreed. "But everything's controlled from the cockpit."

"And with the door shut and locked—"

"We can't get in. Exactly. But . . ." Kit trailed off, thinking. "Hey, Molly . . ."

The flight attendant turned, arms raised, helping hold up a section of insulation.

"Where's the ISPS switch?"

"Uhhh . . ." Molly's eyes narrowed as she tried to envision the galley. "Check the circuit breakers over the coffeepot— No. Try the top of the crew panel. I think there."

Kit stood on her tiptoes. "Got it," she said into the cabin. She lifted the large red cover to reveal a silver toggle switch underneath.

"What's it do?" Will asked.

"It's the emergency cutoff for the power outlets and USB ports under the seats."

Will waited for Kit to say more, but she just stared at the switch.

"You're worried if we shut it off, we'll lose what power we do have," Will said.

"Exactly."

"Then we turn it back on. It's a switch."

"No. It's an emergency shutoff. It can only be reset with circuit breakers in the cockpit. Once it's off, it's off."

Neither of them said anything for a few moments. There was another loud crack as another bin was ripped from the ceiling. Ryan guided the bin down into a submerged row and let it fill with water until it sank out of the way.

Will watched the passengers working while studying the tangle of wires dangling above their heads. "We can't gamble that those wires don't control the emergency lights. I mean, it hasn't exactly been our lucky day. We can manage in the dark. Electrocution, not so much."

Kit nodded, chewing on the inside of her cheek. "Okay," she said after a few moments. "My plane, my call. Whatever happens is on me."

"Guys, hold up—" Will said, extending a hand. The passengers paused, looking over. Everyone waited.

Reaching up to the toggle, Kit took a deep breath and flipped the switch, and the entire plane plunged into darkness.

CHAPTER TWENTY-THREE

SPARKS FLEW AND METAL SCREECHED ON THE DECK OF THE USS *POWELL* AS SAYID AND Noah—assisted by coastguardsmen—made modifications to the Falcon. It was loud and chaotic, but even with all that, the group huddled around the monitors arguing on the other side of the deck pulled focus.

"You said the plane was on the edge of a cliff," Feeny said.

"It is," Tanner replied.

"No," Chris said. "It's ass-up like a skinny kid on a teeter-totter on the edge of a cliff. Big fucking difference. We can't dock this thing like that. We need resistance. The plane's gotta be stable and secure. If not, all we'll do is push it over."

"Okay, okay. So . . ." Rogers said quickly, trying to defuse the situation. He was stuck somewhere in the middle. Officially military, unofficially adopted by Chris's team of misfits. "What about a tail stand? Something to go underneath the plane. To brace it. Prop it up."

Feeny ran a finger down the sloping angle of the plane on the TV. "Too steep. We'd tip it forward off the ledge. But . . ." He widened his stance and frowned at the screens. "What if we attached cables to the tail, then ran the cables down to anchors we'd drill into the reef—"

"No drilling," Tanner said. "That's nonnegotiable."

No one said anything for a while. Both out of respect for what had happened and because no one had anything to contribute.

"What if we laid it flat?" Chris said finally. She let the idea percolate. "Something over the tail, to tip it back down. A weighted cable? A top-over lashing approach. You know, how lumber or pipes are secured for transport."

"Didn't Will say the tail was too weak?" Tanner asked. "He said we'd snap the tail and flood the plane."

"Too weak to lift the plane, yes. But not to anchor it down," Chris said.

"What if we weight it from below?" Feeny said. "Pull it down from underneath."

"How?" Rogers asked.

"We . . ." Feeny paused, figuring out exactly how it would work. "Wrap a sling around the tail. Attach a cable to the sling. So instead of lifting the cable . . ."

"We drop it," Chris said.

"Slowly. It pools on the seabed. The weight of the cable pulls the tail down."

"Airplanes are light," Rogers said. "Twenty feet of two-inch cable would be heavy enough."

"But if we lay it flat," Tanner said, "won't the air pocket flood?"

Chris shut her eyes and slowly tilted her head to the side and back up, trying to visualize the inside of a water-filled plane.

"It won't flood . . ." she said, letting the statement linger as she finalized her thought. "It'll spread. But if we lay the plane down slow . . . controlled . . . then the air bubble will only spread across the top of the cabin. If they know it's coming, they can plan for it." She paused. "Do we know how much air they have?"

"We had a rough estimate before we tried to lift it," Tanner said. "I'm not sure about now. We can ask your husband."

"I've got two updates."

Everyone turned to see Fitz coming down the stairs.

"One," he said. "We're not going forward with your plan. The Navy's got another idea. It's viable. We're going with that."

Everyone glanced at Chris but she just stared at him calmly.

"And two?" she said, her voice pinched.

"We've lost contact with the plane."

3:07 p.m.

3 hours and 6 minutes after impact

Approximately 2 hours of oxygen inside plane

CHAPTER TWENTY-FOUR

WILL TURNED THE FLASHLIGHT TO THE BACK GALLEY. KIT WAS PUNCHING BUTTONS ON the MedLink phone. Holding it to her ear, she looked up, shook her head, and put the phone back in its cradle.

Andy shoved Will from behind and the beam of light spun around as the flashlight flew from his hand.

"The fuck did you do?" Andy snarled.

Will wasn't a natural-born fighter, but today he'd had enough.

Andy took a swing. Will managed to dodge it. Will countered, his fist connecting painfully with the meat of Andy's left cheek. Andy stumbled momentarily before lurching forward, off balance. Ramming his shoulder into Will's chest, he drove Will backward up against the door while Will repeatedly pounded his fists into Andy's sides. Everyone screamed at the two to stop as they grappled and stumbled around the galley, knocking into the metal carriers.

"Hey! *Hey!*" Kit yelled as she and Kaholo tried to get in between them. When they finally did, Kit shoved Will backward across the galley as Kaholo pushed Andy to the other side. Pinning him against the door, Kaholo forced Andy back every time he tried to move forward, while Shannon wrapped her arms around her father on the other side of the plane. The young girl glared at Andy, seemingly challenging him to just try it. Just try to hit a man while his daughter clung to him.

The men breathed heavily as the fight de-escalated. After a moment, Will unwrapped Shannon's arms and Andy begrudgingly held his hands up in surrender.

"Once we're out of here, feel free to beat the shit out of each other," Kit said, alternating glares between the two men. "But you"—she said to Will—"have better uses for your energy. And you"—she turned to Andy—"stop being such a dick."

The men continued to stare each other down, but neither challenged Kit or the other.

"Look," Kit said, addressing the group. "We have enough problems here. Blaming doesn't help. We have to stay together. Yes, we lost the lights. We lost communication. But the plan hasn't changed. They know where we are and they're coming for us. So let's focus on being ready when they get here."

As their eyes continued to adjust to the dark, they returned to the task of removing the insulation from the ceiling. Will and Kit stood at the back of the plane shining their flashlights up at the wires.

"Well," Kit said, rubbing her face with an exhausted sigh, "at least we know the electricity's off."

CHAPTER TWENTY-FIVE

THE DOOR OPENED WITH SUCH FORCE THAT IT SLAMMED AGAINST THE WALL.

"Are the passengers okay?" Chris asked, barging into the room.

Larson, from the far side of the room, turned slowly. "Truthfully, we don't know. The ROVs show the plane in place and intact, but we don't see lights in the cabin anymore. We assume their electrical went out but there's no reason to believe they're not okay."

"What happened?"

Fitz had come into the room, the last to enter after Feeny, Tanner, and Rogers. "We don't know that either," he said. "The line just went dead."

"And that's it?" Chris said. "You have no other way to reestablish contact."

"It's a plane at the bottom of the ocean," Larson said. "We were lucky to communicate at all."

Larson and Fitz stared at Chris, waiting for her to say something else, but she just shook her head, fuming.

"What's this about other plans?" Chris asked, finally.

Larson pressed a button on one of the TVs. The paused image began to move, replaying the footage from earlier where the ROV camera moved around the nose of the plane, the fish scattered, and the captain's dead body appeared.

"Why are we watching this again?" Chris asked.

Someone pressed pause. Caputo, the Navy's lead diver, approached the screen and pointed at the frozen image of the broken cockpit window.

"This is our way in," Caputo said.

Chris looked from Caputo to Larson. "I don't get it."

"The cockpit door is locked to the passengers inside the plane. But it's not locked if you're inside the cockpit."

Chris, again, looked from Caputo to Larson. "You're saying you want to open the cockpit door from the inside? You want to break the airtight seal that has been the *only* thing keeping those people alive?"

"That's what we thought," Larson said as she spread several pieces of paper out on the table. "Until we got the design specs from Airbus. Which is when we noticed . . ."

Chris picked up one of the pages, studying the architectural design for the cockpit door.

"It's not airtight."

"We can open that door with no repercussions to the air pocket," Larson said. "We can get inside that plane."

Milton slid images across the table.

"They're called SEIE suits," Fitz said. Chris and Feeny studied the pictures of the bright red, full-body submarine rescue suits. "Two divers will swim down, enter through the broken cockpit window, open the door from the inside, and we're in the cabin. Divers will bring the suits down one at a time. The passenger making the ascent will be briefed and suited up. Then the divers will escort them through the cockpit, out the window, and they'll free-ascend to the surface together."

The images of the submarine escape immersion equipment suits were from a military training manual that described how the suit allowed for individual free ascents from sunken submarines. It was designed as an option of last resort and it was viable to depths of six hundred feet. The concept, essentially, was to seal a person inside a watertight, full-body suit outfitted with a self-contained breathing apparatus.

Chris flipped one of the images around. "You got some in kid's sizes?"

Larson rattled off some of the potential ideas for modifications, but Chris cut her off. "This isn't a sub full of trained sailors. We're not rescuing some goddamn Navy SEALs. These are regular people. Old folks. Children. What about injuries?"

"Well—" Larson said.

"Forget the physical," Chris kept on. "After what these people have been through, you think they're in any condition psychologically to pull this off?" Chris tossed the pictures on the table. "This is suicide."

"What's the training for these?" Feeny asked. "Can this just be shown and done?"

"All submariners go through a multiday training course that—" Caputo said.

"They don't have multiple days," Chris said.

"Isn't the failure rate something crazy?" Rogers asked. Larson glared at him and he shut up.

"Thirty-two percent," Tanner answered, looking down at the floor.

"Right," Feeny said. "So you want to run a plan that—for trained military—has a thirty-two percent failure rate—"

"Success rate," Tanner said, correcting him. "Only thirty-two percent of trained submariners complete the SEIE training successfully." He looked up at Fitz. "You know these civilians can't make it."

"Not everyone will make it," Caputo said flatly. "We need to accept that. This isn't a perfect plan because there *isn't* a perfect plan."

Chris took slow, methodical steps toward him. "Is that what you're going to tell the families? 'Sorry for your loss, but your grandma was factored into our imperfect plan.' Is that what you're going to tell me after you get my daughter killed?"

Feeny put a hand on Chris's shoulder. She shook off his grip, and that would have been it if she hadn't seen Caputo's eye-roll as he turned away. Chris lunged forward and Feeny had to wrap his arms around her waist, struggling to hold her back.

Chris untangled herself from Feeny, her hands raised. "Are the suits even here?"

"They will be soon," Larson said. "They're collecting them on base."

Chris shook her head and moved for the door. "Well, I'm here now. And I'll be ready when your plan goes bad," she said, already halfway down the hall.

CHAPTER TWENTY-SIX

WILL STARED UP AT THE ROOF OF THE AIRCRAFT, WONDERING HOW THE HELL THEY WERE going to cut that last wire.

"First class," Will said, turning to Molly. "Doesn't first class use real silverware?"

"It's a dull butter knife," Molly replied. "Barely cuts the chicken."

"No one has a Swiss Army knife?" Andy asked.

"Yeah, I've got one right here," Will replied. "TSA had no problem with it."

Andy rolled his eyes, one of which now had a nice shiner.

Having angled three flashlights, two cell phone flashlights, and the clip-on portable reading light Ryan had found, they'd managed to keep working. They'd removed all the insulation. The plane's aluminum skin was now exposed, along with the even pattern of metal stringers that covered the airframe as structural supports.

Then they hit a roadblock: the dense network of wires that ran from the front of the plane to the back—the circulatory system of the modern aircraft.

They'd managed to move most of the wires out of the way by ripping them out of their plastic brackets and sliding them down the sides of the aircraft—but one wire refused to budge. Of course, it ran straight down the center of the plane.

Molly looked to Kaholo. "What about the survival kit?"

"Hold on," Jasmine said. "You got something called a survival kit and y'all just bringing it up *now*?"

Kaholo was already opening a bin at the back of the plane. "It's for survival on the water, not under it. Things like flares. A whistle. A mirror. Shit like that. Stuff we don't need. Unless . . ."

Tossing a yellow plastic bundle to Ryan, Kaholo jumped down from the seat with a splash. Kaholo unzipped the pack and started to rifle through it with his good hand as Ryan steadied it.

"Unless," Kaholo said, holding up a rudimentary metal tool. He rotated a piece of metal outward and a small, dull blade latched into place anticlimactically.

"'Cause that'll work," Andy said.

"Beats a butter knife," Kaholo said, hopping up on one of the aisle chairs. Biting down on the knife's handle to free up his uninjured hand, Kaholo's movements were so casual and easy everyone just assumed he knew what he was doing. He took the knife in his good hand and laid the blade across the wire, ready to muscle through it.

"What are you doing?" Ira said, freezing Kaholo. "Aren't you going to test it?"

"Test it?" Kaholo said.

"To make sure it's not hot."

"Hot?"

Ira rolled his eyes like the grumpy old man he was. "Maybe check that it doesn't have an electric charge, you know, before you cut into it with a metal knife while standing over a pool of water. Just a thought."

"Isn't that why we're in the dark?" Kaholo asked, looking to Will.

"I mean, yes," Will said. "In theory that shouldn't be a live wire."

"In theory?"

"Just test it," Ira said.

"How do I—"

"My god, do men these days know how to do anything?" Ira waded into the water for a closer look. "You'll want to cut the insulation on the wire first. Then touch the blade to the ground. So touch it to, uh, to that," he said, pointing at one of the aluminum stringer supports attached to the roof. "So you touch the blade to that, *then* touch the blade to the wire. If there's a small spark, you know it's hot."

Kaholo hesitated, his eyes darting from the old man to the wire and back. He looked to Will.

"Hey, Will's not the only brain here, you know," Ira said. "Just do what I said."

Kaholo adjusted his grip on the knife, holding it to the blue plastic insulation around the wire. "This blue stuff. That's what you mean by—"

"Oh for Christ's sake."

"Ira, no," Ruth said as Ira stood on the aisle seat on the other side of the plane. The water came up to the bottom of the armrests, just above his ankles.

"Ruth, it's fine. Pass it," Ira said, holding out his hand.

Kit stepped forward. "Maybe someone else should—"

"Goddamn it, stop treating me like an old man!"

"Look, I can do it if you—" Kaholo said.

"Gimme the knife, kid." Ira held out his hand.

Kaholo reluctantly passed him the yellow metal handle and Ira reached up to the wire. He was shorter than Kaholo and couldn't reach.

"Ira. This is a bad idea . . ."

"Ruth," Ira mumbled, biting down on the knife's handle while he steadied himself with one foot on each armrest. Water dripped from the bottom of his pants.

Reaching up, he took the wire in one hand and the knife in the other with a practiced ease. His thumb rested on the back of the blade as he sliced through the insulation to reveal the copper wire underneath.

Everyone in the plane was looking up, silently watching him work.

Ira let go of the wire and readjusted his grip on the knife. Looking up to the ceiling, he raised the blade toward the metal bar. It was just out of his reach, so he went up on his tiptoes.

"Oh, Ira," Ruth whispered.

With a small grunt, Ira extended his reach and touched the blade to the metal support. Everyone held their breath as they watched him move the knife down to the wire.

The moment the knife touched the wire was the moment he slipped.

His left foot slipped first, then the right. Ira reflexively grabbed for the wire and the palm of his hand met the exposed section of metal just as his feet hit the water. Ira jerked with violent spasms as a jolt of electricity coursed through his body. Letting go of the wire, he dropped the knife and fell into the water, unconscious.

Ruth cried out as she went to Ira, but the passengers screamed at her to stop. She ignored them, splashing into the water to wrap herself around her husband while calling out his name. Will and Kaholo rushed forward, carrying Ira out of the water to the back of the plane, where they laid his unresponsive body on the floor in the back galley, his gray hair floating in the standing inches of water.

"Molly—" Kaholo yelled.

"I got it!" Molly said, already digging through an overhead bin.

"No pulse," Bernadette said, her fingers wrapped around his wrist. She began chest compressions as Molly dropped to her knees on the opposite side of Ira's body. The flight attendant was clutching a red package labeled with a cartoon heart and a pulse line running through it.

"Is that a defibrillator?" Bernadette asked breathlessly while her hands pumped rhythmically into Ira's chest.

"Yes," Molly said, unzipping the automated external defibrillator. She held it flat, looking for a place to set it down—but water covered everything.

"We can't—" Bernadette said.

"I know," Molly said, getting to her feet, spinning around, trying to figure out how to make this work. She knew they couldn't use electric shock paddles to restart the heart of a man who was soaking wet and lying in a pool of water.

"Lay him on the galley countertop—" Kaholo said.

"It's metal," Molly said.

"Just get him ready," Kit said, grabbing Will's arm. "We'll figure it out."

"Go over there and hold this," Molly said, passing Jasmine the defibrillator.

Jasmine stepped carefully over Ira's body while Bernadette blew two long breaths into his mouth. Dropping to her knees by Ira's head, Jasmine held the AED out like it was a platter.

"Get me something dry. Dry cloth," Molly said as she ripped Ira's buttoned shirt open, revealing a ribbed white tank underneath. "Where's the knife?"

Kaholo rushed forward with the knife while Andy rifled through the pile of clothes. Shannon and Maia hugged each other, watching the adults scramble while Will and Kit tried to figure out a way they could support Ira's body from underneath if they laid him across the seat backs of the last two rows.

"Ira, honey . . . Ira . . ." Ruth muttered to herself. Ryan's arm was wrapped around her, supporting nearly all her weight.

Molly cut into the neck of the tank top and ripped it all the way down to the bottom hem, exposing Ira's bare chest, while Bernadette continued the compressions.

"Push that button," Molly said to Jasmine, nodding toward the device. "I need something dry!" Andy rushed forward and thrust a T-shirt into her outstretched hand.

Jasmine pushed a circular green button and lights came on across the front of the AED.

Molly rubbed the T-shirt across Ira's chest to dry the skin. Throwing the shirt over her shoulder, she grabbed a plastic pouch from the medical device, ripped it open, and removed the flexible pads inside. Stretching out the cord that connected to the bottoms of the pads, she plugged the plastic end into the device, and moments later, a robotic male voice began to speak.

"Apply pads to patient's chest," the voice said in a calm, even tone.

Bernadette blew into Ira's mouth as Molly carefully peeled the adhesive pads off the holder. Using the descriptive drawings on the back of the pads as a guide, she placed one diagonally across the right side of Ira's chest directly under the collarbone, and the other she stuck to the lower-left side of his chest.

"Move, girls," Will said, ushering the children out of the way.

Wrestling with the lav door, he kicked it open, then struggled to remove the overhead bin lids they'd placed inside.

"We're good, Molly. Ready for him soon," Kit said, taking the first of the plastic lids from Will. Laying it across the back of the seats like a bridge between the rows, she nodded. "Get the other," she said quietly to Will, and he started trying to remove the other lid from the tight space.

"Analyzing heartbeat," the robotic voice said. "Do not touch the patient."

"I'm clear, you're clear," Molly said, scooting back while waving her hands across the space as she'd done so many times in training but never in real life. Bernadette stopped giving compressions and rocked back on her heels.

"We're set," Kit said. "Tell us when you're ready to move him."

Molly nodded, never taking her eyes off Ira's chest. Bernadette breathed heavily and sweat dripped down her forehead. Ruth kept repeating Ira's name. But everything went silent and still as the machine's voice began to speak.

"No heartbeat detected. Shock not advised."

CHAPTER TWENTY-SEVEN

CHRIS DIDN'T LIKE THE LOOK OF THE STORM CLOUDS GATHERING ON THE FAR SIDE OF Molokai. She checked her watch.

The SEIE suits still weren't here. So as far as Chris was concerned, they should proceed like the suits weren't coming.

"This is her from the inside," Rogers said, pointing to the monitor.

The Falcon was remotely operated and Rogers was the best ROV pilot they had. A makeshift control center had been set up on deck near the back of the launching module. Five monitors displayed video feed of the Falcon—two from the inside, three on the outside—and next to it were the controls Rogers would use to pilot the vessel.

"This is where the passengers will sit," he said, drawing a finger up the long benches on the screen. PRM INTERIOR 1 was displayed in the lower right-hand corner. The monitor next to it was labeled PRM INTE-RIOR 2. That angle showed the same space, but from the opposite side. Bright overhead lights illuminated pipe-lined walls inside the cylindrical vessel. It was as austere a design as could be imagined. Nothing was superfluous or built for comfort.

"She can fit sixteen adults and two attendants. Space won't be an issue," said Rogers.

"Feeny's one attendant," Chris said. "Who from your team is going in?"

"Harris," Tanner replied with a nod at the diver. She nodded back.

From the stern, Sayid whistled. He lifted his chin at Chris, and she excused herself.

"We should start getting ready," Sayid said. "Noah's attaching the last piece."

"I'll let them know," Chris said. The SEIE suits still hadn't arrived. Her team was going to be ready first. She started walking backward, headed for the group. "Ask if a few of the military guys can help set up our gear."

There was a loud metallic screech and then a heavy clang.

"*Fuck!*" Noah screamed from the back of the ship.

When Chris and Sayid rounded the corner, Noah was ripping off his gloves in frustration. The final attachment lay broken in two pieces on the ground under the transfer skirt. Noah kicked the side of a column, then walked to the railing, his fingers interlaced and resting on top of his head.

"Was it the weld or the piece itself?" Chris asked him.

"The piece," Sayid said, answering for Noah. He bent to pick up the broken toggle attachment.

Chris swore. Fixing the weld would have been quick. Fabricating another piece would take a lot more time.

"Make another," she said, trying to not let bitter anger color her words. "Don't rush. We need it done right. But do it fast."

Noah put his gloves on and started back toward the equipment. Chris patted his shoulder as he passed and noticed her hand was shaking.

Was this it? Was that one moment, that one stroke of bad luck, going to be the difference between Shannon and Will's surviving or not?

"Get ready to dive anyway," Chris said to Sayid, but his face stopped her. She turned. Navy helicopters were on approach.

All three of them walked to the railing on the far side of the ship, where down below, three hard-bottomed inflatable speedboats full of Navy divers in full gear were riding out to position themselves directly above the plane. As the helicopters neared, the doors slid open. Piles of bright red SEIE-suit bags were stacked inside.

The hovering choppers began dropping the suits into the water, where the divers loaded them into the boats. Payload drop completed, the helicopters headed back to land.

"They're gonna try," Chris said in disbelief as she watched two divers descend into the water with one of the suits, headed for the plane. "And they're gonna learn the hard way."

CHAPTER TWENTY-EIGHT

RUTH KNELT ON THE FLOOR OF THE GALLEY NEXT TO IRA'S BODY. BRINGING HIS LEFT hand to his chest, she covered it with her own, their matching gold wedding bands resting on top of one another.

Will tried to look away. All the passengers had. Out of respect. Out of a desire to give her time alone with him. Out of discomfort at the thought of their own mortality. But there was nowhere to go, and somehow it seemed more intrusive to deny the moment. So everyone came closer. A hand on a shoulder. Fingers intertwined. Leaning against one another, they grieved together.

Death had been their constant companion all day. But they were no longer strangers. It was no longer "*I* am afraid to die." Or "*That person* just died." It was "We've lost *one of our own*." There was no twisted metal, no flames, no blood, no screams. The scene was tender and small, just one little old man and the little old woman he had loved. In the quiet, the dread of mortality had never felt closer.

"We had our first big fight on our first anniversary," Ruth said. "I never could remember what it was about. We were twenty-year-old kids. We didn't know how to fight. We had no clue how to be married, no idea what we were doing."

She paused, wiping her eyes.

"So we're fighting. I'm exhausted. Finally, I say, 'Forget this, I'm leaving.' I grab a suitcase. Throwing who knows what into it. I'm screaming, he's screaming. And after a while, he grabs the bag. It's a mess, clothes falling everywhere. And he takes this big breath"—Ruth took a deep breath—"and says, 'You can't leave me! You don't know how to make the coffee!' He's dead serious. And I swear I looked at that man . . ."

Ruth looked down at Ira.

"I looked at that stupid man holding that stupid suitcase . . . and I started laughing. Then he starts laughing. And we couldn't stop. We couldn't stop laughing."

Tears streamed down her face.

"What do I do now? You never taught me."

Ruth sobbed.

Shannon wrapped her arms around Will's waist and laid her head against his stomach. He stroked his daughter's hair and watched Ruth weep while he thought about Chris. Chris, sitting at the kitchen table, bathed in morning light, blowing into her coffee mug, reading the news.

Molly grabbed some tissues from the lav and passed them around.

"Ruth," Kit said, her voice unsure. "Is there . . . Do you have a preference for what—"

"What we do with his body?" Ruth asked, placing Ira's right hand on top of his left. She considered, looking around the plane. Her eyes fell on Ryan, the other widower. "I think he should be with your wife and the others we've lost today. An aisle seat, if there is one. He preferred the aisle."

Ryan nodded.

It was macabre, the idea of carrying a dead body into the water, dragging it under, and belting it into a seat. But what felt normal or acceptable had shifted over the course of the day.

The men in the group looked at each other, wordlessly communicating how the next part should go. Whatever conflict still simmered between Andy and Will cooled, for the moment. The two moved together and forward but stopped when Ryan, still watching Ruth, bowed his head as she began to pray.

"*Shema Yisrael, Adonai eloheinu, Adonai echad.*"

With her hands covering her eyes, Ruth rocked back and forth. Everyone bowed their heads, but Maia watched the prayer recitation with a child's curiosity. Ruth then said something quietly to herself before voicing aloud: "Amen."

"A-main," Maia whispered to herself, repeating the Hebrew pronunciation.

Ruth kissed Ira on the forehead, placed a hand on his cheek, and looked at her husband for the last time.

Ryan helped her up off the floor. She stepped back out of the way as Will, Andy, and Kaholo came forward to join Ryan. There was a gentle stateliness to the way Ira was lifted from the ground, brought out of the galley, and carried down into the water.

Ruth held on to Kit's arm as they watched the procession. The men walked down the aisle, sinking deeper with Ira's body raised high. They stopped once the water hit their chests, conferring quietly among themselves. Will counted softly to three, the men took a deep breath, and then they all slipped under the water.

"Oh!" Ruth cried as she leaned into Kit, watching small waves ripple toward the back of the plane.

A short while later, as Kaholo, Andy, Will, and Ryan came up out of the water, Ruth said thank you, taking each of their hands in both of hers as they passed. Ryan was the last one. Just as Ruth kissed him on the cheek, a noise came from the front of the plane.

Everyone froze.

The noise came again. A banging. Followed by a creaking and then a click. The water's acoustics distorted the sounds; where exactly they were coming from, what they were, what was making them—no one could tell. Will took Shannon by the shoulders and moved her behind him.

Then, near the front of the plane, under the water, came a small light.

The light grew bigger as it came closer and closer. The water in front of them began to move. Everyone retreated backward as the surface of the water was suddenly broken.

The glare of the headlamp was blinding. When it snapped off, standing in front of them was a diver in full gear.

CHAPTER TWENTY-NINE

CHRIS STOOD AT THE SHIP'S RAILING, WATCHING THE NAVY SAILORS BEGIN A PLAN THAT could kill her daughter—and she had no way to stop it. A tightness clutched her throat as she felt transported back to that afternoon at the pool. Watching the paramedics work on Annie. Knowing there was nothing she could do. Fearing it was already done.

Her hands were shaking. Chris put them in her pockets.

She thought of the mother of the other little girl on board and how she must be out of her mind with worry. Chris wished there were a way to talk to her. To tell her that another mother was here, doing everything she could to protect her baby and speak and advocate on her behalf.

Chris turned her back to the water and studied the SRDRS and the broken pieces of metal on the ground.

"What do you want us to do now?" Noah asked, still watching the divers.

Chris thought about it. The wind picked up, bringing with it the smell of smoke. She glanced over her shoulder at the Navy divers.

"We pray that a bunch of red suits start popping up out of the water," she said. "And we be ready in case they don't."

Chris heard her name, and the whole team looked to the stairs. Milton stood at the top, waving them over.

"Got something to show you," he yelled.

"Is that . . . ?" Chris said as she crossed the room.

People parted to let her through. When she reached the monitors, she dropped to a squat, eye level with the screen.

The live feed was from the GoPro cameras on the two divers. They'd not only reached the plane, they were now inside. Assembled on the screen in front of Chris were the passengers.

Chris reached out, her fingers hovering over the image of Will.

He was as Will as ever. Talking with his hands. Wavy brown mop of unkempt hair falling in different directions. She could even see those three deep worry lines on his forehead that he swore had been there since he was twelve.

"No audio?" she asked.

Fitz shook his head.

Chris turned back to the screen and fell forward onto her knees, bringing her face closer.

It was Shannon.

She was alive. And by the looks of it, she was fine. She stood next to the other little girl with a protective arm around her shoulders, seeming to be explaining something to her. Of course Shannon wasn't just okay. She'd found a purpose. The other passengers' faces were full of fear and worry—Will's included. But Shannon looked calm and steady.

As the camera panned around to the rest of the passengers, Chris got up, mouthing "*Thank you*" to Fitz. He smiled.

But then the SEIE suit appeared on-screen. The plastic bundle bobbed on the surface as the diver's hands pointed out different parts on the pack. The passengers' smiles started to fade as they learned the plan. Hope gave way to skepticism, then to outright refusal.

"They don't want to do it," Chris said, directing her comments at Larson. "They know it's not safe."

Larson didn't respond. On the screen, the passengers all shook their heads. But then the focus turned to something off-screen and the camera followed. It landed on a young man in an airline uniform with a bandaged hand. He was nodding and stepping forward, volunteering to go first.

"Watch," Larson said. "The others will see him succeed and come around."

Chris's hand shot toward the screen. "Look at him!"

"Of course Kaholo will be fine," Will said to the divers. "Look at him!"

Kaholo's wet uniform clung to his chiseled abs.

"What about the rest of us?" He turned to the passengers. "No offense."

"Offend away," Jasmine said, holding on to the neck of her life vest.

"This cannot be the only plan," Kit said. "There's children here."

"How can you expect us all to do this?" Ryan asked, still supporting Ruth by the arm.

"And what am I supposed to do?" Jasmine said. "I can't swim."

"You can't *what?*" Kit said.

"The fuck you think I've been wearing this life vest for?" Jasmine said as everyone stared at her. "I don't know how to swim. Okay? So you better figure something else out, because I sure as hell am not getting in one of those suits."

The Navy divers looked around. They had not expected this level of dissent.

"This is what topside's decided," one of them said.

"This is the correct protocol for what to do in a situation like this," said the other.

"When has there ever been a situation like this?" Molly asked.

"What happened to my mom's plan?" Shannon added.

"Her plan was untested. We're going with what we know works."

"Works for who?" Jasmine muttered.

"Topside doesn't know us. But I do," Kaholo said. "I'll go. If I make it"—he paused after the word *if*, as though just realizing that there was a possibility he wouldn't—"I'll tell them if I think the rest of us can, too. If it's not an option, it's just not. I'll make sure they figure something else out."

Will knew his wife. If she wasn't able to get her way with the United

States military, some flight attendant wouldn't stand a chance. But with no alternatives, the passengers conceded.

Kaholo would go first. They'd reevaluate after that.

The back galley was the only location that made sense to get him suited up, but even there, the typically cumbersome task proved near impossible. The SEIE was a watertight, double-layered, full-immersion suit that Kaholo was supposed to step into—a task made harder by the standing water and his injured hand. After kicking off his shoes, he put one leg in at a time, needing help to zip and secure it as he went, but water was still getting in.

At Molly's suggestion, Kaholo hopped up to sit on the galley countertop. He didn't make it on his first attempt and his feet splashed into the water as he dropped back down. He grimaced and swore, holding his injured hand up after it hit the cart door. The second time he jumped higher and with some assistance was able to muscle his way into a seated position on the high countertop.

Will gave Kit a look and glanced at Ruth as if to say, *They're expecting an eighty-year-old to do this?*

Kaholo stuck his legs out straight and the divers pulled the suit over them. Once he was inside, they zipped up the inner layer and tightened the foot and ankle straps. The process continued up his body until he was able to hop back down to finish zipping the inner layer up to his chin. Kit helped tuck his long black hair into the ascent hood's head lining while the divers tightened the polyurethane wrist seals.

By the time he'd been secured inside, all of them were out of breath.

"Okay," said the first diver. "This outer layer"—he lifted the orange plastic with the tarplike texture—"is going to be zipped up all the way. This will seal you inside the suit."

Kaholo nodded.

"Then we're going to swim down into the plane, through the cockpit, and out the broken cockpit window," said the second diver. "We'll both be with you and we'll push or pull or do whatever you need us to do to help get you there, okay?"

Kaholo nodded again. "How do I breathe once I'm zipped up?"

The diver pointed to the front of the suit, which had a circular section of clear plastic.

"That's the ascent hood. It covers your head and keeps the water out. But more important, it keeps the air in. The air from the venting life jacket," the diver said, motioning to the orange sections across Kaholo's chest, "will come in and be trapped. Just breathe normally."

"And I don't activate the suit until I'm outside the plane?"

"Correct. If you do it in here, you'll be stuck. If the suit's inflated, you won't be able to swim down to get out."

Kaholo nodded, clearly not as confident as when the conversation had started.

"Now," the first diver said. "Once we're outside the plane and clear, you'll engage the suit."

"Which means . . . ?"

"The whole suit will act basically like those do," the second diver said, pointing to Jasmine's inflated yellow life vest. "It'll fill with air and you won't have to do a thing except enjoy the ride. You'll float straight to the surface."

"Stop it," Will said through a clenched jaw. "Just stop doing that."

"Doing what?" the second diver asked.

"Making it sound so easy. So simple. It's not! You know it's not!" Will's booming voice echoed through the plane. "You're professional divers. You have extensive training. You're used to swimming at depth. We're not. At all." He turned to the passengers. "Have any of you ever scuba dived?"

Everyone looked around. No one said anything.

"Has anyone ever even snorkeled?"

Kaholo had, and Bernadette shyly held her hand up. They were the only ones.

"Then who's been swimming at the beach when a wave pulls you under?" Will asked. "And for that split second, you think, *I'm never coming up. The riptide's dragging me out. This is it. I'm gonna drown. I am drowning.* Then two seconds later the wave is gone and you stand up and you realize the water's actually waist deep."

Will looked up at the divers.

"That fear, *that fear*, is so intense. You know it. It's terrifying. And that's on the surface. You're three feet from fresh air. We're two hundred feet down. And you want to stick us in these suits and have us just—what was it you said? Enjoy the ride?" Will shook his head. "It'll be dark. And cold. And we're in these thin plastic suits. *Alone.* Children. A woman who can't swim. And once this thing engages it's loud and chaotic and completely out of your control. Right?"

The divers looked to one another.

"Right?"

"Ah, well, we're not submariners."

Will looked between the two. "What does that mean?"

"They only train submariners in the SEIE program."

"Are you saying neither of you has ever done this?"

One of them nodded.

Will slumped back against a row. Everyone began to shift uncomfortably. "I can't. I cannot believe that this—" Will wiped his face, frustrated. "Okay, think of it like this. Imagine NASA taking an eight-year-old little girl off the street and with no training, no nothing, sticking her in the shuttle. Rocketing her into space. And then telling her she's gonna die unless she gets in a space suit that's twice her size and goes on a space walk, *alone.* NASA wouldn't. Of course not. Because it's insane! This is that. This is that insane."

No one spoke for a long time. After a while, one of the divers motioned to Kaholo.

"You still up for this?"

Kaholo stared into the water. "We gotta get out of here," he said. "And we won't know if this is how until we know if it's possible." Kaholo nodded. "I'll go."

"Okay," the first diver said. "Then there's a couple things you need to be aware of."

"Y'all can't be serious," Jasmine said, and laughed. "They haven't even gotten to the fine print. My god."

"It's a tight fit through the cockpit and the window," the diver said, ignoring Jasmine. "We tried to clear the glass from the frame but couldn't get it all. So just keep track of where you are because there's jagged metal and broken glass."

Kaholo blinked. "Okay . . ."

"But the most important thing—"

"The number one rule you can't forget—"

The divers were speaking over each other. Kaholo looked from one to the other.

"You can't hold your breath."

"Either breathe normally, or exhale the whole way up. Those are your two options."

"Try singing. Or scream. The whole time up. A lot of guys do it that way."

"So you hear," Will muttered. The diver shot him a look.

"But no matter what—do not hold your breath."

"Why?" Maia asked.

The divers looked at each other. One nodded to the other—*You explain.*

"Well, in the suit, you'll be breathing compressed gas. At depth," the chosen diver said. "And as you travel up to the surface, the pressure around you will decrease. So if you hold your breath, the air pressure in your lungs will build. Potentially catastrophically."

Kaholo stared at the divers, once again unsure.

"Yeah, see, my earlier objections?" Will said. "I hadn't even gotten to what this actually looks like when it goes wrong."

"What do you mean?" Ryan asked.

"I mean ascending is different on your body than descending," Will said. "Going from less to more pressure tends to be fine. That's what happened when we went down. The plane sank slowly, we could clear our ears, equalize the pressure. But going up? Going from more to less? Different story. You have to ascend slowly. And you have to breathe continuously. If you don't? We're talking major, *major* ramifications."

"But once we're up, there'll be doctors," Andy said.

"Yeah, but death's pretty hard to treat," Will replied. He didn't care if he was scaring people. That was his goal.

Shannon stared quizzically. "I don't get it. The pressure stuff."

"Imagine your lungs as two balloons," Will said. "You take a deep breath and it fills the balloons. But what happens to balloons if you fill them with too much air?"

"They pop," Maia said.

"That's right," Will said.

The group was silent for a moment. Will shook his head and looked to Kaholo.

"But enjoy the ride."

CHAPTER THIRTY

FITZ WONDERED IF THEY WERE ABOUT TO WATCH A MAN DIE.

The room was as silent as the video feed. Kaholo was the most likely to make the free ascent successfully and still the look on his face was one of pure terror. He and the divers slipped under the surface, and the footage became shaky and unclear as the men swam into the tight, dark space.

As the first diver entered the cockpit, everyone could see the captain's dead body that was still strapped to the chair. A moment later, that diver was outside the plane. He turned back and his headlamp illuminated Kaholo just as the flight attendant was starting out the broken window.

Kaholo was moving in a slow, controlled way, just as the Navy divers had instructed, and he navigated the window carefully, followed by the diver behind him. All three men were clear, floating in the open ocean.

The three flashed the "okay" hand sign to one another, then the SEIE suit suddenly disappeared from the screen, replaced by a blur of bubbles.

Everyone headed for the door.

Walking quickly, they reached the railing. All work on deck stopped. All preparations in the Zodiac boats paused. Everyone watched and waited.

It seemed to take forever. Two hundred feet is a long way down. Fitz could only imagine what that was like for Kaholo. No control. No clue when it would be over.

The water was unchanging. Then, bubbles began to burst on the surface. Everyone held their breath. Moments later, a bright red suit popped up out of the water.

Fitz didn't take his eyes off the flight attendant as divers surrounded him, evaluating the young man. When the divers gave a thumbs-up, everyone erupted in cheers. Fitz exhaled, pulled the now-crumpled papers out of his back pocket, found Kaholo's name in the crew section, and circled it.

They watched the boat below, where Kaholo was being unzipped from his suit. The young man was trembling uncontrollably, his head nodding up and down, then shaking left to right. His eyes were wide and his chest was heaving like he was struggling to catch his breath.

Finally, he looked around—at the sky, the sun, the divers—like he was trying to figure out what had happened. Like he was trying to convince himself that he was actually alive.

He nearly collapsed, then righted himself.

Then he smiled.

"He's okay!" said a voice over the radio. "And he thinks the others could do it, too."

Larson slapped the railing. "Let's get those people out of there."

"How will we know if it worked?" Shannon asked.

Will shrugged. "I assume they'll come back down and tell us."

Shannon nodded and kept doing what the others were doing. Which was nothing. There was nothing to do but wait. So they waited. Stared off into space. Nibbled on food from the food cart. No one said much because there wasn't much to say. It was the first time there had been a purposelessness to the group, and he could feel their bottled anxiety rising.

Will saw Kit looking around and could tell she was thinking something similar.

"You know," Kit said to no one in particular, "if this works, we're all going to have to do it." She turned her focus to Jasmine. "I think it's time you learned how to swim."

The group responded as Kit had hoped they would. Jasmine shook her head and waved her arms while everyone cheered her on. Molly started a slow chant—*"Jasmine, Jasmine, Jasmine"*—and everyone joined in.

"I think you have to take that off," Molly said as Jasmine stepped forward.

"But I don't know how to swim," Jasmine said, holding on to the life vest.

"Yeah, that's kinda the point."

Reluctantly, she took it off and passed it to Bernadette. "But I'm putting it back on when this is done."

Jasmine walked down the aisle into the water, muttering in conversation with the Lord baby Jesus. As the water went higher on her body, she raised her arms and shoulders and turned around.

"Okay, now what?" she said, panic all over her face. "What are y'all laughing at? You know what? Nope. I'm out."

She started back up the aisle while everyone tried to convince her to stay in.

"Kick!" Maia said. "Just kick a lot."

"She's right," Will said. "Go deep enough that your feet don't touch the floor. But hold on to the seat backs. Then kick. Like Maia said. After a while, try to take your hands off the seats."

"What if I sink?"

"Grab the seat backs. They're your training wheels."

Jasmine went back down the aisle, sinking deeper into the water until it was up to her neck.

"Oh Lord. Oh Lord. Oooooh Lord," she said, raising her chin up. "Okay. Okay. I'm kicking. I'm kicking!"

Kit looked around at the group as they cheered Jasmine on. Ryan stuck his fingers in his mouth and whistled. Maia jumped up and down on a seat. Even Ruth, racked with grief, smiled.

Kit marveled at the human capacity not only to endure, but to find joy in the midst of suffering. Sure, right now it was calm. But at any second everything could change and they could all be dead. None of them had forgotten that. How could they? But they'd shifted the weight, found a new point of balance, and carried on anyway.

Suddenly it was clear to Kit. It didn't matter if you died in a car crash or peacefully in your sleep at 102 or if you drowned in a plane at the bottom of the ocean. The end result would be the same. And that was all life was. Shifting the balance, every day, to make room for joy and grace in whatever circumstances you've got before your time runs out.

"Okay, now what?" Jasmine yelled breathlessly as her legs churned the water.

"Sorta flap your arms," Shannon said, mimicking with her own.

"Try to push the water down. With your hands," Ryan said, also stroking the air.

In the small waves Jasmine was making, a shoe floated over. It bumped into her face and everyone laughed.

Except Bernadette. Instead, she emitted a low groan. Kit looked over and found the nurse rubbing her temple.

"You okay?" Kit asked.

"Oh, I'm fine," Bernadette said. "Just a bad headache."

"You're probably dehydrated. Go get some water. Eat something, too."

Bernadette didn't argue. Kit watched her head to the galley and saw that Will was watching her as well.

"Remember what I said about carbon dioxide building up?" Will said, coming over. "I don't think Bernadette's dehydrated. I think she's the first to show symptoms of CO_2 poisoning. We're going to need—"

"Hey!" Molly said, pointing toward the front of the plane.

A small light under the water grew bigger with each second. Bernadette came out of the galley and Jasmine sloshed her way to the back of the plane. A moment later a diver surfaced. With a hiss of air, he took the regulator out of his mouth.

"He made it."

The relief was palpable. Some hugged. Ruth and Ryan began to cry. Maia took a video, panning across the crowd.

A moment later, a second diver emerged with the next SEIE suit. Andy rushed forward, grabbed it, and headed to the galley.

"Shocking," Molly muttered with an eye-roll.

"Oh, let him," Jasmine said, wading back into the water. "C'mon. Next lesson."

"Are you Kit? And Will?" one of the divers asked.

"Yeah. That's us," Kit said.

The diver unclipped a dry bag and unrolled the top. He pulled out a black box.

"Christmas came early," Kit said, taking the new comms set from him.

Topside, Chris watched Fitz on the phone with the pilot.

He updated Kit on Kaholo's condition. He explained the suit modifications and additional escorts they were planning for the little girls and how the same added precautions would be taken for Ruth.

They discussed victim recovery of the dead passengers' bodies that were still inside the plane and then he gave a status update on the surface fire, which was fully contained and virtually burned out. Fitz asked what else they needed. Kit replied they were good on food and water and hadn't touched their oxygen bottles yet. But maybe on the next run, a couple extra tanks would be smart, in case the SEIE ascents took longer than anticipated.

Chris tuned out after a while. She was thinking about the suits and the modifications for the girls, imagining all the ways it could go wrong.

"Chris. *Chris.*"

"Hmm?"

"I said, do you want to talk to your husband?" Fitz asked.

She'd forced herself to stop calling Will that after they separated.

But now, hearing Fitz say it, she didn't correct him. Chris took the receiver and watched Fitz cross the room and close the door behind him.
She sat on the table.

"Will?"

"Hiya, Chrissy."

She couldn't help but smile. "How's it going down there?" she asked.

"Oh, just as surreal as you'd imagine. We've got two little girls teaching a grown woman how to swim—"

"One of you can't swim?"

"Well, she couldn't when she boarded the plane. That's gonna have
to change if she wants to get out of it. She wasn't too worried until your
plan got benched. What happened?"

Chris explained the competing missions and personality conflicts
and how it had been essentially a race to the finish line, and they'd come
in second.

"So we're ready," she said in conclusion. "Noah finished the final
attachment just as the first guy popped up in the SEIE suit. But"—she
shrugged—"all dressed up with nowhere to go."

"I'm sorry."

"I just want Shannon back safely."

"Just Shannon?"

Chris paused, running a finger over the tan line where her wedding
ring used to be.

"I still haven't decided," she said. But she knew he could hear the
smile in her voice.

Neither of them said anything for a while. She could hear people in
the background. A child's laugh, but it wasn't Shannon. She heard a low
voice give a briefing on how the SEIE suit worked. It was strange, how
normal it seemed to be when the circumstances were anything but. But
then again, since Annie died, that'd become their whole lives.

"What are you thinking?" Will asked, knowing her well enough to
sense there was more.

"I just—" Chris paused, surprised by the sudden tightness in her
throat. "I'm so glad you're on that plane."

"I know."

"No, you know what I mean. Shannon wanted to go alone. I thought she should." Chris's voice cracked. She could feel Will leaning into the phone, trying to comfort her, wanting to wrap his arms around her as her eyes welled up, something they *never* did. For a while they sat like that, together alone, while he held her from a distance.

"I'm sorry," Will said, finally.

"For what?"

Will took his time, seemingly searching for the right words, something *he* never did. Will always had an answer. Sometimes before the question was even asked. It drove her nuts and was the source of many of their fights, so this was different.

"When Annie died," he said, finally, "I fell apart. I was a mess. And I know you needed me. Shannon needed me. And I couldn't be there. You needed your husband. Shannon needed her father. But I was buried by my own grief. My own pain. So how could I help you? I knew I couldn't. So I didn't. I let you both just . . . figure it out."

He paused.

"We said 'for better or for worse.' And worse than the worst hit. And I'm just . . . so sorry. You deserved more from me. Better from me."

This was different from any conversation they'd ever had about Annie's death or about their marriage. It wasn't the first time they'd grieved together, but listening to Will, Chris realized this was the first time they'd grieved *together*. As all that had been unspoken was finally said, Chris could feel the barriers they'd built up beginning to come down.

"Will, I knew," Chris said, wiping her cheek. "I was your wife. I knew how deep you were in and I should have reached in after you. But I couldn't even pull myself up. Everything I had, and I mean everything, went to being okay for Shannon. And after that, I had nothing left. Not for myself, not for you. And I . . . I couldn't . . ."

Chris sighed, frustrated at how insufficient all the words felt.

"I'm sorry," she said. "I'm sorry, too."

Will breathed into a sensation of relief that was spreading through his chest. This was everything he'd needed to say and needed to hear.

It was the first time in six years he'd felt connected to Chris in the way he remembered, like her existence was an extension of his own, like her heart beat in his body. She was his partner, his soul mate, the person who made this life make sense. And she was here. He was here. They were finally together.

Will felt hopeful. Like he'd set down a massive weight, and only now that he no longer had to carry it could he see how heavy it truly was.

"I've been trying to tell you I'm sorry for six years," he said. "I couldn't figure out how."

"I know. Me too," Chris said.

Will heard movement and out of the corner of his eye saw a pair of white sneakers with pink and orange zigzags. He didn't look over but wondered how long Shannon had been there. How much she'd heard.

"You know," he said into the phone, just a tiny bit louder, "I see how I've messed up with Shannon. How I've . . . how I let fear win. I was so afraid of her getting hurt, too. Of something happening to her. And I tried to protect her so nothing bad could. I just . . . I wanted her safe. But it . . . I think that's what *I* needed. Not what she needed. But I never asked her what she needed. And that wasn't fair."

Will saw the shoes inch a little closer.

"We got a remarkable kid, Chris. Shannon is exactly how I hoped our children would be. She's everything we need more of in this world. She is good and funny and smart and unique and I am missing it." His voice cracked. "I'm missing it, Chris. I've been so focused on what we lost that I'm missing what we have. A kid who's really something."

Shannon's arms wrapped around Will's body, squeezing hard. Will leaned down into her, resting his cheek on her head. Breathing deeply, he held his little girl.

On the other end of the line, Chris was silent. She was with them but letting them have their moment. Will knew she understood what was happening. A mother always knows.

Finally, Will pulled back and squatted, eye level with Shannon.

"I'm sorry that I was so focused on the loss of my daughter that I never saw that you lost a sister."

Shannon nodded but was quiet. She dodged his gaze and, after a beat, looked away completely.

"I miss her," she said finally, her voice barely above a whisper.

Will gently pulled her chin back to him and waited until she looked him in the eye.

"Annie loved you so much," he said. "I know she misses you, too."

With that, she hugged him in such a way that he knew true healing had broken through. For her, for him, for Chris. They were a family again.

Someone cleared their throat. Will and Shannon looked over.

"Sorry," Kit said, "but they're ready."

In the back galley, Andy was now fully inside the SEIE suit and awkwardly making his way into the plane with the divers. Will nodded. Shannon went to join the rest of the passengers.

"They got the next suit ready, Chrissy," Will said. "I'm going to go see him off. But before I go, I just want to say . . . that I . . ."

He fumbled for words for a few moments before Chris finally stopped him.

"Will," she said. "We'll talk more when you get home."

For the first time in six years, Will was looking forward, not back.

CHAPTER THIRTY-ONE

ONE THING WAS ABUNDANTLY CLEAR TO EVERYONE TOPSIDE. ANDY WAS NO KAHOLO.

They could see the whites of Andy's eyes as the divers pulled and prodded him along. He looked nervous and jittery. Every movement was clumsy and labored. It took forever just to reach the cockpit.

Fitz interlaced his fingers and leaned forward, resting his elbows on his knees, praying this time would go as well as the first.

Andy watched the first diver swim through the tight space and slip out the broken window and into the open water. The diver turned around and reached back into the cockpit for Andy's hand.

'Cause it's that easy, huh, asshole? Andy thought, clutching the cockpit doorframe with both hands. The suit was rigid and uncooperative, and every move was awkward and labored. He kept floating up or drifting over, even with the second diver right behind him pushing him forward into the small space.

Andy didn't like it. The guy's hands on his back stressed him out. Made him feel rushed. Sweat covered his face as his cheeks puffed out with each exhale, breathing that was starting to feel difficult inside the plastic suit. A tightening sensation began to crawl across his chest.

The first diver held out his hands, seemingly saying, *It's okay.* Andy wanted to punch him in the face. Fuck that guy. Fuck Kaholo. Fuck Will. Fuck this whole stupid fucking thing.

The cockpit was small and felt like it was getting smaller. Andy

could hear his pulse in his ear. He could feel it throbbing in his neck.
His own breath was loud and ragged and shook just as much as his
hands did. Andy moved cautiously, heading toward the window, the first
diver, and the open ocean. He was almost there.

The suit's clear plastic face mask was beginning to fog to the point
that Andy couldn't see. He rubbed it clear by pressing it against his face
while he drifted slowly forward past the pilots' chairs—

And that's when he saw the captain's dead body.

"Shit," Fitz said as he watched Andy flail backward frantically, bumping
into the cockpit controls and the pilot's lifeless body. Without an audio
feed, Andy's wide-mouthed screams were even more horrifying by their
silence.

The diver behind Andy wrapped his arms around his chest and
held him in place. He clutched Andy to his own chest, restraining him
until the thrashing began to slow. Finally, when Andy seemed in control
of himself, the diver made the "okay" sign. Andy nodded and the diver
eased his grip.

Fitz looked over to Milton. He and Larson both stared at the screen
unblinking. The whole room was transfixed. Chris stepped over to Fitz.

"You can still stop them. Please. There's no way he makes it."

But before Fitz could respond, the operation continued.

Andy's face shield was almost completely fogged over again, but he
wasn't about to fix it. He didn't want to see that fucking half-eaten dead
body again . . . and he didn't want the divers to see him crying.

Andy reached out both hands and the diver in front of him took
hold of them. The second diver was behind him, hands on his back, and
this time Andy just let them carry him out. The first diver was nodding
encouragingly, so Andy nodded back.

———

Chris watched the divers usher Andy through the confined space. Upon reaching the broken window, the diver outside the plane placed Andy's hands on the frame to act as guardrails of sorts as he was guided out past the jagged glass that lined the frame.

Maybe she was wrong. Maybe it was going to be fine. He was almost out.

Andy was halfway through the window—when the dead pilot's right arm, weightless and floating freely in the water, bumped against his leg.

Andy kicked and flailed, obeying everything in his brain that screamed, *Get out*. Both divers grabbed at him, but Andy moved too erratically. He had no control. No awareness. There was only an endless, unstoppable panic and need to flee.

Andy managed to get back to the window and pull himself the rest of the way out of the plane, but as he did, the leg of the suit caught on a piece of twisted metal. He tried to swim forward but couldn't. Andy thrashed in a panicked frenzy, trying to release himself, when with one final kick the tension eased as the metal sliced through the suit—and his leg.

Andy scrambled out the window into the open water, screaming in pain and terror as cold salt water hit the wound and began to fill his suit.

Chris looked away. Fitz didn't blink. No one made a sound as they watched water flood the SEIE suit.

The second diver grabbed Andy's leg. Dark, colorless blood poured from the wound on the grainy black-and-white video feed. The first diver clutched Andy's shoulders, trying to steady him, but Andy was only focused on the water flooding his suit. He kicked his legs as though that would make it stop, and through the clear plastic, everyone could see his eyes welling with tears.

Rogers leaned forward and put his forehead on the table like he was going to be sick. Fitz wished he could do the same. They were about to watch a man drown.

The light from the diver's headlamp gleamed off the rising waterline as it crept up inside the suit's clear plastic face mask. Andy mouthed a single word. *Why? Mom?* Fitz wasn't sure. Andy raised his chin as the water hit it—but then it stopped.

The water rested just below his mouth, creating an air pocket. Everyone in the room held their breath, knowing whatever happened in the next few seconds would determine the outcome of the mission.

"Steady now," Larson said. "Steady."

"Can he still make it?" Chris asked.

"If he doesn't panic," Fitz replied.

But it was clear Andy thought the water was still rising. He panicked, took a huge breath in, and shut his mouth.

"No," Fitz said under his breath as one of the divers engaged the suit and the screen turned to nothing but bubbles and movement.

This time, no one walked. Everyone ran to the railing.

CHAPTER THIRTY-TWO

"AND . . . GO," MAIA SAID.

Shannon pushed the red button.

"Are you recording?" Jasmine asked.

"Yes, go!" Maia said.

Jasmine began to kick her legs under the water. Concentrating, she slowly took her hands off the seat backs. She was treading water. She was swimming.

Breathing heavily with a big smile, she stood up out of the water on the armrests and took a bow.

The comms set buzzed. Will went to the galley and grabbed it, turning around to find Maia and Shannon recording him.

"Hello, Domino's?" he said, picking up the receiver. "I'd like to place an order for delivery. One large Hawaiian, extra pineapple."

The girls giggled.

"Actually, we're pretty hungry, so better make it *two* large—"

Will stopped. Shannon looked up from the screen. Will's smile began to fade.

"So we're going to pause the operation," Fitz said, leaning against the ship's railing, "then figure out how to proceed. I recommend you all do the same."

He only half listened to Will's response, his focus instead on the water below as the Zodiac made its way back to the ship. Andy was laid flat across the bottom of the boat. A team of divers worked hard to try to revive him. He heard Will say goodbye and Fitz disconnected the call.

Fitz went to the decompression chamber at the back of the ship. Once the passengers were topside, they'd be transferred directly to the airtight cylinder, where medics could monitor their vitals as a calculated balance of oxygen and other gases worked to dissolve the excess nitrogen that would have built up in their bodies.

So far, Kaholo was their only patient.

Fitz looked into the chamber through the porthole window on the door. Inside, a padded bench lined one side, while across from it were several padded chairs that didn't look all that comfortable. Kaholo sat on the bench, leaning forward, elbows on knees, staring at his feet. The flight attendant's hand was freshly bandaged, and while he now had a towel and a silver survival blanket draped around his shoulders, he remained in uniform. An oxygen mask covered his nose and mouth, and a blood pressure cuff wrapped his arm. A medic taking his pulse noticed Fitz and came to the door.

The speaker on Fitz's side crackled.

"Yes," came the medic's soft voice. "He knows what happened."

Fitz watched Kaholo's unmoving form for a moment longer before nodding his thanks and making for the ship's interior.

As he climbed the stairs, Fitz studied the growing black clouds over the top of Molokai. There was a bolt of lightning, but the storm was still too far off to know if thunder came with it.

Opening the door, Fitz walked into a heated argument.

"—a fluke accident," Larson said.

"How can you not see that we're asking too much of them?" Chris argued. "These people are in the worst situation imaginable. They have been pushed to their limits. It's them down there, not us. We have no right to demand that they do anything."

"So we modify. We add a towline. We make it a three-diver escort, four or five with the passengers we're worried about."

"But that man wasn't even one of the ones we were worried about!"

Chris responded. "It doesn't matter how you modify. If we keep doing this, more people are going to die."

"Then we change the tactic but keep the plan," Larson said. "We bring them wetsuits and gear and we scuba-dive them out individually."

"From two hundred feet down? That's at the outermost limits of what even professional divers can do. One of them can't even swim."

"You don't have to swim. That's the point of the suit."

Chris stared, incredulous. "Remember that soccer team in Thailand who got trapped in a cave after it flooded?"

"Yes! They put the boys in scuba gear and they swam out. Exactly."

"It took eighteen days to plan and execute the mission. And to do it, they put the kids under general anesthesia. They didn't swim out. They were dragged out unconscious."

Larson didn't have a response.

"We don't have eighteen days to execute a mission. We have to go now," Chris said. "No SEIE suits. No scuba. It doesn't matter what we're capable of, it only matters what they're capable of."

"And I suppose your plan is what you think we should do instead."

"We're ready. It'll work."

Fitz was only half listening. He couldn't stop thinking about the look on Kaholo's face. Fitz knew that look. He saw it in the mirror every day. Fitz wondered which was worse—the survivor guilt Kaholo would have to bear, or the kind of guilt Fitz knew all too well. Guilt that comes from feeling like you didn't do everything you could.

There was a soft knock at the door. Milton entered.

"They tried . . ." Milton said.

It hit hard. Because of them—their plan, their actions—another passenger was dead.

"Do we know what happened?" Larson asked, the edge to her voice softened.

Milton shook his head. "They think a combination of things. An air embolism, for sure. That's the first domino. Then heart attack, maybe. Or a stroke. A catastrophic stroke. Collapsed lung. Probably? And that cut," Milton said, his eyes flashing wide. "Lot of blood. So I don't—they don't—know. Divers think he held his breath. Had a panic attack. His baseline health was—"

"Milton," Fitz said.

"Yeah."

Fitz watched his friend and waited a couple beats. "Breathe."

Milton nodded a few times, then removed his hat with an exhale and ran a hand across his short, buzzed hair.

A coastguardsman knocked lightly on the door. Handing the comms set to Fitz, the officer said, "It's them."

Everyone was quiet while Fitz listened to the other end of the line.

"Hey. Hey—Will," Fitz said a few moments later. "Hold on, I'm putting you on speaker." Fitz held the set out and pushed a button. "Okay. Repeat what you just told me."

"I said we've talked it through down here and we've decided— unanimously—that we're not doing the SEIE suits."

Larson leaned forward. "Will. Hear out our plans for modifications—"

"Ma'am, you're not listening. None of us are getting in those suits."

Chris leaned back in her chair.

Fitz stared at the speaker. "That's final?"

"Yes. Look, we understand there are risks with any plan. But we're most confident in what Chris came up with. It's all of us, all together. We're leaving this plane the same way we've survived being inside it. Together."

Fitz tapped his fingers silently on the table while everyone in the room processed the ultimatum. They couldn't rightfully go down there and force any of them into a suit. And if the passengers were that scared, Fitz couldn't imagine the day ending with only one SEIE-suit tragedy.

Fitz nodded. "Understood." He then looked at Chris. "You're up."

4:14 p.m.

4 hours and 13 minutes after impact

Approximately 1 hour of oxygen inside plane

CHAPTER THIRTY-THREE

IT WAS KIT WHO'D SUGGESTED THE VOTE, NOT HIM. WILL HADN'T SAID A THING. ALL HE'D done was raise his hand like the others. But he also knew most of them had only put their hands up once they saw him do it. Including Shannon.

There wasn't any part of Will that doubted the decision. The SEIE suits would have only meant more tragedy. And his faith in Chris was bedrock. He *knew* it was the right call. But as he looked around at every raised hand, he felt the weight of that responsibility.

There was a soft sniff. Maia looked up, her eyes brimming with tears. "Did his balloons pop?"

"Oh, sweetheart," Kit said, taking the young girl into her arms.

Bernadette giggled.

Everyone turned. Ruth frowned at the disrespect. Then Bernadette's giggling turned to full-on laugher.

"Bernadette—" Kit said.

"Molly," Will said urgently. "Where are the oxygen tanks?"

Everyone looked around, unsure of what was happening. Bernadette began to spin in sloppy circles, singing.

"Come, Josephine, in my flying machine and it's—"

"*Bernadette*—" Kit said more forcefully, setting Maia down.

"Up, she goes!" Bernadette giggled, splashing the water. "Up, she—no. I don't want it."

Molly had an oxygen bottle slung across her shoulder and was trying to slip the yellow cup over the nurse's face, but Bernadette refused.

"Listen," Molly said. "You need—"

Bernadette slapped Molly's hand. Hard. Will and Kit stepped in and tried to restrain Bernadette, but she thrashed and screamed, refusing the air, fighting them off. Suddenly, she began to retch. Kit and Will let her go and Bernadette vomited into the water.

While Bernadette was bent over, catching her breath, Ryan looped his arms up under her armpits from behind and held her back to his chest. Molly pressed the mask to her face while Will and Kit held down her arms and legs. Bernadette protested, kicking at them.

"She's crazy," Jasmine said.

As the fresh, concentrated oxygen entered Bernadette's system, her objections became more subdued.

"She's the canary," Will replied. "It's carbon dioxide poisoning. And if we don't get air, we're next. Where's the extra bottles?"

"Up there," Molly said, lifting her chin toward an overhead bin while still holding the mask to Bernadette's face. Jasmine opened the bin and took one out, passing it down to Shannon, before grabbing another.

"You want all of them?" she asked.

"Yes," Will said. "Topside's bringing spares. Everyone should start now. You don't have to only breathe from the bottle, the air's not that saturated. But we need to stay ahead of this."

From the back galley, the comms set buzzed. Ruth shakily got to her feet.

"Ruth—" Ryan said, still restraining Bernadette.

"I'm old and grieving. I'm not dead," Ruth said as she made her way to the back galley. "Hello?" She listened to the line. "Will. Your wife wants to talk."

Will made sure Bernadette was calm enough before letting go of her legs. Getting up, he adjusted the mask on Shannon's face as he went by.

"Chrissy?"

"Heads-up, a diver's on their way with the oxygen tanks and lineman's pliers and wire nuts to get that last wire out of the way."

She spoke in a clipped tone that Will recognized. Chris was in go mode.

"Now, talk to me about your air bubble," she said.

Will described the scene. The original waterline he'd marked when the plane first settled was nonapplicable. There wasn't anywhere in the plane they could stand that was dry. The most shallow part came up to his knees.

He lowered his voice and turned away from everyone else.

"If I'm being honest, I'm really worried about the air. One of us already has CO_2 poisoning. We're going to start using oxygen bottles but that will only last so long."

Chris was silent.

"Hello?"

"Yeah. I'm here. Listen," she said. "You're going to have to figure something out because there's no way around it—we're about to make your air pocket a lot smaller."

CHAPTER THIRTY-FOUR

"MAYBE WE SHOULD REVISIT THE RED DEATH SUIT IDEA," RUTH SAID.

"No," Will said. "The plan will work. Trust me."

Will went through it again, explaining that in order for the SRDRS to attach to the plane, the plane would have to be stable and secure. Meaning, it couldn't be tilted forward, teetering on the edge, like it currently was. The rescue team was going to drop the tail—which would lay the plane flat—by weighting it down with a heavy cable attached to the bottom of the tail.

Bernadette was nearly back to her old self, albeit a little confused as to what had happened. When they'd told her how she'd been behaving, it was like telling a drunk what they'd done the night before. So far, no one else had succumbed. But as they listened to Will, everyone breathed oxygen through yellow plastic masks. They weren't taking chances.

"Where's a water bottle?" Will asked.

Molly opened a carrier and pulled out a clear plastic water bottle. Will opened it, poured some out, then recapped it.

"Here's us now."

Will held the bottle on its side, representing the plane. Inside, the water sloshed. Will angled the mouthpiece down and the water ran forward while the air slid up to the back.

"This is our air pocket," he said, pointing to the trapped air in the back of the bottle. "This is where we are now, up here in this bubble."

Heads nodded.

"So when they drop the tail . . ." Will slowly brought the bottle level, and the air shifted, spreading into a thin, even layer across the top. "This is what happens to our pocket. Now, there should be enough air for us. But we're going to have to tread water, spreading out down the aisle. Up here, where the air is distributed."

The heads stopped nodding.

"Again," Molly said. "Did you say there *should* be enough air?"

Chris braced herself as she fell sideways with the ship's lean. In her peripheral vision came a bright bolt of lightning, and everyone looked to the darkening thunderhead. She stepped into the other leg of her wetsuit and pulled it up.

Dive gear was strewn about the deck. Prep partners scurried around to assist, but the usual one-to-one ratio was a luxury this mission couldn't afford.

On a table before them, weights held down the Airbus designs. The wind grew more fierce by the minute and any bit of paper not secured flapped around. Fitz clapped his hands to start the ROC—rehearsal of concept.

"All right," he said. "Let's go through it one last time. There is no room for error."

Chris pointed at the top of the aircraft, at the back of the plane, just forward of the tail.

"Here's where the Falcon needs to dock," she said, looking at Rogers. "That's where they're expecting us. That's the only section of interior they've cleared. Did that wire—"

"It's been clipped. No issues," Fitz said. "The diver's on his way back up."

"Good. But, Rogers, it has to be *here*," Chris said, tapping her finger repeatedly on the drawing of the plane. "Anywhere else is a failed mission."

"Understood."

"We'll be under the tail," Tanner said. He pointed to Caputo. "Cap.

Me. Our teams will monitor the cable attachment and drop. We'll be out of your way. Should be no entanglement issues."

"Milton," Fitz said into a handheld radio. "You set up over there?"

The radio beeped. "Roger," came Milton's voice. Everyone looked to the USCG *Angelica*, which had posted up alongside the *Powell*. A thick cable with a hook attached to the end dangled from the deck crane at the ship's stern. A group gathered around, Milton among them. "When you green-light the dive, we drop the cable. You boys'll grab it, then it's all you. We move at your pace. Just tell us what you need."

Tanner and Caputo nodded.

"I start the dive with you at the tail," Sayid said to the military guys, pulling his wetsuit's zipper up his back. "I look for bubbles. They lead me to weak spots and holes. Then I plug-weld. And while I do that, you rig the sling wrap around the tail."

"Roger," Tanner said.

"When Sayid's done, he joins us at the Falcon," Chris said. "Once we're set, we'll signal Tanner and Caputo. You then tell the *Angelica* that we're all ready for the tail drop."

"But we also need to tell the people in the plane," Fitz said. "They'll need a signal."

"Not just for the tail drop, but for when the Falcon docks," Larson added. "It needs to be visual. In case there's issues with the comms set."

Everyone thought for a moment before Caputo said, "Lights. What if we direct a light at the plane and flash it?"

Fitz nodded. "Flash it twice before the tail drop. And don't go until you get a visual thumbs-up from the plane or a verbal acknowledgment through comms."

"Then do it again before you dock," Larson said.

Everyone nodded and Caputo assigned one of his guys to be the signalman.

"Who's my team's tenders?" Chris asked.

Four Coasties raised their hands.

"We'll give you one 'hot.' Flip the knife switches. And leave 'em. We won't be giving a 'cold.'"

The four hesitated. The knife switch—otherwise aptly named the *safety switch*—was the first line of defense in keeping those working in the water out of harm's way. Turning the electricity on only when it was needed drastically reduced the possibility of electrocution. If they never turned it off, Chris's team would be tethered to an electric charge the whole time.

"But, ma'am," one of the assigned tenders said. "That's—"

"Super unsafe," Chris said. "But even a split-second delay waiting for you to turn on our power is a margin this mission can't afford."

A gust of wind kicked up and one of the dive tanks tipped over with a loud clank. A drop of rain fell on top of the plane design, then a few more. Fitz squinted up at the sky.

"Clock's ticking," Fitz said. "We need to get those passengers out now. They're already using oxygen bottles. They've been wet for too long. Exposure will set in soon. And that's if the air doesn't run out first. Anything that felt manageable is now dire. That said, do not rush." He waited a beat. "Do. Not. Rush. One mistake on our part and that's it. I know I don't need to remind you of what a failed mission means here."

Chris took a deep centering breath.

Fitz was about to continue when the loud blare of an airhorn sounded. Everyone looked up. The sound came again, and then several others.

The flotilla of civilian boats that had conducted the surface rescues was passing the ship on their way back to shore. Every diver and serviceman on deck stopped to take in the honking of the horns. The civilians' message was clear.

You got this. We'll see you—and everyone inside that plane—on the other side.

In focusing on nothing except saving the passengers in the plane, Fitz realized he'd lost touch with how big this was. It wasn't just them. It wasn't just Milton and Larson, Chris and the divers and their teams.

It was the hospital staff in the burn units. It was a MedLink operator in Arizona who'd stayed glued to her station long after her shift ended, just in case Flight 1421 called again. It was the families huddled together watching the news, praying to see a glimpse of the loved one they hadn't yet heard from. It was people just waking up on the other side of the world drinking their morning coffee, pointing to their phones and saying, *Bạn có tin điều này?*

Fitz wondered if the passengers inside the plane had any idea how many people were rooting for them. Praying for them. He hoped they knew. Because that knowledge brought maybe the most important part of the mission.

Hope.

CHAPTER THIRTY-FIVE

AS IT WAS ON THE SURFACE, SO IT WAS IN THE PLANE.

The calm before the storm.

It was the moment before battle when a soldier stares at his enemy from across the field. The moment when he wonders—when he woke that morning, was it for the last time? The passengers didn't want to wonder. So they busied themselves. Because if idle, they'd think about it. And thinking about it made it real.

There was a better-than-good chance they were about to die.

Jasmine tugged at her life vest. Everyone was wearing one now. But only hers was inflated.

"You know you don't have to blow it up now," Maia said. "You can swim."

"Insurance," Jasmine replied, adjusting the yellow cup on her face.

Down the plane, Ryan turned to Will. "Why don't they just run an air hose in here?"

"You mean to give us fresh air?" Will said.

"Yeah. Snake it in through the cockpit."

Will shook his head. "It wouldn't make the air pocket any bigger because the pressure wouldn't be enough to force any water *out* of the plane. And by just adding oxygen, you're not scrubbing the carbon dioxide. So it wouldn't even fix that problem. I'd bet they didn't even consider it, because what they fear most is moving the plane. We go over the cliff, well, then none of it matters anyway."

Ryan stared for a moment, seemingly with nothing to say. Finally, he gave a single chuckle and said, "Dude. You could just say it wouldn't work."

"Dad."

Will looked down. Shannon held out a life vest.

"Haven't we done this already today?" he said, taking the vest and tossing it over his head.

"Well, maybe this time we'll actually make it off the plane," Shannon replied.

Molly came from the back of the galley and headed for her position, adjusting Shannon's oxygen bottle as she went.

That was the best they could do. Strap a portable oxygen bottle across their backs like a poor man's scuba tank. Then, when the plane lay flat, if there wasn't enough air, they'd just press the masks to their faces and try to keep the water out. When Will proposed it, to their credit, no one laughed. By this point, they'd all accepted that any plan was going to be scrappy, cobbled together, and a little nuts.

"Okay, listen up," Kit said, disconnecting the comms set. "The divers are on their way as we speak."

She went through the plan step-by-step. Everyone knew their position. They knew what to do if the water rose too high. They knew the signals from the divers. They knew it all.

Maia raised her hand. Kit smiled and called on her.

"What happens if this doesn't work?"

For the briefest of moments, Kit's smile faltered.

"You don't have to worry about that, sweetheart," Ruth said. "It will."

The group fell silent. There was nothing left to say, only what was going to happen—but so much *had* happened. They'd lived a lifetime in a handful of hours, and now these strangers-turned-kin were about to face the final test. Together.

"You know, any one of us could have gotten out of the plane after the crash," Kit said. "Everyone else did. But we stayed. I hate when people say everything happens for a reason." She opened her arms wide and swung them around. "Tell me the reason. Tell me why *this* happened. So I don't know about that. But what I do know is that being here with you has been the privilege of my life. It has been an honor to be your captain."

Ruth rubbed Kit's back like a mother would. Will kissed Shannon on the top of her head.

"Should we, I don't know . . ." Ryan said. "Group hug?"

"Not to be all Andy," Jasmine replied, "but, no, we're not fucking group hug—"

"Sssshhh!" Molly interrupted.

Everyone froze, listening. There was nothing, and then, just as a flash of light swept through the cabin, came a low whirring noise. They all rushed to the windows on the left side of the aircraft.

The rescuers had arrived, slowly descending from above with sharp beams of light sweeping through the dark water.

"There's so many," Shannon said in an awed whisper.

Will tried to count. Near fifteen divers total. Some wore bright red wetsuits, others wore all black. The scene outside their windows was light, bubbles, and slow, graceful movement.

Their world had been only as big as a handful of people so close together they fit in an air pocket. But now, watching the divers, everything felt so much bigger. He'd been so focused on them, here, inside the plane. Will's only concern had been how to save them, how to save Shannon. This was the first time he'd truly considered the scope and scale of it all.

He thought of the huge ships waiting on the surface above them. He thought of the media and how this was surely international news by now. He thought of the families that were desperate for their phones to start ringing with word from their brother Ryan. Their sister Bernadette. Their grandma and grandpa Ruth and Ira. Their daughter Maia.

Those in the water now, were they friends of the diver they'd lost earlier? Had they been down here with him for the first attempt? Will watched one of the divers escorting a thick cable wrapped in a bright yellow sling toward the tail of the plane and wondered, did that man have time to text his wife I love you before they went into the water? Was she at home right now watching the news, praying not for the plane, but for her husband?

"Dad! Look!"

Shannon and Will were next to each other at a window. He followed her finger to see that one of the divers descending with the group near the tail was outfitted differently from the rest.

"Sayid," Will said, knowing he would be the one plug-welding at the tail. Unlike the rest of the divers, who would be scuba diving, Chris and her team would all be using SSA—surface-supplied air.

Sayid—just like Chris and Noah—was attached to an umbilical cable that ran all the way up to the surface. The thick braid of colored-rubber-coated tubes contained lines for communication, pneumatic power, and, most important, their oxygen. Unlike a dive tank, which would eventually run out of air, as long as the compressor on the ship was running, an SSA diver could breathe.

Sayid and the rest of the divers at the back of the plane were only visible for a moment, then dropped out of sight. Soon, the light from his stinger lit up the water. Work on the tail had begun.

Sayid examined the spots where bubbles squeezed out of the metal, rising for the surface. He flipped the welding visor down again and the bright sparks of burning electrodes lit up the water. A couple seconds later, he stopped, flipped up the visor, and saw that bubbles were no longer escaping.

As fast as he could, he surveyed the tail and repeated this action anyplace he could plug a leak or shore up a weakness. The tail section was worse than he'd expected. Not in terms of actual leaks. No, the places where he was able to spot-weld were manageable.

But the integrity of the airframe was compromised.

The consensus was that the plane had hit the water relatively square. But the damage Sayid was seeing indicated that the plane had actually been nose-up on impact. The aluminum on the top of the plane at the tail section was subtly bent inward, like the plane had tried to fold up on itself.

The divers with the sling were waiting for him to finish. Sayid did a once-around and, content that all the spots were plugged, waved them over. With a diver on each end, they draped the bright yellow sling across the top of the aircraft like it was a headband. When they released it, just the weight of the sling alone made the plane rock subtly.

Inside the cabin, the back dipped slightly. The passengers clutched the seats as the water responded, sloshing back to front.

"It's okay," Will said. "That's just the sling going around the tail. They'll tell us before they drop it. See, there, look . . ."

Outside, two divers were escorting a thick metal cable down into the water. At the end of it was a huge red hook. The divers reached neutral buoyancy and hovered in the water, waiting for the tail to be ready for them.

"That's the crane hook," Will said. "They'll clip it to the sling around the tail, and that cable it's attached to? It runs all the way up to a winch on the ship."

As the divers waited, Will saw them exchange a look.

He leaned forward, trying to get a glimpse of the tail to understand what that look meant—but he couldn't from inside the plane. Shannon peered up at him. He faked a smile.

Sayid waved off the divers with the crane hook as he swam over to the plane, leaning in at the bent section across the top. Something wasn't right. Squinting, he moved even closer, his face inches from the aircraft's skin.

Tracks of minuscule bubbles traced hairline fractures in the aluminum. The fissures were so slight that the tiny bubbles clung to the metal, not filled with even enough air to release them up to the surface. A kind of structural weakness that would be invisible to the naked eye. Only a highly specialized metallurgist using a scanning electron microscope would find it. Without the bubbles, Sayid would have never known.

Everyone watched him, waiting for direction. Sayid could feel his heartbeat in his ears.

He ran his hand along the metal and all the tiny bubbles scattered like he was dusting the plane. A flaw like this would normally take an aircraft out of commission until the damaged portions were replaced entirely. This wasn't something to be shored up or fixed. This was something you replaced. And until you did, it was a no-go item.

But deep maintenance wasn't an option. There was nothing they could do.

Sayid motioned to the divers with the sling, instructing them to slide the yellow fabric-covered cable back away from the bent section by about a foot. If the sling stayed in place, no excess weight or pressure would be placed on the compromised metal. If everything went according to plan, this shouldn't be a problem.

Will was trying not to freak out. The divers had taken the hook over, but why had they paused in the first place? He couldn't see what was going on back there, and just as Will was about to grab the comms set, something else pulled his attention.

Everyone stared up as the Falcon came into view. Bright yellow and moving at a glacial pace, the rescue module slowly dropped down from above like a spaceship entering the atmosphere.

"Why's it a big yellow pill in a cage?" Maia asked in a hushed tone. No one laughed, because that was exactly what it looked like. There was a silver rectangular metal frame encapsulating the oblong rescue module. Underneath was an open-bottomed cup—the transfer skirt.

"Look, look, look," Will said, pointing to all the modifications that had been welded to the bottom. "Look at what your mom did. God, she's amazing. Now, you see those sharp—"

"Mom!"

Shannon's face pressed up against the window as her palm slapped the wall, as though she could be heard out in the water.

Chris, her umbilical cable trailing behind, swam over to the plane, right up to their window. Her bright yellow industrial deep-sea diving helmet encapsulated her whole head, while inside, a black rubber breathing mask covered her nose and mouth. Through the bean-shaped face plate, Chris's green eyes lit up at the sight of her baby girl.

"Hi. Hi, Mom," Shannon said, her mouth moving in an exaggerated way so Chris could read her lips.

Fine lines appeared around Chris's eyes, confirming a smile under the mask.

Will fought back tears. Chris was right there. So close. He wanted to take Shannon and thrust her into Chris's arms and say, *Here, you take her. Keep her safe.*

Chris's throat burned as she tried not to cry. She needed to be strong for Shannon, to show her there was nothing to be afraid of. It was all going to be okay.

Shannon leaned in, nearly kissing the window, and mouthed, "*I love you, Mom. I love you.*"

Chris held her gloved hand over the spot on her chest that ached with love and fear, then pointed at Shannon. It was the same spot where a nurse had once laid both Annie and Shannon's warm, naked newborn bodies.

Chris angled her head, looking behind Shannon at Will.

Shannon stepped back. Will came forward. They locked eyes. Neither tried to communicate. They just looked at one another. Will took his hand and pressed it flat against the window. Chris raised a gloved hand and laid it against his. Palm to palm, with an entire ocean in between.

In her peripheral vision, Sayid appeared. He pointed to the Falcon. Turning back to the window, Chris motioned that she needed to go. Will nodded. And that was it.

As she swam up to the Falcon, Chris could feel Will watching her, and her mind went to a memory she hadn't thought of in forever.

It was after their first date. Will had dropped her off at home—and he'd waited to make sure she got into the house okay before he drove off. No one had ever done that for her before. She hadn't even known it was a thing. She'd opened the front door, turned, waved, and stood there watching him drive off.

That was the moment she knew she loved him.

Will watched Chris swim away for a few moments before joining the rest of the passengers. Shannon was staring at him.

"It's weird, huh?" she said. "She's right there."

"I know. Yet so far."

Shannon went back to the group and Will followed, considering what he'd just said and realizing, actually, he was wrong.

They'd never been closer.

Everyone moved into their position down the aisle. Will picked Shannon up and placed her on his hip. Kit did the same with Maia. Ryan wrapped his arm firmly around Ruth's waist. Bernadette, Jasmine, and Molly were a trio spread down the aisle. Molly was the furthest away and last in line.

"All right, everybody," Kit said. "We only get one shot. This is it."

Everyone stared at the windows, waiting silently.

"Think of everything we've survived already," she said. "No reason that should change now."

Will looked at the dark, unforgiving water beyond the window and hated that Chris was out there in it. Part of him wanted to tell her to stop and go back to the surface, where she'd be safe. He'd always been so terrified of losing her. Which was ultimately, ironically, what had made him leave. But beyond his fear, now a big part of him was just so damn proud. That was his girl. And god, was she a marvel.

"Dad?"

Shannon had been watching him. "Yes, jelly bean?"

"She's capable of more than you think."

They were Chris's words, echoing back from just a few hours ago. Will smiled. "I know. That's what scares me."

Suddenly a bright light lit up the plane twice.

4:58 p.m.

4 hours and 57 minutes after impact

Approximately 10 minutes of oxygen inside plane

CHAPTER THIRTY-SIX

FITZ GLANCED UP AT THE CLAP OF THUNDER. AS IF ON CUE, IT BEGAN TO POUR.

"Cable releasing on three," came the winch operator over the radio.

Fitz looked across the water to the *Angelica*. Hanging off the back of the ship was a thick silver cable that extended from a crane down into the water. Two hundred feet below them, that cable was hooked to the lift sling attached to the plane's tail.

"One, two . . ."

Underwater, the cable began to ease.

"Keep it steady," Caputo said. Similar to Chris's team's industrial dive helmets, his regulator was integrated into his full-face mask, so Caputo was able to speak over comms. "We're looking good."

Caputo and Tanner monitored the heavy cable attached to the plane's tail. When enough weight had been released to offset the balance, the plane shifted, gently rocking back as it dropped toward the seafloor in a controlled, even movement.

Shannon's arms tightened around Will's neck as everything shifted. Water from the front flowed to the back, rising on their bodies, taking everything up with it.

Will heard a life vest inflate. To his right, down the aisle on the other side of Kit, Ruth popped up to the surface. Ryan inflated his own and went with her, struggling to hold them both up. Kit's oxygen bottle floated, bumping into her face. She pushed it out of the way, struggling against the water and Maia's tightening grip around her neck. Kit pulled at the little girl's arms until Maia eased her grip.

Will yanked sharply on the red T-handles on Shannon's vest. The yellow pillows inflated and she shot upright before he grappled for his own. The pneumatic hiss as he rose to the surface was loud in his ear. Shannon's hair tickled his face. The taste of salt was bitter on his lips and burned his eyes. Louder, brighter, more intense—everything was heightened.

Down the aisle near the front, Will saw Molly take a deep breath before she disappeared under a wave passing over her head as the water sloshed back again. Next to her, Jasmine cried out between sputtering coughs. Another life vest inflated and Bernadette bobbed to the surface.

Then, with a loud thud, the plane stopped moving.

"Hold!"

Caputo's own voice echoed in his helmet as he watched the cloud of sand slowly dissipate around the seafloor where the section of cable had settled like a coiled snake.

The plane was level. Step one, down.

"Plane is stable," Caputo said. "Falcon, you are clear to dock."

The sloshing inside the plane settled. The passengers grabbed at the overhead bins, which were now eye level. The air pocket had spread evenly and there was less than a foot of clearance between the waterline and the ceiling. Just barely enough room for their heads.

"Everyone okay?" Kit yelled with a hoarse voice.

"Yes," Will said breathlessly while looking at Shannon, who was nodding and rubbing her eyes. All around the plane came a chorus of coughing and similarly weak and cautious confirmations.

———

From underwater, Molly's screams were nothing but rising bubbles that no one noticed.

She pushed off the seats again, trying to rise to the surface—but the oxygen bottle strapped across her body yanked her back. Molly tugged at it, but the strap was caught on a seat. She was trapped underwater and no one knew.

Fitz watched Rogers's hands shake as he adjusted the controls. On the screens in front of them, the Falcon moved in response.

"You got this," Fitz said.

"I think so," Rogers answered.

"Son, that wasn't a question."

Comms for the welding team crackled.

"*Stand by for go for docking,*" Chris said.

Two lights flashed in succession, illuminating the water inside the plane in a ghostly strobe.

"Everybody hold on!" Will shouted. "This is it!"

Kit held a flashlight under the water, angled at the windows. She turned it on and off repeatedly—the signal that they were ready.

Molly's eyes burned from the salt water and she could see nothing but a blur of rising bubbles in the darkness. She struggled with the strap, but it was impossible to free.

Jasmine was closest. Molly reached out, trying to grab her, desperate to get her attention. But her hand found nothing but water.

Will treaded while looking up at the spot they'd cleared of insulation and wiring. He waited for something to happen—but nothing did.

Something was wrong. It'd been too long. Will glanced to the windows under the water. Had they not seen the passengers' signal? Should Kit flash—

BOOM.

The plane shook violently. Deep waves crested around the cabin.

Shaking the water out of his face, Will looked up at the ceiling. Sharp metal slats had pierced the roof and now lay flat against the interior. All except one.

From that point, water sprayed into the cabin.

Rogers's hands hovered over the controls, waiting.

"Did it work?" he asked.

Fitz didn't respond. They'd know soon enough if it had.

"*My side!*" they heard Chris yell. "*Hot!*"

On the monitors, they watched her flip down the helmet's welding shield, and then the whole screen became a blur of sparks and bubbles.

Caputo glanced up at the bright lights coming off the welder's tools before refocusing on his duty: monitoring the tail. Sand and silt filled the area—but he noticed something new.

Bubbles.

Swimming over to the pooled cable, he waved to clear the cloud of debris. The impact from the Falcon's docking had been hard. Much harder than anticipated. It worried him. And as the seafloor came into focus, Caputo realized his fears were warranted.

Tiny bubbles were rising up from subtle cracks in the fragile seafloor. Cracks that hadn't been there before the Falcon docked.

Kit squinted through the water that sprayed into the cabin. Will, holding Shannon, kicked off a seat to move them back out of the way. Without warning, there was a buzzing sound and the whole plane began to vibrate.

Above them, a blade pierced the aircraft skin and sparks began to rain down. As the blade worked, a hole took shape—and the water draining from the transfer skirt began to pour in.

This was expected.

But how *much* water was pouring in was not.

Their heads inched closer to the ceiling as the waterline rose. Kit looked to Will with alarm.

"Here," he said, pushing her oxygen tank toward her. "Shan, get your mask ready."

Molly began to see stars.

She clamped her lips together, trying to hang on to what little oxygen was left in her lungs. Feeling with her hands, she found a seat back pocket and grabbed a safety information card.

Reaching as far as she could, she swept the water with the card. There was nothing—until there was.

A seat? A bag? Jasmine? She didn't know. Molly kept smacking it with the card.

Will turned away from the sparks as the circular blade cut its way through the plane's aluminum skin. As the hole became more complete, the flow of water coming into the cabin slowed. Will knew the skirt must have been close to drained.

"We should be okay!" he yelled to Kit, but then his head brushed the ceiling.

A jolt of fear and adrenaline shot through his body as water continued to trickle out of the makeshift hatch.

"Hell no. Hellll no," Jasmine said, kicking at whatever was touching her leg. She turned—no one was there.

"Molly?" Jasmine spun around. "Molly!"

She looked down into the water and saw Molly's body, not moving. "Shit."

Jasmine dove headfirst—but the inflated life vest refused to let her go under. She fought it, trying again and again to dive down, but it wouldn't work.

She turned toward the group.

"Help! Help me!"

The saw was too loud. No one could hear her.

Jasmine unbuckled her life vest and removed it from around her neck. With a deep breath, she dove under.

Jasmine grabbed Molly's arm and used it as a guideline through the dark water. She pulled up on the flight attendant's body, but it wouldn't come. Jasmine felt for the part that resisted. Grappling around the life vest, she found the oxygen bottle strap pulled taut. Tracing it to the point where it was caught, she tried to push it out the opposite direction, but a row of seats that had broken forward in the crash was pinching the strap.

Jasmine's lungs burned. She kicked for the surface. Breaking the water, she took a huge breath and dove back under.

This time she grabbed the armrest and planted her feet in the aisle. Bubbles escaped her lips as she groaned, lifting the row of seats up. Shifting her balance, she found the strap and wrestled it toward the opening until she felt the fabric slip free.

Jasmine wrapped her arms around Molly and pushed off the floor. She gasped for air at the surface and began to scream.

"Help!"

Jasmine gargled water, choking as she dragged Molly toward the others. "Help us!"

But everyone had their backs to them. They were watching the saw work. Then, just for a second, the blade stopped moving and the noise ceased.

"Help!"

Bernadette turned. "Oh my god!"

The nurse swam over, taking Molly in her arms while Jasmine coughed and tried to catch her breath. Bernadette checked for a pulse.

"Hold her. Here," Bernadette instructed, and Jasmine tried to push Molly's torso up so Bernadette could begin chest compressions. The back of Jasmine's head kept hitting the ceiling. The water was that high. Bernadette shifted to a different position, but she was trying to do CPR on a floating body while treading water.

It was impossible.

Bernadette stopped and looked at Jasmine, out of ideas.

"No," Jasmine said. "No! Do something! You do something!"

Bernadette stared at Molly's closed eyes and parted lips, helplessly looking her up and down . . .

Bernadette took a deep breath, then blew air across Molly's face.

It was instantaneous, like a reflex. Molly drew a huge breath in and began coughing and spitting up water. Lying on her back in Bernadette's arms, she looked up at the nurse once she could take a full breath and whispered in a raspy voice, "Thank you."

Bernadette shook her head. "Jasmine saved you."

Molly looked past her feet at Jasmine, who was treading water. "You can swim."

"Back up, back up!" Will yelled. The hole was almost cut. When it was finished, the circle of aluminum would drop down into the plane.

Kit, holding Maia, swam backward, their heads hitting the ceiling with each stroke. Ryan lifted Ruth with one arm, spitting mouthfuls of water out over the life vest as he tried to keep his head in the air pocket.

Will squinted into the bright sparks, anticipating that satisfying jump of the blade when the beginning and end of the circle met. But as it approached the last half inch, the blade cut into one of the plane's structural reinforcements.

There was a high-pitched squeal, then a loud crack.

With a jolt, the blade broke off and dropped into the water.

CHAPTER THIRTY-SEVEN

MUFFLED VOICES CAME FROM INSIDE THE FALCON BEFORE A SINGLE VOICE ANGRILY screamed out, "*FUCK.*"

Will looked to Kit. Both her and Maia's heads were bumping the roof. The pilot stroked the water, spinning around, looking for anything useful. Her oxygen tank bobbed behind her.

"Shan," Will said, pulling his daughter's arms off his neck. "Swim to Kit." Kit reached out her arm.

Will kicked hard, reaching up for the hanging lip of the cut metal hole. His fingers slipped into the crack and he winced at the biting sting that came when jagged metal sliced open his palm. He ignored it and pulled the oxygen tank off his back. Sticking the tank's opening valve and pressure gauge into the crack, he pushed up on the metal bottle, leveraging it like a crowbar.

The hole opened, just a bit more. Salt water poured into the gash in his hand as it drained from the hole. He choked on the water as it washed over his head.

"Push it through," yelled a voice from inside the Falcon. It was Feeny. With the slit now wider, Will could push the tank deeper into the hole. Once it was firmly in, he levered it upward again. The hole creaked open that much more.

Light from inside the module shone into the plane from the widening crack. Will could see Feeny's feet.

"Stand back, Willy!"

Will swam backward, motioning to Kit to do the same with the girls.

Suddenly there was a loud bang inside the rescue module and everyone startled. The circular flap of cut aluminum moved down slightly.

There was another bang and the hole opened a tiny bit more. A loud grunt came from inside the vessel and the whole plane swayed with the loudest bang of all as the hatch broke free and a man dropped down into the plane, dunking into the water.

A second later Feeny popped up with wild, wide eyes as he looked around the plane like it was the surface of Mars.

"Anybody want to get outta here?" Feeny said.

"Say again?" Fitz hollered.

He could barely hear a thing. The conditions on the surface were deteriorating rapidly as the wind picked up and the rain came down sideways. The intervals between the waves had become shorter—much shorter—and as a result, the ships rose and fell in an uneven cadence. Enormous swells crashed against the sides, spilling over the railings, washing across the deck, taking anything in their path with them.

Over the wind and rain, Fitz made out the message the second time.

"The Falcon has access! Passengers are loading in!"

Will stood on the headrests of two seats, straddling the aisle, with his torso partially inside the transfer skirt. Holding Shannon under her armpits, he lifted her up into the rescue module.

Shannon raised her arms and Feeny, who had already climbed back inside, pulled her up into the Falcon.

Kit passed Maia to Will. Will passed her to Feeny. Within seconds, Maia was also safely inside the Falcon.

Two down.

"C'mon, Ruth," Will shouted. Kit pushed back out of the way, and Ryan and Ruth paddled forward. Ryan stood on the headrests in the row in front of Will's. The men faced each other with Ruth between them while Feeny waited above.

Ruth raised her arms up, reaching for the ladder on the inside of the SRDRS. Ryan and Will wrapped their arms around her body, trying to lift her up. Feeny couldn't get a good grip and none of the men had any leverage.

Ruth struggled, her arms shaking as she tried to pull herself up. The maneuver was difficult enough, but her age and physical condition made it nearly impossible. Letting go, she told the men to set her down.

"I'm holding up the line," she said. "Let everyone else go first. I'll watch how they do it."

At the tail, Caputo watched the cable's tiny movements, which slowly were getting bigger. He didn't like what he was seeing.

A jagged bolt of lightning lit up the sky, immediately followed by a boom of thunder so intense it rattled the instruments on the deck of the *Powell*.

Fitz looked over to the *Angelica*. Waves pounded the considerably smaller vessel, rocking the ship side to side. The cable, dangling from the back of the ship, whipped around in response.

"*Topside!*" Caputo's voice hollered over the radio. "*Hold that cable steady!*"

The section of cable hooked to the plane didn't move. But the excess, the portion pooled on the seafloor, was moving up and down erratically. Each time it hit the seafloor, a cloud of debris and bubbles mushroomed out.

Bernadette went in easily. With her height, Jasmine didn't need much help at all. Molly was so petite it was like helping one of the children.

At Kit's insistence, Ryan was next. But before he left, Ryan looked down into the plane at where his wife's body was.

"I have to go now," he whispered, tears in his eyes. "I'll tell your family that you didn't suffer. That it was over before you knew it happened. I love you. I will always love you."

Before he could change his mind, Ryan reached up for Feeny's hand. Moments later, he was sitting inside the Falcon.

The module hadn't been docked but five minutes and everyone was loaded inside, except Will, Kit, and Ruth.

"Okay, Ruth," Will said. "Let's try it again."

Will had half a foot on Feeny, so he hopped up into the Falcon. He placed his feet on opposite sides of the opening and sat into a deep squat, stretching his arms down into the plane. Kit, feeling her way underwater, helped Ruth's feet find the tops of the seats.

"Stay in a squat until you feel me push you up," Kit said. "Then reach up and grab for the ladder." The old woman nodded.

Kit took a big breath and ducked under the water, centering herself in a deep squat on the seat. She placed her hands under Ruth's behind. The pilot came to a stand, pushing Ruth up.

Ruth reached up and managed to grab on to the second rung of the ladder. Will clamped his hands under her armpits. Kit grunted as she pushed the woman up higher. Will's face turned red while he biceps-curled her up. Feeny grabbed at her from the other side, but the awkward angle made him not much help. Ruth's arms shook. She released a hand, threw it upward, and managed to grab the next rung up. Will grunted, holding on, as she moved her other hand up to join the first.

Kit wrapped her arms around Ruth's dangling legs and tried to lift her, but she didn't have the height. Will adjusted his grip on Ruth's torso and repositioned his feet. She was nearly there. She was going to make it. He rocked back on his feet and began to pull her up into the Falcon.

Topside, Milton stared out to the water and his stomach dropped.

"*Brace!*" he screamed as loud as he could. But his warning was lost to the wind. Milton grabbed on to the railing, staggered his feet, and leaned into it.

The gargantuan wave hit the *Angelica* on her starboard side with such force that the ship nearly capsized. Water poured across the deck as sailors anchored themselves to whatever they could, but for most, there was no time. Bodies slammed the deck as the water swept under them. Milton, clinging to the railing, felt his feet leave the ground.

He struggled to see the cable. The ship's dramatic lean had ripped the line up from the water, pulling it over to the side. As the wave passed and the momentum shifted, the ship began to right itself and the cable began to drop back down.

Caputo watched helplessly as the heavy, thick cable—which had whipped up with abandon and hung weightlessly for a moment—began to drop to the reef.

"Got you," Will grunted as Feeny helped pull Ruth up into the confined space.

Suddenly, a snapping sound came from somewhere outside in the water and the rescue module began to tip. Everyone inside the Falcon fell over.

Ruth slipped out of Will's grasp and fell down into the plane, landing on top of Kit. Both women plunged into the water with a splash.

Tanner and Caputo swam down to the seafloor where the cable had struck the reef, quickly followed by the plane's tail. The water was hazy with sand. But they didn't need to see anything to know what had happened . . .

. . . and what was about to happen.

CHAPTER THIRTY-EIGHT

"*THE SHELF'S GONNA GIVE!*"

Caputo's voice boomed over the radio through the Falcon.

"*Detach! Detach! Detach!*"

Everyone scrambled for a seat on the long benches that lined both sides of the Falcon, buckling themselves in with shaking hands. Shannon pulled her harness straps tight, then laid her hand on the empty seat next to her, looking anxiously at her dad.

A low rumble came from outside and the Falcon began to shake.

Will reached his arms down into the plane. "We gotta go!"

Feeny hopped over to the opposite side of the transfer skirt. "Pass her up!"

Kit grabbed Ruth by the shoulders.

"Ruth," she said to the old woman. "We need to go. No. No, stop! Take my—"

Ruth continued to try to pull away. "I'm staying."

"We're not leaving without—"

"Yes. You are."

"Ruth! This isn't—"

The plane rocked forward. Kit felt the water rise on the back of her neck as it rushed forward. Up above, she heard Maia start crying.

Kit wrapped her arms around Ruth so they were face-to-face and stood up on the chair, trying to lift her toward the opening.

But Ruth refused to help.

"Please," Kit said, choking on the lump in her throat as she struggled against Ruth's deadweight. "We can do this."

Kit looked up. Will and Feeny had stopped trying to reach down.

"Take her!" Kit cried up at them.

"Kit," Will said softly.

"We have to get out. *I* have to get you out," Kit pleaded with Ruth.

Ruth laid a wrinkled hand on Kit's cheek and waited until she had her attention. Ruth tilted her head with a small smile. "Going down with the ship means nothing to those two little girls, sweetheart. This is my choice. Not yours. I choose here. Now. With Ira."

Ruth pulled back, and this time Kit let her go. Kit stood there, numb, watching the old woman swim away, heading deeper into the plane.

Before Kit knew what was happening, she was being lifted up into the transfer skirt. Kit called after Ruth while trying to fight Will off, but Feeny grabbed her from the other side, and moments later, Kit was lying on the floor of the Falcon watching Andrea Harris slam the hatch shut.

Will helped her up. She sat on the bench. Somehow she buckled herself in. Someone yelled something into a radio. Muffled noises came from outside the module in the open ocean. The divers started cutting the Falcon free. Will sat down next to her. He squeezed her knee. Kit just stared blankly.

Kit knew that final moment would be with her forever. It would keep her up at night. It would whisper to her when she was alone with her doubt and guilt. It would play over and over in her mind.

The image of a lovely old woman whose survival *she* was responsible for, removing her life vest as she swam deeper into the plane.

CHAPTER THIRTY-NINE

CHRIS IGNORED THE VOICES IN HER HELMET SCREAMING THAT THE CLIFF WAS ABOUT TO give. She focused instead on the stream of bubbles rising up from the blinding light at the end of her torch. There was a snap, and the piece broke off.

They were one piece closer to freeing the Falcon from the plane.

"Let's go, let's go!" she hollered as she swam to the next attachment. Sparks flew as she, Noah, and Sayid circled the rescue module, working as fast as they could.

Will double-checked Shannon's harness and tightened the straps.

"Let's go! Get it done!"

Chris's voice. Here, with Shannon. Will knew that there were still a million ways this could go wrong—only one way it could go right—and stuck in the middle of those odds were Shannon and Chris. His whole world.

Will belted himself in and took Shannon's hand. Running his thumb across her wrinkly, water-pruned skin, he leaned back against the curved side of the rescue module, closed his eyes, and focused on the vibrations from Chris's tools reverberating across his back.

Deep breath in.

Hold.

Hold.

He could feel his heart beating against his chest.

Hold.

Exhale out.

He opened his eyes.

None of it helped.

He swallowed the bitter, metallic taste of adrenaline. His leg bounced up and down involuntarily. The heat and humidity in the small space from their wet bodies was suffocating. The fluorescent lights created weird, misplaced shadows. There were no windows; they had no clue what was happening out there.

Molly sniffed and rubbed her nose. A moment later Will smelled the urine, too. Jasmine leaned over and kissed Maia on the top of her head.

"It's okay, little mama," she said, taking the girl's hand. Maia leaned in and tucked herself under Jasmine's arm.

There was nothing for them to do except stare at each other and wait.

"One Mississippi. Two Mississippi," Bernadette whispered to herself, taking a breath with each count. "Three Mississippi. Four Mississippi. Five Miss . . ."

Bernadette went quiet, as did everyone else. They felt the rumble before they heard it. Will watched his leg bouncing up and down before realizing—he wasn't the one doing it.

On deck of the *Angelica*, the cable attached to the plane began moving.

The winch operator held up his hands and took a step back. "That's not me," he said, shaking his head.

Milton listened to the screaming coming in over the radio. "That's not any of us."

Massive pieces of rock broke off the edge of the cliff and began to fall into the abyss as the shelf started to give. The plane dangled further over the edge. Its tail rose up.

In Chris's peripheral vision, everything was shifting. The plane jostled and dropped. She moved with it. She ignored everything besides that last part of metal weld her cutting torch was closing in on.

"*C'mon. C'mon*," she mouthed to herself, and a moment later, the torch snipped off the last of it. Without pausing, she swam to Sayid and Noah, both of whom were still cutting. As she swam, there was movement to their side. She looked over to see a large chunk of reef break off the cliff and start to sink down into the abyss.

"Done!"

She looked up. Noah's attachment was done. Only Sayid's piece was left. Chris aimed her cutting torch at the opposite side of the attachment, and blazing light and sparks flew around them both as they cut their way toward each other.

"*Are we clear?*" Rogers's distraught voice rang out in her helmet.

"Negative," Chris said, feeling sweat dripping inside the rubber mouthpiece. "Almost."

This was the last attachment. This was it. Once they cut it free, Rogers could pilot the vessel to the surface. It would be over. Shannon would be safe.

Suddenly the torch in her hands began to shake uncontrollably. The line she was working became more jagged. Everything began to move— and she knew it wasn't her.

Inside the Falcon, everything shook. Every voice on the radio was panicked. So too were the passengers' prayers and sobs. A distant rumbling grew louder.

Then Will felt the shift.

They were falling.

CHAPTER FORTY

A LOW GROWL EMANATED FROM THE SHIFTING EARTH. DISTORTED BY THE UNDERWATER acoustics, the noise became something indistinct and animal as the entire shelf finally gave, taking the plane with it.

The divers watched helplessly as sheets of terrain broke free and slid downward into the pitch-black expanse of the abyss. Everyone moved away. Away from the crumbling cliff. Away from the ocean depths. Away from the free-falling plane. Away from the people trapped inside the Falcon, which was still attached to it. Everyone moved away from disaster, protecting their own personal safety.

Everyone except Chris.

Chasing after it with strong, firm kicks, she extended her strokes as both she and the plane descended into darkness. The slack in the length of her umbilical began to pull taut, mirroring the cable that was still attached to the lift sling wrapped around the tail.

Suddenly, there was a subtle snap as the cable attached to the plane hit full extension.

The yellow sling swung around slowly to the top of the tail. Sliding up, it caught on what little remained of the plane's damaged horizontal stabilizer. The aircraft rebounded, pulling back in the opposite direction—with the brunt of the force absorbed by the already weakened portion on the top of the tail. A steady stream of bubbles began to rise out of the widening stress fractures. The bubbles were getting larger and larger by the second.

The plane was now completely vertical. Nose down, it dangled over the abyss, held up by a single cable anchored to the weakest part of the plane's structure. Swaying slowly in the weightless environment, the Falcon remained attached to the roof of the plane.

Everything was sideways inside the Falcon.

Will's body pulled against the harness, pushing him into Kit below while Shannon sandwiched him from above. He struggled to lift his head, trying to see over Shannon to Feeny. The attendant seats were at the very front, perpendicular to the long benches. Feeny's face was bright red and his feet dangled, swinging free, as he white-knuckled the harnesses that cut into his torso. It was the only thing keeping him from falling the length of the vessel.

"Am I go to lift?"

Everyone held their breath. No one moved. They waited to hear their fate, but the question was met with silence. A few moments later, the same voice came again. His desperation told them everything.

"Chris. Are we clear? Can I bring her up?"

No one answered.

Kit kicked the side wall with the back of her heel. Jasmine jumped at the sound. Ryan and Molly just stared forward into space.

A different voice came over the radio, this one sounding as panicked as the last.

"Should we pull the cable up?"

Will leaned his head back and silently bargained with a god he didn't believe in. *I'll do anything. Anything. Just please, God. Let me hear her voice. Let me know she's okay.*

There was a crackling noise and then heavy breathing.

"Stand by."

"Mommy," Shannon said, burying her face into Will's arm. For the first time that day, she began to cry.

Will tucked her under his arm and stroked her hair with a trembling hand. "It's okay, Shan. It's going to be okay. It's going to be okay."

Tears welled in his eyes as he said it over and over. Maybe if he said it enough, it would be true.

"It's going to be okay, Shan. It's going to be okay."

Chris kept kicking down to the plane. There were only three inches of weld on one final attachment left. It would take her less than a minute to finish.

I can do it.

As she reached the Falcon, she kept telling herself that, over and over. *I can do it. I can do it. I can do it.*

The end of her torch lit up in a sparkling brilliance. Placing it against the weld, she began to burn through the metal. Chris didn't blink. She just focused on the bright light as though she could make the machine work faster by sheer force of will.

With a loud creak, the weakened part of the airframe began to fail in earnest. The weight of the fuselage was too much. The tail began to tear off the body of the plane. What little remained of the air pocket inside the cabin bubbled up through the widening separations in the metal as the plane—along with the Falcon—dropped another few feet.

The plane slipped out from under her.

Chris kicked, moving in on that last strip of metal. She reached out her fingers. She was right there!

And that's when her umbilical cable snapped taut.

The breath knocked out of her chest as she was yanked from behind. She kicked and pulled against it, but she could go no further. She dangled there, helplessly grabbing at the Falcon, which was just out of reach, not a foot away. Her mind went to Shannon. And Will. And Annie.

Reaching up to the brass coupling plugs that attached the umbilical to her helmet, she released them and untethered herself.

Instantly, the pressure in her helmet changed as the unlimited supply of surface air disconnected. As she swam down to the Falcon, she reached for her bailout gas and twisted the emergency oxygen bottle open with a puff of bubbles. She knew it only had enough air to get a diver back to the surface. But as the burning electrodes lit up the water, she prayed it had enough air for her to finish the job.

Sayid, Noah, Caputo, and Tanner all kicked down into the darkness toward the single bright light coming from the end of Chris's torch. Rogers's voice begged over the radio.

"*Come in! Can I lift?*"

Before any of them could answer, there was a loud creaking, followed by a sharp snap.

The cable next to them began to move as the thick twist of metal attached to the plane changed from a straight, taut line to a weightless, undulating sway.

The tail had broken completely off the plane.

Chris felt the resistance give as the Falcon dropped out from under her completely. She quickly reached a hand out and slipped her gloved fingers under the lip of the transfer skirt like a rodeo rider holding on to a bull rope. Pulling herself down to the skirt, she kept working.

Inside the Falcon, the rescue module dropped backward and everything went upright. For just a moment, the passengers faced each other right-side up again—and then the balance shifted in the opposite direction.

They were in free fall.

As the plane fell into the abyss, Chris hung on to the Falcon with one hand, cutting through the final attachment with the other. Her heavy breathing began to fog the glass of her helmet. The sparks of light began to blur—but she knew she was right there. She closed her eyes. *See like the blind man.*

A quarter of an inch. An eighth of an inch.

C'mon . . . c'mon . . .

Her hand was rock steady. She'd entered into a flow state of such singular focus that the rest of the world disappeared. There were no distractions. She felt no emotions. She had no thoughts. The whole universe was nothing but that line of fused metal.

She was there. This was it. It was paper thin . . .

The piece snapped off. The Falcon was free.

"Now! Bring her up!"

The Falcon didn't move.

"Go! Now!"

But it just kept sinking.

"Rogers!" Chris's voice was hoarse, she was screaming so loud. "Does anyone read—"

And that's when she realized.

The comms cable was part of the umbilical. No one could hear her.

Will wondered what would kill them first. Would they run out of air? Would they reach crush depth, where the sides would buckle in under the pressure? Or would they land on another shelf—too deep for rescue, just high enough to live—where they'd wait in the cold, starving and dehydrated, dying off one by one?

The Falcon kept dropping. He could feel the changing pressure.

He squeezed Shannon tighter.

This was the end.

Sayid kicked down toward the sinking plane looking for Chris, trying to see the Falcon.

All he saw was darkness.

Suddenly, the bright light of Chris's torch lit up the water, sputtering on and off in an irregular way, almost like a signal. Confused, he squinted into the light and found Chris—and instantly realized he was seeing her through a gap between the plane and the Falcon.

Chris screamed at the top of her lungs as she turned the torch on and off. Praying someone would see it. Someone would understand. Someone would see it was free. Someone would tell them.

But the Falcon wasn't responding. Nothing was happening. And there was literally nothing she could do.

So Chris surrendered and let it in. All of it.

Annie in the car seat in the rearview mirror, smiling with purple Popsicle lips. Shannon's head resting on her stomach as she hugged her goodbye just a few hours ago. Will's hand on the window, pressing against hers.

Chris was going to lose them. She had failed Shannon just as she had failed her sister. A burning tightness filled her chest as the screams no one heard turned to wails . . .

The Falcon stopped moving.

Chris and the massive machine were mirror images, frozen, floating in a weightless suspension. Just holding their position. Then the Falcon began to move in the opposite direction.

Up.

A tingling relief radiated out of every cell in her body, warm and light. Shannon and Will were going to be safe. They were going to be okay. Chris cried tears of relief as she thought of them all together, at home—

The cutting torch's cable snapped taut.

Instinctively, she gripped the tool harder, clutching it with both hands as her body was jerked sideways. Kicking, she flipped herself right-side up—just in time to see the jagged, razor-sharp metal edge where the plane had torn from the tail slice through her electrical line.

"'At first I was afraid, I was petrified.'"

Jasmine's voice sang out over the cheering and the crying. It was the perfect soundtrack for the moment: an iconic disco anthem that declared an unwavering commitment to one thing and one thing only.

Survival.

"C'mon now," Jasmine said. "I know y'all know it."

Voices joined hers, remembering the words to varying degrees.

"'—you're back! From outer space!'"

Will clasped Kit's hand. She was staring morosely at the floor and he could tell she was still with Ruth. And Ira. Andy. The diver who'd tried to save them. The passengers who'd gotten off the plane. The singing continued, and a tear slid down the pilot's cheek. Will squeezed her hand.

Kit sighed. And as she began to sing softly, she squeezed his hand back.

"*You guys gotta hear this,*" came Feeny's voice.

Sayid couldn't help but laugh as the sound of singing began to play in his helmet. Watching the bright yellow rescue vessel move by him as it slowly headed for the surface, a lump came to his throat. Shannon and Will were right there, safe inside. It was over.

As the rescue module continued up, it moved past all the floating divers watching it go. There was a cautious relief and triumph to the moment. Not an outright celebration. For them, nothing was over until the passengers were topside. But it was impossible not to savor the fact that the Falcon was headed to the surface.

As Sayid kicked to meet the other divers and follow the Falcon up, he saw the umbilical cable. Dangling. Loose. Unattached.

It took him a second to put it together. When he did, he spun in the water, panicked.

"Chris!"

There wasn't an answer.

He looked down, just as the plane sank deep enough that it disappeared completely into the black void of the ocean.

That's when he saw her.

"Shit, this is long, cut to the chorus, y'all," Jasmine sang, leaning her head back, her long braids shaking. "'I will survive!'"

Maia and Shannon laughed and danced in their seats, not knowing the song everyone else belted out at the top of their lungs. Will's voice broke on the high notes. Or, perhaps, it was the lump in his throat.

But then he heard something else. Something beyond Gloria Gaynor's immortal lyrics. Voices that weren't singing.

"Hey . . . hey! Hey, stop!"

He waved his arms until everyone quieted down. Only then could they hear the panicked voices coming in over the radio.

"Get her up! Get her up now!"

CHAPTER FORTY-ONE

SAYID KICKED AS HARD AS HE COULD TOWARD CHRIS'S SINKING BODY, KNOWING NOAH was right behind him. The two of them would chase her to crush depth before they would surface without her.

Chris was plummeting, facedown. She wasn't moving. No bubbles rose from her helmet. She wasn't breathing. Or her bailout bottle was empty. If she'd even used it. When had she untethered? How long had she been out? The answers were the difference between life and death.

Sayid's breathing rattled loud and labored in his helmet. It was supernatural, how fast he was swimming. He'd packaged the team's gear for transport, so Sayid knew his own umbilical was longer than hers—but not by much. She was getting closer. He was almost there. And just as he began to feel his own umbilical tightening, he grabbed her unresponsive body by the torso, flipping her over.

"Chris!" he screamed to no response. Through the glass of her helmet, he saw her eyes were closed and the breathing mask pushed up high on her cheeks.

Sayid immediately kicked for the surface while he reached around to the tank strapped to her back. Finding the valve on the emergency bailout gas, he went to twist it open—but realized it already was.

Noah appeared at his side and immediately went for the quick-release feature on Chris's harness. He removed the excess weight and drag with a click, and the nylon around her body went slack. As the men kicked for the surface together, Noah untangled the harness from Chris's body and let it drop before pulling up on her bailout bottle to check the pressure gauge.

"She's in the red," Noah said.

Sayid took a deep breath and grabbed at the brass coupling plugs on his own helmet. He released, feeling the pressure inside his helmet shift, and passed his own umbilical to Noah. Noah attached the line to Chris's helmet while Sayid twisted open his own bailout bottle. As the men kept kicking for the surface, both watched Chris for any changes.

She remained unresponsive.

Noah and Sayid flanked her body, each with one hand clutching her arm while the other tipped her head back to create as open and unobstructed an airway as possible. But the massive metal dive helmets they all wore were designed for protection, not mobility. Chris's neck barely angled back at all. But they did it anyway, even though both men knew it might not matter.

They might already be out of time.

Will stroked Shannon's hair with a shaking hand, whispering *shhhhh*. The shushing wasn't for her. Her crying was calm and even as her body trembled in his arms. It wasn't for himself either, although it did force him to breathe.

He shushed to cover the sounds that were coming in over the radio.

Everyone was talking at once. Emergency commands. Calls for medical air support. Details of what had happened. What would happen next. No one seemed to know much. Nothing seemed to make sense. It was loud and chaotic. It was out of control.

Will shushed louder, desperately trying to drown it all out. He looked over to Feeny.

Feeny's hands clutched the harnesses that cut into his broad barrel chest like he was strapped to a roller coaster. He was a full-grown man looking like a tiny little boy, lips parted, eyes rimmed with tears. He looked at the wall, as though trying to see through it to Chris out in the water, and then looked to Will.

They were helpless. There was nothing they could do but wait.

Sayid's chest and throat burned as he began to hyperventilate. Emotion was a luxury Chris couldn't afford and certainly would never have given in to herself. So he forced himself to relax. To meet the situation like he knew Chris would.

The Falcon was far below them now. But as they'd passed, Noah and Sayid had locked eyes. They didn't need words to know they were both thinking the same thing.

Will, Shannon, and Feeny were right there. Chris, Sayid, and Noah were here on the other side. It was exactly what they'd worked for all day. To get everyone back together. To make their weird, chosen dysfunctional family whole. That was how Chris ran the business. That was why she'd hired all of them. That was why they'd all worked there forever and assumed they always would. It wasn't a job. It wasn't a business. It was family. And Chris wasn't just the boss. She was the glue that held them all together. The Wendy Darling to their Lost Boys. First one in the water, last one out. No one worked harder, no one cared more.

Losing Chris wasn't an option.

The dive computer on Sayid's wrist vibrated a warning. He ignored it. He also ignored the red numbers blinking across the computer's rectangular screen. He knew the decompression alerts would keep going off all the way to the surface, but he also knew they'd ignore every single one of them.

They didn't care about safe diving practices or what could happen to them. Sayid prayed for decompression sickness, he prayed for the bends. He prayed to find Noah, himself, and Chris camped in recompression chambers. He prayed he would need physical therapy, prayed for restrictions on when they could dive again. He prayed for nerve damage. He prayed for never being the same again. He prayed for pain and suffering and agonizing misery—because it would mean they'd survived.

CHAPTER FORTY-TWO

THE WORST OF THE STORM HAD PASSED, BUT THE RAIN WAS STILL BEATING DOWN AS
the Falcon broke the surface.

This was the moment they'd worked for, waited for, hadn't been
sure would or even could actually happen: the moment the rescue team
returned to the surface triumphantly with the passengers from the plane
safe and alive.

But no one was celebrating.

Overhead, a local news chopper circled. It was barely dusk, but the
storm had darkened the sky prematurely, and so the helicopter aimed its
large searchlight down on the water as it filmed the scene. The Falcon
had arrived, but all focus was elsewhere.

On Chris.

Servicemen in one of the Zodiacs worked to drag her body out of
the water. They laid her flat across the bottom of the boat and unbuckled her dive helmet. Sliding it off, they found her unresponsive, eyes
shut, skin gray.

The news helicopter peeled off after the call came to clear the area.
The sailors in the boat were beginning CPR just as the distant sound of
a USCG chopper was heard.

At the back of the *Powell*, the hydraulic power unit for the handling
arm rotated forward and down toward the water to grab the Falcon and
lift it on deck.

As that process began, the rescue helicopter arrived. The door on the side of the chopper slid open, and with sickening familiarity, a rescue basket was lowered to the water.

Fitz stood next to Larson, alternating his focus between the raising of the rescue module and the medical attention Chris was receiving.

"Bravo Zulu, Fitz," Larson said with a sadness to her voice that didn't usually accompany the traditional naval shorthand for "well done." She held out her hand and Fitz took it in his.

"Bravo Zulu, ma'am."

Fitz told himself it was over. That it was done. They had worked together, overcome incredible odds, and brought the passengers home safe. Mission accomplished.

But watching the rain fall on Chris's unresponsive body as they loaded her into the rescue basket, he felt no relief.

By the time the Falcon was attached and hoisted on deck, the helicopter carrying Chris was already en route to the hospital in Honolulu. Fitz, Milton, Larson, Tanner, Caputo, and all the rest of the divers and sailors stood around the rescue module as they prepared to open the hatch.

While they waited, the rain eased to a soft patter, and then after a few moments, nothing.

Fitz looked up at the sky just as the clouds began to part before the final moments of a magnificent Hawaiian sunset. Milton, standing beside him, spoke only loud enough so that Fitz could hear.

"If there's a fucking rainbow when they come outta there, I swear to god . . ."

The hatch opened. One by one, the passengers began to emerge from the Falcon.

Everyone on deck cheered. Kaholo was right at the front, clutching each of them in a tight hug as they came out. Fitz smiled as Kaholo took Maia into his arms and set her on the deck.

Stretchers were set up nearby and medics waited to see what they were dealing with. The passengers were shaky and weak, and would be immediately transferred to the hyperbaric chamber, but everything they would face from here on was manageable.

Shannon was one of the last out. As soon as Kaholo set her down, Maia wrapped her arms around Shannon in a tight hug. But Shannon wasn't focused on Maia. She was looking around the deck anxiously.

Will appeared next, and what little was left of Fitz's smile disappeared completely. Kaholo tried to hug him, but Will pushed him away. Medics came forward, but Will moved right past them. His chest heaved as he spun around, searching for Chris. When he didn't see her, he turned to the nearest person in uniform.

"Fitz," Will said. "Who's Fitz?"

Fitz had already started that way, and as the coastguardsman pointed him out, Will began to jog toward him. His legs gave out and Will fell to the ground. People ran over, helping him to his feet.

"Sir, your body is—"

"Where is she?" Will said, pushing hands off him, his legs continuing to shake.

Fitz grabbed his arm to steady him. "Will, you need to go to the hyperbaric—"

Will slapped his hand away. "Where is she?"

Everyone on deck turned. Fitz watched the tears stream down Will's face. The cocky engineer, so sure of himself, was gone.

"She's at the hospital in Honolulu. She was transported by helicopter as soon as she came up."

"What happened?"

Shannon appeared at his side, watching Fitz with a clear, steady gaze, so different from her father's emotional outburst. *She's just like her mother*, Fitz thought. Shannon listened, seeming to understand everything that was happening like an adult would. Feeny came up behind her and placed his hands on the child's shoulders.

Fitz looked to Will, feeling out whether he should keep going. Will waited.

"We don't know all the details. But at some point she untethered from her umbilical. And after she cut the Falcon free, something—we think most likely the section of fuselage where the tail ripped off—sliced her electrical line."

He looked down at the little girl. Tears welled in her eyes, but they didn't fall.

"Chris received an electric jolt."

"How big of a jolt?" Will asked.

"We don't know," Fitz said. "And we don't know if it was that or lack of oxygen that made her black out first."

"What about her bailout gas?" Feeny asked.

"Noah said it was empty by the time they got to her. Sayid gave her his own umbilical, but we don't know how long she was out. They both went to the hospital with her."

"Is Sayid—"

"Fine. They'll both be fine," Fitz assured them. "The hospital put them in a recompression chamber, just like you all need to—"

Will interrupted, stammering questions that had no answers, until Fitz stopped him.

"Look," Fitz said, putting a hand on Will's arm. "Let's get you and Shannon in with the rest of—"

"No," Will said, pulling his arm away. "You get me a helicopter. I need to go to the hospital. I need to see my wife."

"You won't be able to. They're working on—"

"I need to see her! She's . . . she's . . ."

Will started to sway. His eyelids drooped and his head began to bob. Feeny stepped up quickly and wrapped an arm around his waist.

"Easy, Willy," Feeny said, nodding to Shannon.

This time Will didn't protest or try to fight it. Fitz assumed that even in this condition, Will knew there was nothing he could do for Chris right now and he still had to take care of his daughter. Will took Shannon's hand, and with Feeny's help, they headed for the recompression chamber.

The other passengers were already inside, sitting silently as the medical staff evaluated them. They all wore the same look of shock as the one on Will's face. The adrenaline was wearing off and reality was setting in. They barely even looked up as Shannon and Will entered. Before an attendant shut the door, Fitz cleared his throat.

"Will."

Will turned.

"I promise you," Fitz said. "I *promise* the second we know anything about Chris, you will know."

There hadn't been a thing Will didn't have a counterargument to the whole day. He had challenged every word that had come out of Fitz's mouth. Now he just stared at Fitz with nothing to say.

Will walked into the chamber and the door was shut behind him with a loud, airtight thud. Fitz watched through the porthole window as Will slumped down onto a bench next to Shannon. Someone came over with a blood pressure cuff and an oxygen mask. Will sat there letting them move him around like he was a doll. After a few minutes, Fitz pushed a button on the door.

"Hey, Will," he said, hearing his tinny voice on the other side. Everyone in the chamber looked over. Will slowly turned his attention to Fitz. "You were right. About everything. And so was Chris. You were both right, and you're all alive because of it."

Will listened, but Fitz wondered if he'd heard. Either way, the engineer didn't react. He just looked at something up above Fitz's head for a few moments before lying down on the bench.

Fitz turned to leave, and that's when he saw what Will was looking at.

A full double rainbow stretched across the sky.

CHAPTER FORTY-THREE

IT WAS DARK. BUT WHY?

Chris didn't know if it was night, or a dark room, or if her eyes were just closed. Nothing was clear. Nothing made sense. She tried to move but couldn't. It was as though her body was no longer connected to her brain.

Was she dead?

It felt possible. This wasn't what it felt like to be alive. Whatever this was felt like some sort of in-between. A vague floating sensation. Floating through nothingness. A kind of weightless freedom. Like diving.

She heard something. A low vibration. A sound she recognized. She tried to focus, to hone in on it. Something primal connected, and the noise became clearer.

It was a voice.

Will.

His voice was distant. Distorted. Like he was underwater. Or she was.

"You'd have been so proud," Will was saying. "She never lost her head. She was everything you've raised her to be."

The thought of Shannon brought a radiating warmth. It was a powerful sensation and it covered the feeling that was already there, one that she hadn't noticed until now. Pain.

"She's everything you are, Chrissy. The very best of you."

Chris wanted to smile. She tried to smile. But wherever her body was, it didn't comply.

There was a long pause. A moment. A year. A lifetime. Chris didn't know. Chris didn't care. She wanted to stay here forever. Quiet and calm. No fighting. No anger. No resentment. No grief. Just love. Just him. He was home. They were home.

When Will spoke again, his voice was broken, humble. He was changed.

"I always thought we'd have time. I thought we'd work it out. But then I blinked, and all this time passed. Now I see it. I understand."

He paused.

"Time is luck. You grab it. You hold on tight. And you *be* there. You have to *be there* for it. It's going, with or without you. And no one knows for how long. No one knows."

Something in Chris stirred. Faint, like a tap on the shoulder trying to get her attention. She ignored it. Instead, she leaned into her desire to climb into Will's lap and feel small and safe with his arms wrapped around her. She wanted time. With him. With Shannon. Living a today. A tomorrow. Not longing for a yesterday that could never come back.

They wanted more time. Chris needed more time.

"Shannon's going to be fine," Will said, his voice breaking. "Because of you. But I've got her now. You can rest."

Will's voice started to drift away as that stirring returned. This time, Chris couldn't ignore it. It was too strong. A sensation of peace slowly crept closer as a warm tingling that started at the tip of her toes began to fill her feet, her legs, and up and up as Will's voice shrank away, getting softer. *Come back*, she tried to say, but her thoughts found no words, and as his voice grew dim, another appeared. Faint and sweet, the voice was exactly as she remembered, calling Chris's name, beckoning her closer.

Mom . . . Mom . . .

Will and Annie's voices overlapped, blurred by an understanding that she was so loved. And as that feeling consumed Chris's whole body, Will's voice disappeared entirely . . .

. . . and Annie was there.

A hazy shimmer encompassed them both. Mother and daughter, together, at last. That pink swimsuit. Those purple Popsicle lips. The smell of chlorine and the warmth of the sun.

Chris kneeled, eye level with her little girl. Every freckle, every hair. The sound of her breath, the smell of her skin. It was hers—Annie was here. Or maybe Chris was there. It didn't matter. They were together.

Annie held out her arm. Chris took it in her hands. And as she rubbed sunscreen into soft skin her fingers remembered, Chris felt her pain start to dissolve.

"I've missed you," she said.

Annie smiled. That bottom tooth, it still hadn't come in.

Chris finished with one arm and moved to the next. Then her legs. Her neck. Her chin. Her cheeks. Annie closed her lips and shut her eyes tight while Chris attended to every inch of her baby's face. Covering her, protecting her, enshrouding her in a mother's love. When she finished, when there was nothing left, Chris stopped, and Annie opened her eyes.

"It doesn't hurt," Annie said.

Chris smiled, relieved. "Are you sure?"

Annie nodded. Her brave, brave little girl.

Chris took her daughter in her arms for the first time in six years, feeling Annie's warm body pressed against hers. As their bodies melted together, their hearts beat in sync. Their breath flowed as one. Mother and child, one indistinguishable from the other.

Forgiveness. Acceptance. Peace. And love. Concepts became sensations became knowledge became known. And as Chris felt this understanding expand from her body to a place beyond, everything else faded away.

ONE YEAR LATER

WILL LOOKED UP AT THE NIGHT SKY.

Chris always said the moonless nights were her favorite because the darkness made the stars twinkle a little bit brighter. She wasn't wrong.

"I wish Bernadette could have been here," Molly said as she stared into the fire. A breeze came in off the ocean and blew the smoke in her face. She closed her eyes and turned her head, but the wind shifted quickly.

"I couldn't sleep the night before I flew out," Ryan said. "I almost didn't come, either."

"No, I get it," Molly said. "I just wish she was here. They should've had the ceremony in San Francisco or something."

"I think they wanted to make a point," Kaholo replied. "The airline. Like, *After all that, we still think it's safe to fly.*"

"I don't," Jasmine said. "But a free first-class ticket, a free hotel, a six-figure settlement. Well, I'll let Xanax do the work."

Shannon sat in the sand, leaning back against Will's chair. Maia sat next to her, and the girls looked at a phone, watching the montage of pictures and videos that had been played at the ceremony—all pictures and videos that the two official historians of Flight 1421 had taken on the plane.

"It was nice to meet Ruth and Ira's family," Kit said. She was leaning forward, her elbows resting on her knees, watching the flames. She smiled. "Is Rachel an exact younger version of Ruth or what?"

"I was surprised no one from Andy's family came," Will said, still looking up at the sky.

Molly scoffed. "I wasn't."

Will looked down. "Why?"

"You don't know?" Kaholo asked.

"Know what?"

"That when he was in Hawaii, his family thought he was in Denver on a business trip. Dude was in Honolulu with another woman."

"You're kidding," Will replied.

"Nope," Molly said. "His family watched all the crash coverage having no clue that he was on the flight."

"Didn't he have kids?"

"Three boys," Kit said.

Will shook his head. "I don't want to speak ill of the dead, but—"

"What an asshole," Jasmine said.

Everyone laughed.

It felt good to laugh. It felt good to be together. The past year had been hard. Processing the trauma. Trying to understand what had happened. Why they had lived when so many hadn't. If they were all honest, there hadn't been much laughter in their lives since the crash. But here, with each other, with no one else around, they didn't have to explain anything or justify themselves. They could just be.

Molly unzipped her purse, reached inside, and pulled something out.

"No way," Kaholo said. "No way!"

"When we were getting ready for the Falcon to dock, I remembered it," Molly said, twisting the sticker-covered water bottle so the notes inside mixed together.

"What do they say?" Jasmine said.

"I didn't read them!"

"Oh, I definitely would have."

Molly unscrewed the bottle and shook the papers out onto the sand. Kaholo sat next to her and the two sorted through the notes, passing them around to the right people. Once the notes were all handed out, with Bernadette's put back in the bottle, three remained on the sand, unclaimed.

The group went silent as they read. And then the group stayed silent as they thought about what they'd read. After a while, Ryan was the first to talk.

"Anyone want to share?" he asked.

No one volunteered at first, but then Maia stood up and read hers word-for-word like she was at the front of the class. Everyone smiled, remembering her letter since she'd already read it out loud as she'd written it. They knew she'd had shaved ice, they'd already heard about the sea turtle, and earlier in the day they'd all met the grandparents she'd had such a good time in Hawaii with.

"Your turn," she said to Shannon as she sat down.

Shannon looked around sheepishly. "Is it okay if I don't stand?"

Everyone nodded, while Will leaned over and kissed the top of her head.

"Um, okay, so I wrote: 'I don't think I have any regrets because I don't really even know what that means? But I think that's a good thing, to not understand something that's bad. Maybe that's the good thing about dying as a kid. For Annie, too. We only ever figured out the good stuff.'"

Will leaned his head back against the chair and stared at the sky as the stars went blurry through his tears.

"'I love my dad,'" Shannon said before her voice got quieter. "'I love my mom. And I love when we're a family together.'"

There were a few sniffles around the fire. Molly wiped her face.

Jasmine chuckled, shaking her head. "Well, mine's not deep like that, but . . ." She leaned toward the firelight to read her tiny handwriting on the back side of the boarding pass. "It says . . . oh wait, no, I'm not saying that." She paused. "Oh, I'm not saying that either." Everyone chuckled. "Okay. Now, here we go, here we go. 'But, if there was one thing in life I *would* have done differently . . .'"

She looked up as everyone waited expectantly.

"'. . . I would have learned to swim.'"

Once the group had settled down from another round of deep, healing laughter, Molly read hers. Then Ryan, then Kaholo. All of them cried. All of them talked about family. All of them were low on regrets and high on gratitude. Even Ryan. That seemed to be the consistent theme—here, in this moment, and also then, as it was happening.

If it was the end, how lovely it had been.

"Wait, where's yours?" Kaholo asked Kit.

The pilot shook her head. "I never wrote one."

"Why?" Shannon asked.

"I was the captain. That was my plane. You were my passengers. And I felt . . ." She stared into the flames. "I felt like if I wrote a goodbye letter, it would be betraying that. I'd be admitting that we were out of options. I'd be giving up on getting us out of there. On surviving. I'd be giving up on you. And I just couldn't do that."

The fire crackled as everyone nodded.

"But I did write one in my head." Kit laughed. "I kinda made a mental note of what I *would* write if I was to write one."

"And . . . ?" Molly said.

"I would have written that I was disappointed in myself for not being brave enough to live the life I wanted."

"Is that why you quit?" Kaholo asked.

Kit nodded. "Look, I loved being a pilot. I did. But I'd always told myself I had become a pilot because my dad was a pilot. And that he had always wanted me to be a pilot, like him. But when we were down there, for the first time I realized what I think I'd always known. That I'd *really* only become a pilot because he didn't think I could. And I wanted to prove him wrong. And I told myself that if we did get out of there, I wouldn't waste my whole life, my one shot at, at *this*"—Kit waved her arms around at the ocean and the stars—"trying to prove something to someone else."

"Good for you," Molly said.

"So what are you doing now?" Will asked.

"Figuring out what to do now," she said, and laughed. "But I will."

Jasmine raised her chin at Will. "What about yours?"

Will thumbed the slip of paper in his hand before tucking it into his pocket.

No one asked again.

After a few moments, Kaholo nodded to the three notes that were left.

"What do we do with those?"

No one answered immediately as thoughts of Ruth, Ira, and Andy lingered. Their absences loomed now, as they had all day during the ceremony and reception and media interviews with the rest of the survivors from Flight 1421.

"I think they'd like it if we read them," Molly said.

No one disagreed, and so Kaholo picked one up. Unfolding the paper, he read it, and laughed.

"Well. Safe to say this was Andy's."

Kaholo turned the paper around to face everyone.

" 'I have no regrets.' "

"No," Molly said.

"That's it?" Kit said.

Will clapped, his head thrown back in laughter as Kaholo crumpled the note and tossed it into the fire.

"Final words." Jasmine laughed. "What an asshole."

Ryan motioned to the slips of paper and Molly passed one to him. He opened it, turned it right-side up, and read.

" 'To the kids: Be good to one another. You're all you got now. Stick together and you'll be fine. We are so proud of you. To Ruth: Making your coffee every morning was the greatest privilege of my life. I never once wanted anything more.' "

Tucked in Ryan's fingers, Ira's paper moved with the breeze. No one spoke for a long while; they just watched the flames dance as the wood crackled and the waves crashed.

Kit motioned and Molly passed her the final note. Unfolding it, Kit read aloud Ruth's looping cursive handwriting.

" 'Something tells me we're not going to make it out of here.' "

Kit's cheeks was already trembling. Kaholo put a hand on her shoulder.

" 'And that's okay. Your father and I are both okay with that. After all, it's why we . . .' "

Kit trailed off, her brow furrowing. Her eyes moved faster as she read ahead for a few moments. A pained look covered her face before she cleared her throat and continued, her voice breaking.

"'After all, it's why we came to Hawaii. You should know, the cancer's come back. The doctors said this time there was nothing they could do. Months. If I was lucky. Your father and I didn't come to Hawaii for our anniversary. We came for one final adventure together. I wanted to spend what time I had left feeling alive. Experiencing grand and unexpected things. Well. I'd say I got my wish.'"

The group stared at Kit, riveted by Ruth's every word.

"'I hope this brings you comfort, knowing that the inevitable is happening in a way I wanted. This was my choice. I wanted it this way. And I hope that when you think of me now, you'll do so while looking up at the sky, remembering just how bright and special it was. My life. Our lives. The love we shared and the adventures we had. Together.'"

No one spoke for a very long time. Kit stared into the fire, processing the pain. The grief. The relief. And the gratitude. After a while, she looked up. They all did.

The waves continued to crash, the fire continued to crackle, the embers continued to glow. And one by one, brilliant sparks of light floated up, disappearing as they headed to the stars.

Will and Shannon drove back from the beach in silence. The neighborhood was dark and quiet. As they passed, Will looked through the front window of the Allens' old place. The family that lived there now was just sitting down for dinner.

"How you holding up?" Will asked.

"I'm okay," Shannon said.

The car wound up the mountainous foothills for a few minutes before either spoke again.

"I feel bad," Shannon finally added.

Will nodded. "There were a lot of big feelings today."

"No. I feel . . . like, guilty."

Will took a deep breath. "A lot of people died, Shan. We were lucky. Survivor guilt is—"

"No. Well. I mean, yes. I get that. I know. But I feel guilty not just 'cause, like, we're here. And, you know, others aren't . . ."

Shannon trailed off. Will waited.

"But . . ." he prompted after a long time.

"But because I'm kinda glad it happened."

Will turned into the driveway and the headlights shone onto the house's wide, honey-colored wood siding. He put the car in park, not knowing what to say. "Okay. That's okay," he said finally. "But . . . why?"

Shannon got out of the car, then leaned back in. "Because it brought you home."

She closed the door and Will watched her cross the lawn to the front door. Shutting off the car, he followed her into the house, locking the door behind him. Emptying his pockets, he put his phone and keys on the entryway table and then unfolded the note. Rereading it, he smiled.

"How was it?"

He turned and watched Chris come down the stairs. Laying the note down, he crossed the entryway to meet her at the bottom. She stood a couple steps up so they were eye level. Brushing his hair back, she kissed him on the forehead.

"It was good," he said. "It was what we needed."

She smiled. Looking past him, she nodded to the note.

"What's that?"

He glanced over his shoulder, turned back, and wrapped his arms around his written promise.

"I'll tell you later."

ACKNOWLEDGMENTS

Drowning covered some familiar ground, but was far more uncharted territory. I had to study and learn things I knew absolutely nothing about, so my endless thanks to those who knew what I didn't and were patient in teaching me. Jack Sayers, Caltech Research Professor of Physics (pass the Watergate salad, please). Curt Cunningham, Undersea Special Mission Systems—Submarine Escape and Rescue, for providing a curious civilian with all the information on submarine rescue equipment that she was allowed to have. Phoenix Scuba, for my scuba certification. Kelli White, for all things emergency response. Syd Alperowicz, for showing me new ways to look at the questions that don't have answers. Marty, my engineer brother-in-law, for helping translate my thoughts when I had no vocabulary. And my dad, Ken, for a whole bunch of "What's this called again?" moments.

My same crew of phone-a-pilot friends proved invaluable once again: Mark Bregar, Fabrice Bosse, Brian Patterson, and Jaimie Rousseau. Not once have any of you ever laughed at or dismissed my questions—and there were some wild ones this time around. Thank you for always taking the flight attendant with the big imagination seriously. And special thanks to Captain Patterson. From milkshakes at LAX in T1 after missed commutes to here. Who'd a thought?

Speaking of flying—the support I've felt from the aviation

community has blown me away. Seeing your pictures of my book with a crew, on the plane, being read in the jump seat—it's all made me feel like I was still part of an industry I love and respect so deeply. Any time I have a reader say: *I never really knew what flight attendants did, I have so much more respect for them*, I'm always filled with pride. I'm no longer flying, and seeing how brutal the past few years have been for frontline aviation employees, I should probably say I'm glad. But the truth is, I miss it. Maybe that makes me a little masochistic . . . but who are we kidding? You gotta be to work for an airline.

Also, a quick note to my Virgin America family: the way you've supported and encouraged me has proven why it'll *always* be Redwood forever.

To my friends: I miss you. We all know I've been busy. Writing. Editing. Making the most of fleeting, once-in-a-lifetime opportunities. Hanging on for dear life as I try to figure out which end is up amidst all the change. I've had to say "no" a lot more than I've said "yes." I've frequently dropped the ball on responding to texts. Calling back. Getting together. I've prioritized the needs of my circumstances and never, not once, did any of you make me feel like that's not exactly what I should be doing. Never, not once, did I doubt that our friendship wasn't still foundationally solid. To have an inner circle made up of people so selflessly committed to one another's happiness and fulfillment is a profound wealth. I love you and appreciate you more than you know. You all know who you are (especially you, Julia Scinto, Sheena Gaspar, and Brian Shuff). I can't wait to get back to giving more than I take. Thank you for giving so much to me.

To my family: What can I say? No, I'm serious. How can I possibly distill down to a paragraph all you've done for me, for this book, to make any of it possible? And everything in my life is only possible because you show me, every single day, how to show up. It may be as simple as leaving a hot meal at my door when you know I don't have time to cook or even grocery shop—but what I *feel* and what I'm *shown* is grace. Understanding. Support. Selflessness. Trust. Belief. Belonging. Acceptance. Or, more simply: love. Marty, Kellyn, Davis,

Grant. My mom Denise, and my dad Ken. I love you so much. Thank you for being my people.

Now, about the nuts and bolts of this book.

Wrangling this story from sheer chaos to organized chaos was a herculean task, and early reads by Abby Gewanter were crucial in narrowing the focus. Thanks for not sugarcoating, Abby. Your notes were brutal. But they helped the most.

Publishing books in the last couple of years has meant unique challenges crop up near daily and I'm grateful I've been with a publisher who was game to rise to the occasion. Avid Reader, your passion and drive paved the way. Deep thanks to the whole team, but specifically: Carolyn Kelly, who came through in a pinch more than once. Gary Urda and the entire sales force, for getting the book out there. David Kass, for getting my story out there. Alison Forner and David Litman, for working with Shane to create covers more awesome than I could have ever hoped for. Meredith Vilarello, for, somehow, keeping all the plates spinning. And my editor and publisher, Jofie Ferrari-Adler, for a steady hand and a deep commitment to this book's success.

As for The Story Factory—my literary agency—boy, am I ever proud to be one of your authors. It's a small but mighty crew that makes these books happen, and of the group, special mention is warranted . . .

Ryan Coleman: for the myriad ways you helped make this book better. Next Costco slice is on me. Steve Hamilton: for always picking up the phone and having the right answer, even with the three-hour time difference. Don Winslow: for the support you've shown me and other authors. It has meant the difference between bestseller or not. I am so grateful. Dervla McTiernan: for flowers that said what I needed to hear from someone I actually wanted to hear it from. And Deborah Randall: please tell Shane to call me. I'm sure I'm waiting to hear back on something or other.

Which leads me to my final thanks.

I've never met anyone who works as hard as my agent, Shane Salerno. I thought I knew what hard work was. I thought I understood committing to a goal. But until I witnessed Shane's tireless pursuit of excellence and his outright refusal to accept anything less than the absolute best something can be, I had no idea.

None of what's happened to me the last few years would have happened without this man. Trust me, I am so acutely aware of this. And what he sacrifices for me, for all his authors, for every project he touches, seems a grossly unfair deal. See, when you work way, way behind the scenes (happily out of view, as I know he prefers) no one *really* gets to see or appreciate the scope of what you do. And that's a shame. Because it's a lifetime's worth of knowledge and insight applied in ways you wouldn't believe. It's nothing short of magic.

Shane, you've always expected more of me than I thought I was capable of. And every time I say *No, I can't*, you're right there saying *Yes, you can*. And the thing is, I trust you. And so I give it a shot. And then . . .

Well. We both know how much you love to say *I told you so*.

Every day, you're either out in front, by my side, or watching my back. We got some battle scars, now, you and I. Each hard won. But there's no one, and I mean *no one*, I'd rather ride out with.

You and me, Shane. Big things.

ABOUT THE AUTHOR

T. J. NEWMAN is a former bookseller and flight attendant whose first novel, *Falling*, became a publishing sensation and debuted at number two on the *New York Times* bestseller list. The book was named a best book of the year by *USA Today*, *Esquire*, and Amazon, among many others, and has been published in more than thirty countries. *Falling* will soon be a major motion picture from Universal Pictures. T. J. lives in Phoenix, Arizona. *Drowning* is her second novel.

Read on for the first
chapter of ...

FALLING

CHAPTER ONE

GIVING THE DUVET A SHAKE, CARRIE SMOOTHED THE CREASES WITH HER HAND. A whiff of fresh-cut grass drew her glance to the open window. The neighbor across the street mopped his face with the bottom of his shirt before closing the trash can full of lawn clippings with a clunk. Dragging it into the backyard, he gave a wave to a passing car, the loud music fading as it drove on. Behind her, in the bathroom, the shower shut off.

Carrie left the room.

"Mom, can I go outside?"

Scott stood at the bottom of the stairs holding a remote control car.

"Where's your—" Carrie said, making her way downstairs.

The baby crawled into the room, blowing wet raspberries as she went. Reaching her brother's feet, Elise grabbed onto his shorts and pulled herself up to a stand, her little body jerking subtly as she tried to find balance.

"Okay, did you bring your dishes to the sink?"

"Yup."

"Then you can, but only for ten minutes. Come back before your dad leaves, okay?"

The boy nodded and ran for the door.

"Nope," Carrie called after him, placing Elise on her hip. "Shoes."

The "whoops" baby ten years after the first kid had been overwhelming in the beginning. But as the family of three learned how to be four, Bill and Carrie realized the age gap meant big brother could do little things like watch-the-baby-while-I-get-dressed-and-make-the-bed. Things became more manageable after that.

Carrie was wiping the remnants of sweet potato and avocado off the high chair when she heard the front door open.

"Mom?" Scott hollered, a pinched alarm to his tone.

Hurrying around the corner, she found Scott staring up at a man she didn't know. The stranger on the front porch wore a startled look, his hand frozen on its way to the doorbell.

"Hi," Carrie said, shifting the baby to her other hip as she moved to place herself subtly between her son and the man. "Can I help you?"

"I'm with CalCom," the man said. "You called about your internet?"

"Oh!" she exclaimed, opening the door wider. "Of course, come in." Carrie cringed at her initial reaction, hoping the man hadn't noticed. "Sorry. I've never had a repairman come on time, let alone early. Scott!" she yelled, her son pivoting at the end of the drive. "Ten minutes."

Nodding, the boy ran off.

"I'm Carrie," she said, closing the door.

The technician set his equipment bag down in the entryway and Carrie watched him take in the living room. High ceilings and a staircase to the second floor. Tasteful furniture and fresh flowers on the coffee table. On the mantel, family photos over the years, the most recent taken on the beach at sunset. Scott was a mini-me of Carrie, their same chocolatey-brown hair blowing in the sea breeze, their green eyes squinted with wide smiles. Bill, nearly a foot taller than

Carrie, held a then-newborn Elise in his arms, her lily-white baby skin a contrast to his Southern California tan. The repairman turned with a small smile.

"Sam," he said.

"Sam," she said, returning the smile. "Can I get you something to drink before you get started? I was just about to make myself a cup of tea."

"Tea would be great, actually. Thanks."

She led him into the other room, bright, natural light filling the kitchen that opened into the toy-dotted family room.

"Thanks for coming on a Saturday." Carrie sat the baby back in the high chair. Pounding her fists on the table, Elise giggled through a sparsely toothed grin. "This was the only appointment I could get for weeks."

"Yeah, we're pretty busy. How long has your internet been out?"

"Day before yesterday?" she said, filling a tea kettle with water. "English breakfast or green?"

"English breakfast, thanks."

"Is it normal," Carrie asked, watching the stove's pilot light ignite to a full flame, "for our house to be the only one having issues? I asked a few neighbors who also have CalCom and theirs is fine."

Sam shrugged. "That's normal. Might be your router, maybe the wiring. I'll run diagnostics."

From the front room, heavy footsteps made their way down the stairs. Carrie knew the next sounds well: a suitcase and messenger bag set by the door, followed by hard-soled shoes crossing the entryway. In a handful of strides, he was in the kitchen, polished black dress shoes, crisply ironed pants, suit coat, and tie. Wings above his breast pocket displayed the Coastal Airways insignia, BILL HOFFMAN engraved boldly below. A matching pair adorned the front of the gold-trimmed hat he laid softly on the counter. His entrance felt oddly dramatic and Carrie noticed how much of a contrast his aura of authority made to the rest of the house. She'd never noticed it before; it wasn't like he came to dinner in uniform. And it was probably only because there was another person in the room, a man who didn't know him, didn't know their family. But for whatever reason, today, it was conspicuous.

Bill placed his hands in his pockets with a polite nod to the technician before settling his attention on Carrie.

Lips pursed, arms crossed, she stared back.

"Sam, would you mind . . ."

"Yeah, I'll, uh, get set up," Sam said to Carrie, leaving the couple alone.

The clock on the wall ticked the seconds. Baby Elise banged a drool-covered teething ring on the tray before it slipped out of her fingers, falling to the floor. Bill crossed the kitchen and picked it up, rinsing it off in the sink and drying it with a dish towel before returning it to his daughter's eager hands. Behind Carrie the tea kettle began a soft whistle.

"I'll FaceTime when I get to the hotel to hear how the game—"

"New York, right?" Carrie cut him off.

Bill nodded. "New York tonight, Portland tom—"

"There's a team pizza party after the game. With the three-hour time difference, you'll be asleep before we get home."

"Okay. Then first thing—"

"We're getting together with my sister and the kids tomorrow morning," she said, and shrugged. "So, we'll see."

Bill straightened with a deep inhale, the four gold stripes on his epaulets rising with his shoulders. "You know I had to say yes. If it'd been anyone else asking I wouldn't have."

Carrie stared at the floor. The kettle began to screech and she shut off the burner. The noise gradually softened until it was only the clock making noise again.

Bill checked his watch, cursing under his breath. Giving a kiss to the top of his daughter's head, he said, "I'm gonna be late."

"You've never been late," Carrie replied.

He put on his hat. "I'll call after I check in. Where's Scott?"

"Outside. Playing. He's coming back any minute to say goodbye."

It was a test and she knew Bill knew it. Carrie stared at him from the other side of the unspoken line she'd drawn. He glanced at the clock.

"We'll talk before I take off," Bill said, leaving the room.

Carrie watched him go.

The front door opened and closed a few moments later and a hush settled over the house. Crossing to the sink, Carrie watched the leaves on the oak tree in the backyard flutter in the breeze. Distantly, Bill's car started up and drove off.

Behind her, a throat cleared. Wiping her face hastily, she turned.

"Sorry about that," she said to Sam with an embarrassed eye roll. "Anyway. You said English breakfast." Tearing open the tea bag, she dropped it in a mug. Steam rose from the kettle as she poured the hot water. "Do you need milk or sugar?"

When he didn't reply, she looked back.

He seemed surprised by her reaction. He had probably imagined she would scream. Maybe drop the cup. Start to cry, who knows. *Some kind of drama* he surely expected. When a woman, at home, in her own kitchen, turns to find a man she's known for a mere handful of minutes pointing a gun at her, a big reaction would seem natural. Carrie had felt her eyes widen reflexively, like her brain needed to take in more of the scene to confirm that this was actually happening.

He narrowed his eyes, as if to say, *Really?*

Carrie's heartbeat pounded in her ears while a cool numbness trickled down from the top of her spine to the back of her knees. Her whole body, her whole existence, felt reduced to nothing but a buzzing sensation.

But that was for her to know. She ignored the gun and focused on him instead, and gave him nothing.

Puckering and cooing, baby Elise threw her teething ring back to the floor with a squeal. Sam took a step toward the baby. Carrie felt her nostrils flare involuntarily.

"Sam," Carrie said calmly, slowly. "I don't know what you want. But it's yours. Anything. I will do anything. Just please"—her voice cracked—"please don't hurt my children."

The front door opened and closed with a slam. Panic seized her throat and Carrie drew breath to yell. Sam cocked the gun.

"Mom, did Dad leave?" Scott called from the other room. "His car's not here, can I keep playing?"

"Tell him to come in here," Sam said.

Carrie bit her bottom lip.

"Mom?" Scott repeated with childish impatience.

"In here," Carrie said, and closed her eyes. "Come here real quick, Scott."

"Mom, can I stay outside? You said I could go—" Scott froze when he saw the gun. He looked at his mom and back at the weapon and back at his mom.

"Scott," Carrie said, and motioned for him. The boy never took his eyes off the firearm as he crossed the kitchen to her, where she deliberately tucked him in behind her.

"Your children may be just fine," Sam said. "Or they may not. But that's not up to me."

Carrie's nostrils flared again. "Who is it up to?"

Sam smiled.

Bill could feel people watching him.

It was the uniform. It had that effect. He stood a little taller.

Bill was many things but the consensus seemed to be that he was first and foremost *nice*. Teachers and coaches growing up, girls he dated, his friends' parents. Everyone knew Bill as the nice guy. Not that he minded. He *was* nice. But when he put on the uniform, something changed. *Nice* wasn't the default description. It still made the list. But it wasn't the only word on it.

Passengers' heads popped up as he bypassed the never-ending line for security at Los Angeles International Airport, but it only took a peek at that hat and tie to dissolve indignation into curiosity. People didn't dress like that anymore. It harkened back to a time when air travel was a rare privilege, a major event. Purposefully unchanged, the uniform kept a certain antiquated mystique alive. It elicited respect. Trust. It proclaimed a sense of duty.

Bill approached the lone TSA agent seated at a small podium set discreetly off to the side of passenger security. Scanning the barcode on the back of his badge, the machine beeped and the computer went to work.

"Morning," Bill said, handing the woman his passport.

"It's still morning?" she said, studying the information printed next to his picture. Comparing it to the information on his badge, she slid the passport under a blue light, holograms and hidden print appearing in the document's blank space. Glancing up, she verified that the face in front of her matched the one on the IDs.

"I guess it's not technically morning," Bill said. "Just morning for me."

"Well, it's my Friday. So the day needs to hurry up."

Bill's badge photo and information popped up on the computer screen. After triple-checking all three forms of identification, she handed back the passport.

"Safe flight, Mr. Hoffman."

Leaving the crew security checkpoint, he walked past the passengers tugging their shoes back on and returning liquids and laptops to their carry-on bags. On his last trip, Bill flew with a flight attendant who refused to retire simply because she didn't want to give up her crew security clearance. She turned up her nose at the thought of having to travel like a mere mortal; waiting in line, liquid restrictions, limited to two carry-ons—which would be searched every single time, not just occasionally at random. Watching a man in his socks being patted down, Bill had to admit she had a point.

Claiming privacy at an unoccupied gate, Bill dialed home as promised. Watching a catering truck outside on the tarmac down below dodge about while rampers in neon vests loaded and unloaded bags from the cargo hold, he listened to the other end of the line ring over and over. An aircraft taxied out to the runway and in the distance, another took off.

He and Carrie didn't fight often. Which was why when they did they were so bad at it. She had every right to be upset. Today was Scott's Little League season opener and Bill had promised him he would be there. He made sure he didn't have a trip on his line for the day of the game and the two days before and after. But when the chief pilot calls to ask you to fly a trip as a personal favor, you don't say no. You can't say no. Bill was the third-most senior pilot flying. When he was a new hire, no one was sure the company was even going to make it. Startup airlines almost never do. But he stuck it out nonetheless. And now, nearly twenty-five years later, the airline was a total success with both passengers and shareholders. Coastal was his baby. So when your boss says the operation needs you? You say yes. No isn't even an option.

He had told Carrie as much. But he didn't tell her that Scott's game hadn't crossed his mind when O'Malley asked if he was available. Or that even if it had, it wouldn't have made a difference.

The phone rang and rang before finally, "Hi! You've reached Carrie. I can't come . . ." Ending the call, he saw a family photo appear on the phone's home screen before he pocketed it.

Catching a glimpse of his reflection in the window, Bill surveyed his dark, full hair. A betraying gray salted his temples. His eyes, a vibrant, deep blue.

Bill slapped the bell in the middle of the coffee table.

"Eyes. My eyes."

"Final answer? This is for the win."

"She said they're like night swimming. When you can't see the bottom. But it's exciting. So, yes. My eyes. Final answer."

Carrie's jaw dropped.

Bill leaned forward. He could smell the beer on his own breath. "I overheard you say that to a friend on the phone once. I never told you, though. I love you so much, baby." He blew Carrie a kiss.

The wives cheered, the husbands ribbed.

"All right, Carrie," the party host said. "'His eyes.' Was that your answer for what your favorite part about your husband is?"

Her cheeks turned pink. With a giggle she held up a piece of paper, her answer scribbled out: His butt.

The room erupted. Bill laughed hardest of all.

He adjusted his tie. *I'm a good man,* he reminded himself without wavering. His mind flashed to the image of Carrie's look of disappointment as he walked out of the kitchen. He blinked, glancing away to follow a plane as it took off.